BEST WEST INDIAN STORIES

BEST WEST INDIAN STORIES

KENNETH RAMCHAND

NELSON CARIBBEAN

Thomas Nelson and Sons Ltd
Nelson House Mayfield Road
Walton-on-Thames Surrey KT12 5PL
51 York Place Edinburgh EH1 3JD
P O Box 18123 Nairobi Kenya
YiXiu Factory Building Unit 05–06
5th Floor 65 Sims Avenue Singapore 1438

Toppan Building 10/F 22a Westlands Road
Quarry Bay Hong Kong

ISBN 0–17–566251–7

NCN 500–6673–1

First published 1982
Reprinted 1984

Composition in Sabon by
Filmtype Services Limited,
Scarborough, North Yorkshire

Printed in
Hong Kong

CONTENTS

The Short Story – an introduction

for Gillian, Natalie, Emma and Michael, with love

THE SHORT STORY – AN INTRODUCTION

THE LITERARY FAMILY

The short story is a piece of prose fiction of a certain brevity. It can be shorter than *The Bridge* and *I Used To Live Here Once*; and it can be longer than *Ilyushin '76* or *Let Them Call It Jazz*. But these may be used as lower and upper limits. The short story, then, may be differentiated from the novel simply on the grounds of length, a yardstick which allows us to describe intermediate cases as 'long short story' and 'short novel'. The criterion of length is safe and reasonably objective; it does not, however, depend upon any recognition or analysis of essential qualities.

The term 'novella' has been used to describe material that might have been covered by the terms 'long short story' and 'short novel', and attempts have been made to show that the novella has special qualities and possibilities that mark it off clearly from the novel and the short story. Some of these attempts succeed with respect to particular carefully selected novellas, but the most that can be said here, as a general rule, is that novellas sometimes work like novels, and sometimes work like short-stories, and sometimes combine properties associated with both.

The words 'tale' and 'fable', used in connection with pieces of prose fiction of about the same kind of length as that associated with the short story, also need to be looked at. In his theory, Edgar Allan Poe used the word 'tale' as if it were the same as 'short story', although in his practice it is plain that for him, as for many other writers and readers, the tale is an account of strange happenings with a supernatural colouring. Had this been all, it would have been possible to think of the tale as a particular kind of short story. But the word has also been used to describe writings like D.H. Lawrence's *The Ladybird* or *The Fox* which may be said to deal in strange happenings (even if these are not located in the supernatural or in the external world). These very works have been referred to as 'fables' because like the animal stories from which the name comes, they have a didactic motive, and their characters and situations are carefully shaped to stand for or to signify specific meanings deliberately intended by the author. So we don't just have quite separate things called 'tales' and 'fables', there are instances when one work is called by both names.

A handy solution to these kinds of difficulties might be to note that the term short fiction includes tales, fables and short stories; and to hope that when we come across examples, they will fall into one of these categories.

When they don't it will probably be because they are a blend of two or more.

Before leaving the literary connections of the short story it might be useful to mention the 'sketch'. This is a form which seems to lie between the essay (which is non-fiction), and the short story (which is fiction). The sketch usually has a recognisable narrative element but its main emphasis is not on what happens; it is usually concerned to describe people, places and things, with a certain element of nostalgia since the things described are caught at the moment of arrest or decay, and with a vein of humour or irony in the author's voice. Examples of sketches are *Oxford in the Vacation* (Charles Lamb); Walter Pater's *The Child in the House*; George Orwell's *Shooting an Elephant*, and many of the items in Washington Irving's *Sketch Book* (1820)[1]. A modern West Indian practitioner of the sketch is the Trinidadian Anthony Milne.

ORAL CONNECTIONS

Part of the distinctiveness in the form and in the flavour of the short story comes from its obvious connections with narratives belonging to the oral sphere. In almost every country the short story draws upon the following: the folk tale (in the West Indies, anancy stories with their trickster heroes and their conflicting commitments to morality and survival); fairy stories (a sinister type in the Caribbean including la diablesse, obeah, soucouyant and devil stories); the humorous tale (usually in dialect, and to be found trying to burst into print as early as in late 19th century newspaper accounts of the doings of the lower orders); the tall tale (boasting and grandiloquence, as well as the dead-pan lie of the slave who cannot understand how the stones he put in his shirt have turned into his master's potatoes); and the anecdote, ballad or local colour story (akin to the calypso which used to reflect the mores and the sensibility of the society with much more relish, wit, and range of interest than in recent times).

These oral elements have given to the short story a strong regional flavour; and it has kept the literary form close in tone and tempo to oral narration. Samuel Selvon's famous *Brackley and the Bed* illustrates the latter point, and many of the stories in this collection further exploit such possibilities (see *At the Stelling* and *Let Them Call It Jazz*).

The West Indian short story, which pre-dates the West Indian novel, may be seen as the bridge between the oral tradition and the highly literary appearance of the West Indian novel. Once the bridge is put in place, the subtle connections between the West Indian novel and the oral tradition should be obvious to those who would like to see the novel returning to a more folksy relation to oral sources.

SOME CHARACTERISTIC FEATURES

All the characteristics to be noted here are not to be found in any one story; and at different stages in the history of the genre, some would have been regarded as more important than others. The first and enduring appeal of the short story, as can be seen in its Biblical, Oriental, Classical and Medieval ancestors is that it tells a story. Its brevity does not allow suspense of the type achieved by digressions, descriptive passages or multiple plots. Nor can the writer of a short story keep us asking what happens next. There just are not so many events in a short story. Instead of suspense and curiosity about the chain of events, the short story writer works at surprise, revealing something unexpected in the character or event. What this tells us is that although the short story is a narrative, story is not its only concern. There are many modern stories especially where (as in many modern novels) it is the reader who constructs a story out of what has been presented – see *Her House* and V.S. Naipaul's *A Flag on the Island* (1967), and that formally daring example, the delightful *The Night-Watchman's Occurrence Book*. Sometimes, as in *My Girl and the City*, and *Enchanted Alley*, the events are not a sequence in narrative but carry a mood or feeling that is the story's raison d'etre.

There are short stories with a strong narrative line and clear signs of the author's control of the plot of the story. V.S. Naipaul's *B. Wordsworth* is the classic of this conventional type, it shows that we must not hurry to dismiss a work of art simply because it does not seem innovatory. In this collection, *Drunkard of the River*, *Crazy Mary* and *Cane is Bitter* are examples of this type. There is a danger that stories like these might seem to readers to be little different from extracts or sections of a novel.

But novels *are* different. A novel of the conventional type usually gives a picture of a whole society or a world within a society. It contains many characters of whom more than one are presented in depth and over a period of their lives. In such a novel we are always aware of the authorial voice interpreting, summarising, looking forward and in other ways guiding the reader through the successive episodes. Of the stories listed above, only *Cane is Bitter* attempts to make a broad social statement, though even here as in the other stories, there is a notable absence of the direct authorial voice, and the focus is on one character in an isolated state at a particular point in his life.

The short story is a concentrated form. It focuses on a single character at a critical point in his or her life, or in the grip of a particular mood or emotion; what it says about a society comes not from an attempt to portray a society, but from its penetration of an event or character or situation. Instead of explanation through the omniscient author's voice, it prefers to work through a strict description of scene, action, and a strategic representation of dialogue. Wilson Harris's initial reluctance to allow *Banim Creek*, a fragment of a novel, to be used in this collection arose partly from the novelist's sense of the difference between novel and story. The editorial cuts in the story, made with the author's permission, were aimed at reducing authorial voice, and putting the brake on the material's tendency to explode outwards into multiple points of interest, too many perhaps to be accommodated within what was expected to pass as a short story. Given the tendency of the form towards economy and concentration it is not surprising that there are stories in which the language, too, approaches the intensity and figurative density of language usually associated with poems. Some commentators indeed, responding to content, form and linguistic texture, have gone so far as to see the short story as 'the romantic prose form', which in its 'normally limited scope and subjective orientation ... corresponds to the lyric poem as the novel does to the epic.'[2] And in a more general way, it is sometimes held that the short story is closer to the poem than to the novel.

BEST WEST INDIAN STORIES

Some of the best. I have omitted *La Divina Pastora* and *Triumph* by C.L.R. James, was tempted by E. Snod's *Maroon Medicine* (1905), thought hard about Shiva Naipaul and Seepersad Naipaul; and could not obtain permission to include *B. Wordsworth* and *The Night-Watchman's Occurrence Book*. Without these one really cannot claim to have captured the best. I agonised over Lamming and Austin Clarke but I came to abide by the rule not to give any story the benefit of the doubt. Late in the day I wondered whether too much indulgence was shown to *Ilyushin '76* but gave in again to its energy. Other stories by writers in the collection presented themselves, and perhaps in another mood the choices might have been different. In the end, there is something arbitrary in making an anthology but one hopes that all these stories give pleasure and encourage thought and feeling.

The stories have not been arranged in chronological order nor has there been an attempt to put them in groups. The sequence in which they have been placed, however, has not been done carelessly.

The editor is grateful to the authors of the stories and their agents and publishers for unusual cooperation. John Hearne and Earl Lovelace have been specially generous. Mr Barrie McWhirter, the publisher's editor, has worked on this book in the way one is told American editors do.

Kenneth Ramchand
St Augustine and Newhaven, Conn. 1981

FOOTNOTES

1 Examples cited by Ian Reid in *The Short Story* (1977)

2 *The Short Story*, p 28

SELECTED BIBLIOGRAPHY OF THE SHORT STORY

Bates, H.E. *The Modern Short Story* (1941)

O'Connor, Frank *The Lonely Voice* (1963)

Reid, Ian *The Short Story* (1977) This work contains a useful bibliography, and interesting discussion.

MICHAEL ANTHONY

Michael Anthony was born in Mayaro, Trinidad in 1932 and attended the Junior Technical School in San Fernando.

He left Trinidad for England in 1955 where he worked in factories, for the railways and as a tele-graphist.

His literary career began with contributions to *BIM*, the Barbadian magazine. His first novel, *The Games Were Coming*, was published in 1963, and his most famous, *The Year in San Fernando*, in 1965.

He now lives in Trinidad.

This is one of the earliest of the short stories I ever wrote and it was inspired by the memory of an incident, or several incidents of the kind I experienced when I began going to the Junior Technical School in San Fernando. The period was from September 1944 to September 1946. Although I wrote the story in England in 1958, it sprang from these nostalgic memories. In the story the boy was younger than I would have been at that time, but I think his response was more or less the same as mine.

I believe that this story, which came at the very start of my writing career, reflected feelings about San Fernando which were to be expressed later in the novel, *The Year in San Fernando* – although the setting of the book was earlier, in 1941.

The 'enchanted alley' I referred to in this short story is not really an alleyway but a narrow street – Mon Chagrin Street, or part of it. It ran off the High Street and I believe I sometimes took a short-cut, just to get to know San Fernando better, and to take in the sights and sounds, and who knows, to eat some *barah* and *channa*!

Michael Anthony

ENCHANTED ALLEY

Leaving for school on mornings, I walked slowly through the busy parts of the town. The business places would all be opening then and smells of strange fragrance would fill the High Street. Inside the opening doors I would see clerks dusting, arranging, hanging things up, getting ready for the day's business. They looked cheerful and eager and they opened the doors very wide. Sometimes I stood up to watch them.

In places between the stores several little alleys ran off the High Street. Some were busy and some were not and there was one that was long and narrow and dark and very strange. Here, too, the shops would be opening as I passed and there would be bearded Indians in loincloths spreading rugs on the pavement. There would be Indian women also, with veils thrown over their shoulders, setting up their stalls and chatting in a strange sweet tongue. Often I stood, too, watching them, and taking in the fragrance of rugs and spices and onions and sweetmeats. And sometimes, suddenly remembering, I would hurry away for fear the school-bell had gone.

In class, long after I settled down, the thoughts of this alley would return to me. I would recall certain stalls and certain beards and certain flashing eyes, and even some of the rugs that had been rolled out. The Indian women, too, with bracelets around their ankles and around their sun-browned arms flashed to my mind.

I thought of them. I saw them again looking shyly at me from under the shadow of the stores, their veils half hiding their faces. In my mind I could almost picture them laughing together and talking in that strange sweet tongue. And mostly the day would be quite old before the spell of the alley wore off my mind.

One morning I was much too early for school. I passed the street-sweepers at work on Harris' Promenade and when I came to the High Street, only one or two shop doors were open. I walked slowly, looking at the quietness and noticing some of the alleys that ran away to the backs of fences and walls and distant streets. I looked at the names of these alleys. Some were very funny. And I walked on anxiously so I could look a little longer at the dark, funny street.

As I walked it struck me that I did not know the name of that street. I laughed at myself. Always I had stood there looking along it and I did not know the name of it. As I drew near I kept my eyes on the wall of the corner shop. There was no sign on the wall. On getting there I looked at the other wall. There was a sign-plate upon it but the dust had gathered thickly there and whatever the sign said was hidden behind the dust.

I was disappointed. I looked along the alley which was only now beginning to get alive, and as the shop doors opened the enchantment of spice and onions and sweetmeats emerged. I looked at the wall again but there was nothing there to say what the street was called. Straining my eyes at the sign-plate I could make out a 'C' and an 'A' but farther along the dust had made one smooth surface of the plate and the wall.

'Stupes!' I said in disgust. I heard mild laughter, and as I looked before me I saw the man rolling out his rugs. There were two women beside him and they were talking together and they were laughing and I could see the women were pretending not to look at me. They were setting up a stall of sweetmeats and the man put down his rugs and took out something from a tray and put it into his mouth, looking back at me. Then they talked again in the strange tongue and laughed.

I stood there awhile. I knew they were talking about me. I was not afraid. I wanted to show them that I was not timid and that I would not run away. I moved a step or two nearer the wall. The smells rose up stronger now and they seemed to give the feelings of things splendoured and far away. I pretended I was looking at the wall but I stole glances at the merchants from the corners of my eyes. I watched the men in their loin-cloths and the garments of the women were full and many-coloured and very exciting. The women stole glances at me and smiled at each other and ate the sweetmeats they sold. The rug merchant spread out his rugs wide on the pavement and he looked at the beauty of their colours and seemed very proud. He, too, looked slyly at me.

I drew a little nearer because I was not afraid of them. There were many more stalls now under the stores. Some of the people turned off the High Street and came into this little alley and they bought little things from the merchants. The merchants held up the bales of cloth and matched them on to the people's clothes and I could see they were saying it looked very nice. I smiled at this and the man with the rugs saw me and smiled.

That made me brave. I thought of the word I knew in the strange tongue and when I remembered it I drew nearer.

'Salaam,' I said.

The rug merchant laughed aloud and the two women laughed aloud and I laughed, too. Then the merchant bowed low to me and replied, 'Salaam!'

This was very amusing for the two women. They talked together so I couldn't understand and then the fat one spoke.

'Wot wrang wid de warl?'

I was puzzled for a moment and then I said, 'Oh, it is the street sign. Dust cover it.'

'Street sign?' one said, and they covered their laughter with their veils.

'I can't read what street it is,' I said, 'What street this is?'

The rug merchant spoke to the women in the strange tongue and the three of them giggled and one of the women said, 'Every marning you stand up dey and you doe know what they carl here?'

'First time I come down here,' I said.

'Yes,' said the fat woman. Her face was big and friendly and she sat squat on the pavement. 'First time you wark down here but every morning you stop dey and watch we.'

I laughed. 'You see 'e laughing?' said the other. The rug merchant did not say anything but he was very much amused.

'What you call this street?' I said. I felt very brave because I knew they were friendly to me, and I looked at the stalls, and the smell of the sweetmeats was delicious. There was *barah*, too, and chutney and dry *channa*, and in the square tin there was the wet yellow *channa*, still hot, the steam curling up from it.

The man took time to put down his rugs and then he spoke to me. 'This,' he said, talking slowly and making actions with his arms, 'From up dey to up dey is Calcatta Street.' He was very pleased with his explanation. He had pointed from the High Street end of the alley to the other end that ran darkly into the distance. The whole street was very long and dusty, and in the concrete drain there was no water and the brown peel of onions blew about when there was a little wind.

Sometimes there was the smell of cloves in the air and sometimes the smell of oil-cloth, but where I stood the smell of the sweetmeats was strongest and most delicious.

He asked, 'You like Calcatta Street?'

'Yes,' I said.

The two women laughed coyly and looked from one to the other.

'I have to go,' I said, – 'school.'

'O you gwine to school?' the man said. He put down his rugs again. His loin-cloth was very tight around him. 'Well you could wark so,' he said, pointing away from the High Street end of the alley, 'and when you get up dey, turn so, and when you wark and wark, you'll meet the school.'

'Oh!' I said, surprised. 'I didn't know there was a way to school along this alley.'

'You see?' he said, very pleased with himself.

'Yes,' I said.

The two women looked at him smiling and they seemed very proud the way he explained. I moved off to go, holding my books under my arm. The women looked at me and they smiled in a sad, friendly way. I looked at the chutney and *barah* and *channa* and suddenly something occurred to me. I felt in my pockets and then I opened my books and looked among the pages. I heard one of the women whisper – 'Taking, larning . . .' The other said, 'Aha . . . ' and I did not hear the rest of what she said. Desperately I turned the books down and shook them and the penny fell out rolling on the pavement. I grabbed it and turned to the fat woman. For a moment I couldn't decide which, but the delicious smell of the yellow, wet channa softened my heart.

'A penny channa,' I said, 'wet.'

The woman bent over with the big spoon, took out a small paper bag, flapped it open, then crammed two or three spoonfuls of channa into it. Then she took up the pepper bottle.

'Pepper?'

'Yes,' I said, anxiously.

'Plenty?'

'Plenty.'

The fat woman laughed, pouring the pepper sauce with two or three pieces of red pepper skin falling on the channa.

'Good!' I said, licking my lips.

'You see?' said the other woman. She grinned widely, her gold teeth glittering in her mouth. 'You see 'e like plenty pepper?'

As I handed my penny I saw the long, brown fingers of the rug merchant stretching over my hand. He handed a penny to the fat lady.

'Keep you penny in you pocket,' he grinned at me, 'an look out, you go reach to school late.'

I was very grateful about the penny. I slipped it into my pocket.

'You could wark so,' the man said, pointing up Calcutta Street, 'and turn so, and you'll come down by the school.'

'Yes,' I said, hurrying off.

The street was alive with people now. There were many more merchants with rugs and many more stalls of sweetmeats and other things. I saw bales of bright cloth matched up to ladies' dresses and I heard the ladies laugh and say it was good. I walked fast through the crowd. There were women with saris calling out 'Ground-nuts! *Parata*!' and every here and there gramophones blared out Indian songs. I walked on with my heart full inside me. Sometimes I stood up to listen and then I walked on again. Then suddenly it came home to me it must be very late. The crowd was thick and the din spread right along Calcutta Street. I looked back to wave to my friends. They were far behind and the pavement was so crowded I could not see. I heard the car horns tooting and I knew that on the High Street it must be a jam session of traffic and people. It must be very late. I held my books in my hands, secured the paper bag of *channa* in my pocket, and with the warmth against my legs I ran pell-mell to school.

CLAUDE McKAY

Claude McKay was born in Jamaica in 1890 and educated there and in the United States. He is now regarded as one of the earliest exponents of a truly West Indian literature and his writing gives a valuable insight into social life in Jamaica during the last years of the nineteenth century. *Crazy Mary* comes from *Gingertown*, a collection of short stories published in 1932.

His other publications include *Songs of Jamaica* (1912), *Banana Bottom* (1933), *Spring in New Hampshire* (1920), and *Home to Harlem* (1928). He died in 1948.

Crazy Mary is taken from *Gingertown* (1932), a collection of McKay's stories which is not as well-known as it ought to be. Some of the stories are set in the United States, and some in Jamaica.

McKay's evocation of village life is precise and economical. At one level, Church and School represent the norms. Beyond in the city, are to be found Law, Government and Medicine. There is a major crisis when the schoolmaster is accused of having had intercourse with a precocious schoolgirl called Freshy. The Church meetings called to judge the matter keep breaking up in disagreement and disorder.

The village has seen and approved of the courtship of the genteel Mary by the schoolmaster, expects there will be a marriage soon, and so is surprised by the development around Freshy, but the narrating voice conveys the impression of a broad tolerance in the village. This appears again later when Mary returns and begins to act strangely; she roams the village barefooted, picking each day a bouquet of flowers which she nurses like a baby. Soon the village accepts her as crazy but harmless.

McKay is not interested in stressing distinctions between the authentic feeling of the village as against its colonised conscience. The schoolmaster's flight once the decision is taken to settle the Freshy affair with the help of the doctor and the law courts, causes Mary's breakdown and prolonged grieving; his return many years later as a respectable married man, at last breaks Mary's waiting heart, and inspires the final burst of crude disrespect which precedes her suicide. It is Mary's grief and her sense of having been betrayed that McKay is really interested in. The disciplined objectivity of a narrating voice that neither explains nor blames is the means by which McKay subtly and powerfully renders the emotion of the experience.

Kenneth Ramchand

CRAZY MARY

Miss Mary startled the village for the first time in her strange life that day when she turned herself up and showed her naked self to them. Suddenly the villagers realised that after many years of harmless craziness something was perhaps dangerously wrong with Mary, but before they could do anything about it she settled the matter herself.

For a long time she had been accepted as an eccentric village character.

Ever since she had recovered from her long sad illness and started going round the village with a bunch of roses in her arms.

Before that she had been the sewing-mistress of the village school. She was a pretty, young, yellow woman then. Her parents, following the custom of those peasants with a little means, had sent her to a sewing-school in Gingertown. She had gone away in short frocks, with her hair down and a bright bow pinned to it.

When she returned for good after three years she was in long skirts, with her hair up in what the villagers called a 'Chinese bump.'

Her father bought her a Singer, finer than those of the other peasant women, a foot-working one similar to that owned by the village tailor. She subscribed to *Weldon's Ladies' Journal* and the *Home Magazine*, and opened a little school in her home for girls to learn to sew and design and cut. Her girls called her Miss Mary, and a few superior folk, such as the parson and family, the schoolmaster, and the postmistress, called her Miss Dean.

The schoolmaster's wife was the sewing-mistress then. But two years later the schoolmaster left for a better-paying school. He was succeeded by a bachelor, and Miss Mary applied for and got the sewing-mistress's job. The sewing-mistress went to the school twice a week for two hours during the afternoon session.

Miss Mary sometimes took two or three of her bigger girls along to help teach the tots to sew.

Girls came from other villages to learn Miss Mary's art. She was much admired, for she was charming. She was nice-shaped, something like a ripened wild cane, and could look a perfect piece of elegance in a princess gown.

Naturally much of Miss Mary's spare time was spent with the schoolmaster. Often they went out walking together in the afternoon after school until twilight. And sometimes they rode horseback to Gingertown together. The villagers got to liking to see them together. The parson approved of it. So did Miss Mary's parents. And everybody thought the two would certainly get married ...

The schoolmaster was a pure ebony, shining and popular. He played cricket with the young men. He was of middle size, stocky, and an excellent underhand bowler. He organised a cricket club, and during the short days let school out earlier than usual to go to field practice.

Sometimes the schoolmaster and Miss Mary took tea together at the parsonage. And the schoolmaster would talk about the choir and new anthems with the minister's wife, who was the organist. Miss Mary was not in the choir, for she hadn't a singing voice nor any knowledge of music.

As a constant visitor to the Dean home the schoolmaster became almost like one of the family. The villagers indulged in friendly gossip about the couple, anticipating a happy termination of the idyll. Nothing could enrapture the people more than a big village wedding with bells and saddle horses and carriages.

But bang came the scandal one day.

The girls who attended Miss Mary's sewing-classes at home were nearly all girls just out of elementary school, between fourteen and fifteen years. There were a few younger who for some reason had not finished school, and also a few older who were considered and treated as young ladies.

Among those who accompanied Miss Mary to the school was a little bird-brown one, plump as a squab, just turned thirteen, curiously cat-faced and forever smiling. They called her Freshy because she was precocious in her manners.

Sometimes the schoolmaster would tell one of the girls to do something in the teacher's cottage. To do a little cleaning up or prepare a beverage of bitter oranges or pineapple or a soursop-cup during the recreation hours. And it seemed that Freshy, always forward, had got herself asked to do things many times.

And one morning while the classes were humming with work, the schoolmaster at his desk, the mother of Freshy, with her bluejean skirt tucked high up and bandanna flying as if for war, rushed into the school and slapped the schoolmaster's face and collared and shook him, bellowing that he had ruined her little daughter.

The schoolmaster was in a pitiful state, trying to hold his dignity and the woman off, until the monitors interfered and the woman was at last mastered and put out.

The village was shaken as if by an earthquake. Of course, the schoolmaster denied that he had ruined Freshy, but the girl maintained by the mouth of her mother that he had.

The village midwife, after seeing Freshy, insisted that she had not been ruined. But the midwife was the sister of Miss Mary's father, who was a leader in the church.

The parson was constrained to relieve the schoolmaster of his duties and put his wife in temporary charge of the school. For the protection of his pastorate, he said. Then there was the religious side. The school-master being a member of the church and a lay preacher, a church meeting was called to air the affair.

The village was divided for and against the schoolmaster. Curiously, it was the older heads who were more favourable to him. The young folk and chiefly the bucks were already calling the man a rogue and turning the whole thing into a salacious song. It began to be bruited that the schoolmaster was secretly a wild one who abused the innocence of schoolgirls. But there were some who maintained that even at her age Freshy had already passed the age of innocence with the apples of her bosom so prettily tempting.

Freshy was very conscious of the notoriety she had attained, and, fortified by the aggressiveness of her mother, when she went about the village she tossed her head and turned her lips in scorn like a petulant little actress at those who whispered and stared at her.

The first church meeting, with the parson presiding, broke up in a babel of recriminations, when Freshy's mother became bellicose and abusive to those who had dared to insinuate that her daughter was not a mere child.

It was then that Miss Mary acted. Freshy had not returned to the sewing-school since the day the trouble began. Meeting her in the lane one afternoon, Miss Mary took her home. And alone with Freshy in a room she third-degreed her until the girl cried out that the schoolmaster had not touched her.

At the next church meeting Miss Mary gave an account of Freshy's confession. Speaking quietly in her refined way and holding all attention with her pretty personality, she was almost convincing the whole meeting. But Freshy's mother jumped up, interrupting her, and related how Miss Mary had prevailed upon her child to confess, accusing her of being a little woman and having been with the boys. In her turn Freshy's mother charged Miss Mary with being the schoolmaster's mistress, and in a rage she threatened to box her ears and made a rush for her. Women shrieked as if filled with the spirit for a public fight, but some men held back Freshy's mother and she was put out.

Again the church meeting broke up. The young men especially did not want to believe that a person so nice as Miss Mary could say dirty things to Freshy. But the women shook their heads dubiously and repeated the saying, 'Still river run deep.' The declaration of Freshy's mother started a big gossip, for it was locally conceded that Miss Mary was a virgin. There was nothing dishonourable in the fact that girls were deflowered at a tender age and young virgins were few in the country, nevertheless the village folk took a pride-like interest in any young woman of whom it could be said she was a virgin up until the time of her marriage.

It seemed as if the church and the village were going to rags over the affair, until a member named Jabez Fearon suggested taking the case to the law courts and having Freshy examined by a doctor from Ginger-town. Jabez Fearon was the local tax-collector, commonly called the bailiff. His outstretched hand carried much weight among the peasants, but they had never considered his mind of any weight at all.

Now, however, his opinion appeared intelligent and worth acting upon. How strange that nobody had thought of the legal course before! After all the church-meeting bickering and disagreement! The younger church members thought that was the most excellent way of settling the trouble. A doctor's examination and the decision of a judge.

But before any step was taken and another church meeting called, the schoolmaster quietly disappeared.

And a few weeks after his disappearance Miss Mary went to the city and stayed there a long time. Her people said that she had had a breakdown from nervous trouble and they had had to take her to a doctor in the city.

But the weeks became months before she returned. And then she was confined to the house for as many months more. The village thought she was surely consumptive. Especially when they glimpsed her so tiny and strange in the portico of the house or on the barbecue.

Then at long last, when she could not be detained at home and away from people any longer, she came out, and the village became aware that she was not consumptive, but a little crazy. Her parents stayed away from the church and were never the same charming folk again. Their village respectability became a sour thing.

Miss Mary went about with her hair down like a girl. And it was lovely hair, thick, black and frizzly. The first day she went out she gathered a bunch of flowers and took it to the schoolhouse and placed it on the teacher's desk without a word, and walked out. The new schoolmaster was a married man. The parson said that he would never engage an unmarried man again.

Miss Mary got rid of her shoes too and went about barefooted like a common peasant girl. Every day she gathered her flowers, and there was always plenty of red – hibiscus, poinsettias, dragon's-blood. And she had a strange way of holding the bouquet in her arm as if she were nursing it. Sometimes she talked to herself, but never to anybody, and when anyone tried to talk to her she answered with a cracked little laugh.

Her people kept her clean. And the village folk settled down into familiarity with her as a strange character. Nobody thought that she should be sent to the madhouse, for she was harmless.

And the months turned into years, the village changed schoolmasters again, and even the parson was called to a church in a little town where he earned more money. The village had long ceased from wondering about the disappearance of the schoolmaster, and Freshy had had three children for three different black bucks before she was nineteen.

Then one day the schoolmaster returned. He had been away in Panama. He was a changed man after being so long free from semi-religious duties, a little dapper with a gait the islanders called 'the Yankee strut.' He was married to a girl he met over there, a saucy brown dressed in an extreme mode of the Boston dip of the day.

It was on a Sunday and they went to church. And after the service the schoolmaster and his wife stood in the yard, surrounded by an admiring group of old friends and young admirers who wanted to hear all about the life and prospects in Colón and Panama.

Nobody had thought of Miss Mary, poor crazy thing in that social centre of the village, where new acquaintances were introduced and sweethearts met and children skipped about.

But she must have heard of his arrival somehow, for suddenly she appeared in the churchyard and, pushing through the folk around the schoolmaster, she threw the bouquet of flowers at him and, turning, she ran up the broad church steps and turned herself up at everybody, looking at them from under with a lecherous laugh.

There was a sudden bewildered pause. And then a young church member dashed up the steps after Mary and the church crowd recovered from the shock, remembering that she was crazy. But before he could reach and seize her she had jumped down the steps, shrieking strange laughter, and started running towards the graveyard.

Just outside the gate she turned again, repeated her act, and laughed. The young villager gave chase after her, followed by others. Mary ran like a rabbit in a mad zigzag. And whenever she saw herself at a safe distance from her pursuers she performed her act with laughter.

She ran past the graveyard and, striking the main road, she headed straight for the river. A little below where the river crossed the road there was a high narrow waterfall that from the churchyard looked like a gorgeous flowing of gold.

Mary ran down a little track leading to the waterfall. Her pursuers stopped in the road, paralysed by her evident intention, and began shouting to her to stop. And watching from the churchyard, the folk began to bawl and howl.

But Mary kept straight on. On the perilous edge of the waterfall she halted and did her stuff again, then with a high laugh she went sheer over.

Again one of the earliest of my stories. It was written in 1960. *Drunkard of the River* is set in Mayaro, where I was born, and although the incident itself is imaginary, it was written about a man and family that I knew well. The man was quite a drunkard and did cause his family pain – especially on Saturday nights. It was a fairly large family, though to suit my purpose in the story (fiction after all) I had him as having just a wife and son. In a way this story is very meaningful to me because it has made me notice that the drunkard of the river meant more to my literary life than I thought. I used him again as Mr Gidharee in my novel *Green Days by the River* and I used his children – Kitsin, Molly, Amy, Coots – in another of my short stories, *The Patch of Guava*. These, by the way, are real names. I can make bold to say that now because so much water has passed under the bridge.

One thing about that story is that in a sense it is the most imaginary of my stories, for, since the incident is not real I cannot even place it in a time-scheme. Yet I think in the story the man is true to character – in a drunken state – and I think his wife was even truer to character. If this incident was going to happen at all – and I am glad it did not, for the boy's sake – if it was going to happen at all, it would have happened in the early 1940's just before I left Mayaro for San Fernando. The man and his wife are now dead.

Michael Anthony

DRUNKARD OF THE RIVER

'**W**here you' father?'

The boy did not answer. He paddled his boat carefully between the shallows, and then he ran the boat alongside the bank, putting his paddle in front to stop it. Then he threw the rope round the picket and helped himself on to the bark. His mother stood in front of the door still staring at him.

'Where you' father?'

The boy hid his anger. He looked at his mother and said calmly, 'You know Pa. You know where he is.'

'And ah did tell you not to come back without 'im?'

'I could bring Pa back?' the boy cried. His bitterness was getting the better of him. 'When Pa went to drink I could bring him back? How?'

It was always the same. The boy's mother stood in front of the door staring up the river. Every Saturday night it was like this. Every Saturday night Mano went out to the village and drank himself helpless and lay on the floor of the shop, cursing and vomiting until the Chinaman was ready to close up. Then they rolled Mano outside and heaven knows, maybe they even spat on him.

The boy's mother stared up the river, her face twisted with anger and distress. She couldn't go up the river now. It would be fire and brimstone if she went. But Mano had to be brought home. She turned to see what the boy was doing. He had packed away the things from the shopping bag and he was now reclining on the couch.

'You have to go for you' father, you know,' she said.

'Who?'

'You!'

'Not me!'

'Who you tellin' not me,' she shouted. She was furious now. 'Dammit, you have to go for you' father!'

Sona had risen from the couch on the alert. His mother hardly ever hit him now but he could never tell. It had been a long time since she had looked so angry and had stamped her feet.

He rose slowly and reluctantly and as he glanced at her he couldn't understand what was wrong with her. He couldn't see why she bothered about his father at all. For his father was stupid and worthless and made their life miserable. If he could have had his way, Mano would have been out of the house a long time now. His bed would have been the dirty meat-table in front of Assing's shop. That was what he deserved. The rascal! The boy spat through the window. The very thought of his father sickened him.

Yet with Sona's mother it was different. The man she had married and who had turned out badly was still the pillar of her life. Although he had piled up grief after grief, tear after tear, she felt lost and drifting without him. To her he was as mighty as the very river that flowed outside. She remembered that in his young days there was nothing any living man could do that he could not.

In her eyes he was still young. He did not grow old. It was she who had aged. He had only turned out badly. She hated him for the way he drank rum and squandered the little money he worked for. But she did not mind the money so much. It was seeing him drunk. She knew when he staggered back how she would shake with rage and curse him, but even so, how inside she would shake with the joy of having him safe and home.

She wondered what was going on at the shop now. She wondered if he was already drunk and helpless and making a fool of himself.

With Sona, the drunkard's son, this was what stung more than ever. The way Mano, his father, cursed everybody and made a fool of himself. Sometimes he had listened to his father and he had wanted to kick him because he was so ashamed. Often in silence he had shaken his fist and said, 'One day, ah'll ... ah'll ... '

He had watched his mother put up with sweat and starvation. She was getting skinnier every day, and she looked more like fifty-six than the thirty-six she was. Already her hair was greying. Sometimes he had looked at her and, thinking of his father, he had ground his teeth and had said, 'Beast!' several times to himself. He was in that frame of mind now. Bitter and reluctant, he went to untie the boat.

'If I can't bring 'im, I'll leave 'im,' he said angrily.

'Get somebody to help you!'

He turned to her. 'Nobody wouldn't help me. He insult everybody. Last week Bolai kick 'im.'

'Bolai kick 'im? An' what you do?'

His mother was stung with rage and shock. Her eyes were large and red and watery.

The boy casually unwound the rope from the picket. 'What I do?' he said. 'That is he and Bolai business.'

His mother burst out crying.

'What ah must do?' the boy said. 'All the time ah say, "Pa, come home, come home, Pa!" You know what he tell me? He say, "Go to hell, yuh little bastard!"'

His mother turned to him. Beads of tears were still streaming down the sides of her face.

'Sona, go for you' father. Go now. You stand up there and watch Bolai kick you' father and you ain't do nothing? He mind you, you know,' she sobbed. 'He is you' father, you ungrateful ... ' And choking with anger and grief she burst out crying again.

When she raised her head, Sona was paddling towards midstream, scowling, avoiding the shallows of the river.

True enough there was trouble in Assing's shop. Mano's routine was well under way. He staggered about the bar dribbling and cursing.

Again and again, the Chinaman spoke to him about his words. Not that he cared about Mano's behaviour. The rum Mano consumed made quite a difference to Assing's account. It safeguarded Mano's freedom of speech in the shop.

But the customers were disgusted. All sorts of things had happened on Saturday nights through Mano's drunkenness. There was no such thing as buying in peace once Mano was there.

So now with trouble looming, the arrival of Sona was sweet relief. As Sona walked in, someone pointed out his father between the sugar bags.

'Pa!'

Mano looked up. 'What you come for?' he drawled.

'Ma say to come home,' Sona said. He told himself that he mustn't lose control in front of strangers.

'Well!'

'Ma send for you.'

'You! You' mother send you for me! So you is me father now, eh ... eh?' In his drunken rage the old man staggered towards his son.

Sona didn't walk back. He never did anything that would make him feel stupid in front of a crowd. But before he realised what was happening his father lunged forward and struck him a blow across his face.

'So you is me father, eh? You is me father, now!' He cried, and threw a kick at the boy.

Two or three people bore down on Mano and held him off the boy. Sona put his hands to his belly where his father had just kicked him. Tears came to his eyes. The drunkenness was gripping Mano more and more. He could hardly stand by himself now. He was struggling to set himself free. The men held on to him. Sona kept out of the way.

'It's a damn' shame!' somebody shouted.

'Shame?' Mano drawled. 'An' he is me father now, 'e modder send him for me. Let me go,' he cried, struggling more than ever. 'I'll kill 'im. So help me God, I'll kill 'im!'

They hadn't much to do to control Mano in this state. His body was loose and weak now, his bones seemed to be turning to water. The person who had cried, 'It's a damn' shame!' spoke again.

'Why you don't carry 'im home, boy? You can't see he only making trouble?'

'You'll help me put 'im in the boat?' Sona asked. He looked calm now. He seemed only concerned with getting his father out of the shop, and out of all this confusion. Nobody could tell what went on below the calmness of his face. Nobody could guess that hate was blazing in his mind.

Four men and Sona lifted Mano and carted him into the boat. Sona pushed off. After a while he looked back at the bridge. Everything behind was swallowed by the darkness. 'Pa,' the boy said. His father groaned. 'Pa, yuh going home,' Sona said.

The wilderness of mangroves and river spread out before the boat. They were alone. Sona was alone with Mano, and the river and the mangroves and the night, and the swarms of alligators below. He looked at his father again. 'Pa, so you kick me up then, eh?' he said.

Far into the night Sona's mother waited. She slept a little on one side, then she turned on the other side, and at every sound she woke up, straining her ears. There was no sound of the paddle on water. Surely the shops must have closed by now, she thought. Everything must have closed by this time. She lay anxious and listened until her eyes shut again in an uneasy sleep.

She was awakened by the creaking of the bedroom floor. Sona jumped back when she spoke.

'Who that – Mano?'

'Is me, Ma,' Sona said.

His bones, too, seemed to be turning liquid. Not from drunkenness, but from fear. The lion in him had changed into a lamb. As he spoke his voice trembled.

His mother didn't notice. 'All you now come?' she said. 'Where Mano?'

The boy didn't answer. In the darkness he took down his things from the nail-pegs.

'Where Mano?' his mother cried out.

'He out there sleeping. He drunk.'

'The monster,' his mother said, getting up and feeling for the matches.

Sona quickly slipped outside. Fear dazed him now and he felt dizzy. He looked at the river and he looked back at the house and there was only one word that kept hitting against his mind: Police! Police! He knew what would happen. He felt desperate.

'Mano!' He heard his mother call to the emptiness of the house, 'Mano!'

Panic-stricken, Sona fled into the mangroves and into the night.

EARL LOVELACE

Earl Lovelace was born in Trinidad in 1935, he was educated there and in the United States where he attended Howard University. His first novel *While Gods Are Falling* was published in 1965. He has also written *The Schoolmaster* (1968) and *The Dragon Can't Dance*.
He now lives in Trinidad and teaches at the University of the West Indies at St Augustine.

This story was first written in about 1962 before I wrote
While Gods are Falling. It lay around for a long time
and I did nothing about it until 1979 when I re-wrote it
for the present anthology. I used the same characters
except for the girls who are new, and I kept the incident
about Britto and the rum, and the donkey-cart. The tone
was changed and it succeeded.

One of the things about this story is that it is a *story*,
not an attempt to make any point. I didn't set out to
write about Time. The story speaks for itself because the
characters are true.

Earl Lovelace

SHOEMAKER ARNOLD

Shoemaker Arnold stood at the doorway of his little shop, hands on
his hips, his body stiffened in that proprietory and undefeated
stubbornness, announcing, not without some satisfaction, that if in
his life he had not been triumphant, neither had the world defeated him.
It would be hard, though, to imagine how he could be defeated, since he
exuded such hard tough unrelenting cantankerousness, gave off such a
sense of readiness for confrontation, that if trouble had to pick someone
to clash with, Shoemaker Arnold would not be the one. To him, the
world was his shoemaker's shop. There he was master, and, anyone
entering would have to surrender not only to his opinion on shoes and
leather and shoemaker apprentices, but to his views on politics, women,
religion, flying objects, or any of the myriad subjects he decided to
discourse upon, so that over the years he had arrived at a position where
none of the villagers bothered to dispute him, and to any who dared
maintain a view contrary to the one he was affirming, he was quick to
point out, 'This place is mine. Here, I do as I please, I say what I want.
Who don't like it, the door is open.'

His wife had herself taken that advice many years earlier, and had
moved not only out of his house but out of the village, taking with her
their three children, leaving him with his opinions, an increasing taste for
alcohol, and the tedium of having to prepare his own meals. It is possible
that he would have liked to take one of the village girls to live with him,
but he was too proud to accept that he had even that need, and he would
look at the girls go by outside his shop, hiding behind his dissatisfied
scowl a fine appraising, if not lecherous, eye; but if one of them happened
to look in, he would snarl at her: 'What do you want here?' So that
between him and the village girls there existed this teasing relationship of
antagonism and desire, the girls themselves walking with greater flourish

and style when they went past his shoemaker's shop, swinging their backsides and cutting their eyes, and he, scowling, dissatisfied. With the young men of the village, his relationship was no better. As far as he was concerned none of them wanted to work and he had no intention of letting them use his shoemaker's shop as a place to loiter. Over the years he had taken on numerous apprentices, keeping them for a month or two and sometimes for just a single day, then getting rid of them; and it was not until Norbert came to work with him that he had had what could be considered regular help.

Norbert, however, was no boy. He was a drifter, a rum drinker, and, exactly the sort of person that one did not expect Arnold to tolerate for more than five minutes. Norbert teased the girls, was chummy with the loiterers, gambled, drank too much, and, anytime the spirit moved him, would up and take off and not return for sometimes a month. Arnold always accepted him back. Of course he quarrelled, he complained, but the villagers who heard him were firm in their reply: 'Man, you like it. You like Norbert going and coming when he please, doing what he want. You like it.'

More than his leavings, Norbert would steal Arnold's money, sell a pair of shoes, charge people and pocket the money, not charge some people at all, and do every other form of wickedness to be imagined in the circumstances. It must have been because Norbert was so indisputably in the wrong it moved Arnold to exhibit one of his rare qualities, compassion. It was as if Arnold needed Norbert as the means through which to declare not only to the world, but to himself, that he had such a quality, to prove to himself that he was not the cantankerous person people made him out to be. So, on those occasions when he welcomed back the everlasting prodigal, Arnold, forgiving and compassionate, would be imbued with the idea of his own goodness, and he would feel that in the world, truly, there was not more generous a man than he.

Today was one such day. Two weeks before Christmas Norbert had left to go for a piece of ice over by the rumshop a few yards away. He had returned the day before. 'Yes,' thought Arnold, 'look at me I not vex.' Arnold was glad for the help, for he had work that people had already paid advances on and would be coming in to collect before New Year's Day. That was one thing he appreciated about Norbert. Norbert was faithful, but Norbert had to get serious about the right things. He was faithful to too many frivolous things. He was faithful to the girl who dropped in and wanted a dress, to a friend who wanted a nip. A friend would pass in a truck and say, 'Norbert, we going San Fernando.' Norbert would put down the shoes he was repairing, jump on the truck without a change of underwear even and go. It wasn't rum. It was some craziness, something inside him, that just took hold of him. Sometimes, a week later he would return, grimy, stale, thin, as if he had just hitchhiked around the world in coal bins, slip into the shop, sit down and go back to work as if nothing out of the way had happened. And he could work when he was working. Norbert could work. Any shop in Port of Spain would be glad to have him. Faithful worker. Look at that! This week when most tradesmen had already closed up for Christmas there was Norbert working like a machine to get people's shoes ready. Appreciation. It shows appreciation. People don't have appreciation again, but Norbert had it for him. Is how you treat people, he thought. You have to understand them. Look how cool he here working in my shoemaker shop this big Old Year's Day when all over the island people fêteing.

At the door, he was watching two girls going down the street, nice, young, with the spirit of rain and breezes about them. Then his eyes picked up a donkey cart approaching slowly from the direction of the Main Road which led to Sangre Grande, and he stood there in front of his shoemaker shop, his lips pulled back and looked at the cart come up and go past. Old Man Moses, the charcoal burner, sat dozing in the front, his chin on his chest, and the reins in his lap. To the back sat a small boy with a cap on and a ragged shirt, his eyes alert, his feet hanging over the sides of the cart, one hand resting on a small brown and white dog sitting next to him.

Place dead, he thought, seeing the girls returning; and, looking up at the sky, he saw the dark clouds and that it was going to rain and he looked at the cart. 'Moses going up in the bush. Rain going to soak his tail,' he said. And as if suddenly irritated by that thought, he said, 'You mean Moses ain't have no family he could spend New Year's by,' his tone drumming up his outrage. 'Why his family can't take him in and let him eat and drink and be merry for the New Year instead of going up in the bush for rain to soak his tail? ... That is how we living in this world,' he said, seating himself on the workbench and reaching for the shoe to be repaired. 'That is how we living. Like beast.'

'Maybe he want to go up in the bush,' Norbert said. 'Maybe he going to attend his coal pit, to watch it that the coals don't burn up and turn powder.'

'Like blasted beast,' Arnold said. 'Beast,' as if he had not heard Norbert.

But afterwards, after he had begun to work, had gotten into the rhythm of sewing and cutting and pounding leather, and had begun the soft waxing of the twine, the sense of the approaching new year hit him and he thought of the girls and of the rain, and he thought of his own life and his loneliness and his drinking and of the world and of people, people without families, and on pavements and in orphanages and those on park benches below trees. 'The world have to check up on itself,' he said. 'The world have to check up ... And you, Norbert, you have to check up on yourself,' he said broaching for the first time on the matter of

Norbert's leaving two weeks before Christmas and returning only yesterday.

'I not against you. You know I not against you. I talk because I know what life is. I talk because I know about time. Time is all we have, boy. Time ... A time to live and a time to die. You heard what I say, Norbert?'

'What you say?'

'I say, it have a time to live and a time to die ... You think we living?'

Norbert leaned his head back a little for a few moments and he seemed to be gazing into space, thinking, concentrating.

'We dying,' he said, 'we dying no arse.'

'You damn right. Rum killing us. Rum. Not bombs or cancer or something sensible. Rum. You feel Rum should kill you?'

Norbert drew the twine out of the stick and smiled.

'But in this place, Rum must kill you. What else here could kill a man? What else to do but drink and waste and die. That is why I talk. People don't understand me when I talk; but that is why I talk.'

Norbert threaded the twine through the stitch with his smile and in one hand he held the shoe and with the other he drew out the twine: 'We dying no arse!' as if he had hit on some truth to be treasured now.

'We dying, no arse!'

'That is why I talk. I want us to check up, to put a little oil in your lamp, to put a little water in your wine.'

Norbert laughed. He was thinking with glee, even as he said it, 'We dying no arse, all o'we, everybody. Ha ha ha ha,' and he took up his hammer and started to pound in the leather over the stick, 'Ha ha ha ha ha!'

Arnold had finished the shoe he was repairing and he saw now the pile of shoes in the shoemaker shop. 'One day I going to sell out all the shoes that people leave here. They hurry hurry for you to repair them. You use leather, twine, nails, time. You use time, and a year later, the shoes still here watching you. Going to sell out every blasted one of them this new year.'

'All o'we, every one of us,' Norbert chimed.

'That is why this shoemaker shop always like a junk heap.'

'Let us send for a nip, nuh,' Norbert said, and as Arnold looked at him, 'I will buy. This is old year's, man.'

'Rum?' Arnold paused, 'How old you is, boy?'

'Twenty-nine.'

'Twenty-nine! You making joke. You mean I twenty one years older than you. We dying in truth. Norbert, we dying. Boy, life really mash you up.' And he threw down the shoes he was going to repair.

'We have three more shoes that people coming for this evening,' Norbert said, cautioning. 'Corbie shoes, Synto shoes and Willie Paul sandals.'

Arnold leaned and picked up the shoe again. 'Life ain't treat you good at all. I is twenty one years older than you? Norbert, you have to check up,' he said with desperate urgency. 'Listen, man, you getting me frighten. When I see young fellars like you in this condition I does get frighten ... Listen. Norbert, you tell me something! I looking mash up like you? Eh? Tell me the truth. I looking mash up like you?'

Norbert said, 'We dying no arse, all o'we, every body.'

'No. Serious. Tell me, I looking mash up like you?'

'Look, somebody by the door,' Norbert said.

'What do you want,' Arnold snapped. It was one of the village girls, a plump one with a bit of her hair plastered down over her forehead making her look like a fat pony.

'You don't have to shout at me, you know. I come for Synto shoes.'

'Well, I don't want no loitering by the door. Come inside and siddown and wait. I just now finishing it.' He saw her turn to look outside and she said something to somebody. 'Somebody there with you?'

'She don't want to come in.'

'Let her come in too. I don't want no loitering by that door. This is a business place.' He called out, 'Come in. What you hanging back for?'

The girl who came in was the one who reminded him of rain and moss and leaves. He tried to look away from her, but he couldn't. And she too was looking at him. 'You fraid me?' And he didn't know how his voice sounded, though at that moment he thought he wanted it to sound tough.

'A little,' she said.

'Siddown,' he said, and Norbert's eyes nearly popped open. What was he seeing? Arnold was getting up and taking the chair from the corner, dusting it too. 'Sit down. The shoes will finish just now.'

She watched him work on the shoe and the whole shoemaker shop was big like all space filled with breathlessness and rain and moss and green leaves.

'You is Synto daughter?'

'Niece' she said.

And when he was finished repairing the shoes, he looked around for a paper bag in which to put them, because he saw that she had not come with any bag herself. 'When you coming for shoes you must bring something to wrap it in. You can't go about with shoes in your hand just so.'

'Yes,' she said. 'Yes.' Quickly as if wanting to please him.

He found some old newspaper he was saving to read when he had time and he folded the shoes in it and wrapped it with twine and gave it to her and she took it and she said 'thank you' with that funny little face and that voice that made something inside him ache and she left, leaving the breathlessness in the shoemaker shop and the scent of moss and aloes and leaves and it was like if all his work was finished. And when he caught his breath he pushed his hand in his pocket and brought out money and said to Norbert, 'Go and buy a nip.' And they drank the nip, the two of them, and he asked Norbert, 'Where you went when you went for the ice?' And he wasn't really listening for no answer for he had just then understood how Norbert could, how a man could, leave and go off. He had just understood how he could leave everything just so and go.

'You had a good time?' Though those weren't the right words. A good time! People didn't leave for a good time. It was something more. It was out of something deeper, a call, something that was awakened in the blood, the mind. 'You know what I mean?'

'Yes,' Norbert said, kinda sadly, soft, and frightened for Arnold but not wanting to show it.

Arnold said, 'I dying too.' And then he stood up and said sort of sudden. 'This place need some pictures. And we must keep paper bags like in a real establishment', and with that same smile he said, 'Look at that, eh. That girl say she fraid me a little. Yes, I suppose that is correct. A little. Not that she fraid me. She fraid me a little.'

When they closed the shop that evening they both went up Tapana Trace by Britto. Britto was waiting for them.

'Ah,' he said, 'Man reach. Since before Christmas I drinking and I can't get drunk. It ain't have man to drink rum with again. But I see man now.'

They went inside and Britto cleared the table and put three bottles of rum on it, one before each one of them, a mug of water and a glass each, and they began to drink.

Half an hour later the parang band came in and they sang an *aguanaldo* and a *joropo* and they drank and Norbert started to sing with them the nice festive Spanish music that made Arnold feel he wished he could cry. And then it was night and the parang band was still there and Britto wife and family came in and a couple of Britto friends and the women started dancing with the little children and then Josephine, Britto neighbour, held on to Arnold and pulled him onto the floor to dance, and he tried to dance a little and then he sat down and they took the gas lamp and pumped it and Britto's wife brought out the portion of *lappe* that she had been cooking on a wood fire in the yard and they ate and drank and with the music and the children, and the women, everything, the whole thing was real sweet. It was real sweet. And Norbert more drunk than sober sitting in a corner chatting down Clemencia sister, picked up another bottle of rum and broke the seal and about to put it to his lips, caught Arnold's eye and hesitated, then he put it to his lips, again. He said 'Let me dead.' And Arnold sat and thought about this girl, the one that filled the world with breathlessness and the scent of aloes and moss and he felt if she was sitting there beside him he would be glad to dead too.

JANICE SHINEBOURNE

Janice Shinebourne was born in Guyana. She was a
teacher in rural Berbice before she moved to the capital,
Georgetown. She attended the University of Guyana and
worked in Georgetown as a bank clerk, newspaper
reporter, librarian and researcher with the Curriculum
Development Unit at the Ministry of Education. She is
currently doing postgraduate research in literature in
London.

THE BRIDGE

The Bridge is set in Guyana, at Rose Hall in Canje. A village once thrived there. It was demolished by Bookers Sugar Estates in the mid-fifties and the inhabitants dispersed and re-settled elsewhere. The story portrays the experience of the character Mannick when he keeps a rendezvous at the bridge over the canal, one of the old landmarks in the desolate landscape. But the vision of childhood which haunts him and other incidents at the bridge impinge on the rendezvous.

   Janice Shinebourne

THE BRIDGE

Mannick stood on the bridge, looking down at the trench in which a few naked boys were swimming. Their bodies were slender and brown. They looked like fishes fighting against pulling lines as they swam with furious strokes, churning up the water.

Mannick thought briefly of how strange it was that he couldn't remember how he used to feel cutting through the water, in that same trench.

He watched, fascinated, at one boy who had climbed out of the water, a length of weed trailing like a dead animal from his hand. The surface of it was a conglomeration of small green leaves. The underside of it resembled a caterpillar's belly; small white roots protruded from the layer of mud beneath. The boy began to spin the weed in the air: water whipped out of it: then he let it go flying through the air. It landed on the back of another boy standing on the rim of a moored punt; he fell, face forward, into the water. Almost at once, he emerged, his hair wet on his face, spitting, gasping, treading water.

Mannick turned away and looked towards the road which disappeared around another bridge in the distance. There high bushes hid the next village where Lizzie lived. He expected to see her coming along the road but it was empty.

The sun was going down behind the line of cane trees hiding the horizon.

Mannick's health was bad. His wife had taken another man into his house; he could see it from where he stood. It was a little way from the distant bridge, at the side of the road, opposite the Anglican church, tall against the trees. Behind him, the sugar factory sprawled out like a sleeping monster: puffs of smoke issued from its chimneys. Further away, white bungalows. He had money once, was lucky with women, blind to problems, happy.

Now he drove the magistrate to court in the village, and at night caught the late bus home. He liked to sit in the dark of the bus and listen to the women talk. When he got home, he found his dinner waiting in the small room on the ground floor of his house.

He could see Lizzie now. She walked towards him steadily, swaying her hips too much. She was very thin, her face was drawn. Mannick looked down at himself: his trousers flapped around his legs. He did not want to go on.

Later, when he and Lizzie came out from under the bridge, they found the boys sitting on the rails. One boy muttered and the others laughed. Then they jumped off the rails and walked off the bridge, towards the village. Mannick watched the boys until they disappeared in the dark which was falling gradually.

ROGER MAIS

Roger Mais was born in Jamaica in 1905 and died there in 1955. As well as being a distinguished author he was a painter, dramatist and poet.

His most famous novels are *The Hills were Joyful Together* (1953), *Brother Man* (1954), and *Black Lightning* (1955).

In the early 1940's, Roger Mais published in Jamaica two collections of his own short stories – *Face and Other Stories*, and *And Most of All Man*. But he only became widely known as a writer later, when his three novels were published in England by Jonathan Cape. Of these novels, the first two, *The Hills were Joyful Together*, (1953) and *Brother Man* (1954) are better known, and Mais's passionate concern in them for the wretched of the Kingston slums and the Kingston underworld have led to his work being described as 'yard literature'. In this mode of writing there is usually an urban slum setting, characters speak deep-level dialect, and the presentation of the conditions under which the mainly black characters vividly spend their brief and violent lives is socially realistic.

The two short stories chosen from *Face and Other Stories* are not 'yard literature', but they show Mais's social consciousness. In 'Red Dirt Don't Wash', which has a suburban setting, a newly-arrived rural character courts a superior maid working in a well-to-do household; and in 'Look Out' a girl from the country is a virtual prisoner in the lower middle-class home of her brother whose wife and child she has to take care of in return for exposure to the larger world of the city.

In the first story, Mais moves, uncharacteristically, towards comedy, making fun of Miranda's pretensions ('She was not a cook, though she made delicious pastries. Not a washerwoman, although she was entrusted with the washing of the doilies and the table-runners and the cushion covers and the table napkins and the handkerchiefs and the silk stockings, and dainty things like that'); and showing up the clumsiness and country boy style of Adrian, out to impress the knowing Miranda. But it isn't long before we realise that Adrian's innocence is preferable to Miranda's experience of the brave new city world. At the end, illumination comes for Adrian who cuts himself free of illusion, recognising 'the cleanness and the wholeness' of the red dirt he had been trying to forget in his dreams of the powdered city girl. There is the obvious contrast between Miranda's powder (intoxicating, illusory) and Adrian's red dirt, but this reader cannot forget in *Red Dirt Don't Wash* the freshness and excitement of Adrian so concisely caught in the simile, 'his heart was like a leaping fish held in the hand', a simile which speaks too of Adrian's roots in the saving red dirt of home and origin.

Kenneth Ramchand

RED DIRT DON'T WASH

He stood awkwardly, shifting his weight from one foot to the other, looking through the open pantry window with the dancing eyes of a boy about to receive a treat of good things. But it wasn't the jam tarts that the maid, Miranda, was taking hot from the oven and putting in a dish that held his gaze rapt. It was Miranda herself, flicking her fingers smartly and putting them to her mouth as the hot baking tin burnt them.

Her trim figure in her blue uniform, chic, neat-fitting, made his eyes swim in his head. It was as though whenever she was in sight he couldn't take his eyes off her. She ravished his senses. And simple country yokel that he was he didn't know how to set about making a girl like Miranda. For Miranda was city-bred, and house-broke, and all the things that he wasn't. She had training. She had refinement, culture. She knew how to lay a table all by herself. Things like that. She knew all the tableware, all the silver, by name. She could tell them over to you, without even stumbling once. He had often helped her polish them, so he knew.

She knew which was a cake fork from a fish fork. She knew a cake server from a cheese server. She knew a tea plate from a breakfast plate, and which one of the shiny mugs was a coffee percolator, and which was for hot water, and which for cream. There wasn't anything she didn't know.

And she had let him help her after his work in the garden was over. She had let him stand near as near to her over the kitchen and wash dishes . . . and feel the presence of her, the delicious, maddening nearness of her go through him like sharp knives, like red hot needles.

He could get the smell of her in his nostrils, standing that near to her; like you get the smell of a ripe fruit in your nostrils when you bite it! She smelt like a lady. Just like any lady. He wondered what it was that gave her that delicious, wonderful, ravishing perfume to her body; and so he had been tempted to stand on tip-toe outside the crack in the window of her room, where the gummed paper just didn't cover it quite and take a good long look at her . . . one day after she had come out from the servants' shower bath. What he had seen had devastated him. He had come away feeling dizzy, faint; as though something was happening inside him, in his stomach.

He had seen all her loveliness in the nude. For one devastating instant he had held within his dull, unimaginative eye, all her loveliness that was without blemish; and his heart was like a leaping fish held in the hand.

But he knew now what it was that gave her body that delicious smell, that mounted to his nostrils like incense, and held his senses within a hazy sort of swoon, and gave him that dry feeling in his throat, and that queer feeling in his stomach. It was powder!

She took powder from a large red tin and dusted it all over her body. Not just dabbing it on her face alone, like other girls did, but all over her body!

Such luxury! Such expensiveness! It made his head reel.

Made him aware of his own grossness, his own inferiority, his own lack of polish and refinement. Made him aware of his own soiled and patched clothes, and his own large bare feet, his own rough red skin, which seemed as though the red dirt of his Clarendon hills had come there to stay, and couldn't even wash off.

When his work was done in the garden, when he had washed down the car, and rubbed it down with a chamois cloth until it shone, she would let him carry the pan in which she washed napkins and doilies and table-runners and handkerchiefs, and small things like that (for you must understand that Miranda was no ordinary servant, but a lady's maid. She was not a cook, though she made delicious pastries. Not a washer-woman, although she was entrusted with the washing of the doilies and the table-runners and the cushion covers and the table napkins and the handkerchiefs and the silk stockings, and dainty things like that). She would let him carry the pan with its heaping foam of white suds from the sink under the standpipe in the backyard to the deal table on the back verandah; and he would just stand and watch her, her arms up to the elbows in suds. Now and then she would look up from her work and smile at him, and he grinned back at her all the time.

He learnt a lot from just standing around talking and joking with her; and helping her through her pantry chores sometimes.

He told her about the place he came from. All about his people up in the mountains. And the ways in which their ways were different from the ways of the people who lived in towns. And she laughed a lot. She was a great one for laughing.

'They are simple, jealous folk, but really the kindest people in the world. We understand each other. We know what makes a man or a woman happy, and what makes them mad. All the people in my district get along together like one big family.'

'My! And I suppose all the girls and the men work together in the fields? Don't tell me that! Really?'

'It just come natural for everybody to pitch in and do whatever work there is to be done – whether in the fields, or about the yard, or in the house – it's all the same. But mostly the men do the heavier work. And women in the family way don't do any but the slightest things.'

'You don't say!' She squealed with laughter.

'They say,' she remarked, twinkling up at him provocatively, 'that all the people are red – like you. Is that true?'

He just grinned back at her for answer.

'Even the dirt is red. All red dirt. They say the people's skins take its colour from the dirt, if they live there long enough – all their lives, I suppose.' She frowned a little, flicking soapsuds from her forearms and hands. 'They say the red dirt gets on them, and even *inside* them, under their skins, and just stays there.'

'Don't know 'bout that. I 'spects it's so! Never give it no thought before.'

'It's true. For no matter where you meet a mountain man you can always know him. I guess it must be true – that red dirt don't wash.'

Once or twice she let him walk home with her, where she stayed with her cousin who was another kind of maid – an office maid – because she got along better with gentlemen, she said.

But always she led him through back lanes, and down through a dry gully course, and always she parted with him at a certain spot some little way from the house. And he never questioned her. He never thought to question anything she did.

He knew this girl was right – just right in everything she did or said. Almost a lady. Much too good for him, just a country boy. Big and clumsy and awkward and halting in speech and gestures. Almost a living caricature of a country boy, he was so bad. But he knew also that he wanted her, even though she was miles too good for him. And at first it didn't trouble him at all, the thought of his wanting her so badly. But after a bit it got to haunting him at nights. Days and nights, so that he got no rest from the thought of her that was sweet torture to him.

He would lie in his bed and remember every sprightly word and vivid gesture of hers. How she looked at him, looking up sideways, like a little bird, and laughing in his face. Well, a girl didn't look at a fellow like that unless she – she kind of liked him. A bit.

He remembered how she put out her hand once and touched his arm – and grabbed hard hold of his arm around the bicep muscle, and said 'My!', admiringly. Meaning how hard and strong he was. He remembered how she let a clothes-pin fall down his back once, and laughing that squealing laugh of hers, ran her hand down after it, and fetched it up slowly from way down at his waist – sky-larking – while he just sat still and let her do what she would with him. He remembered all that, and it was as though things were going on inside him all the time, in his blood secretly.

Once or twice he saw her walking out with nice looking young men – chauffeurs, and such. He envied them. Not alone because she was walking out with them, but because of something they had that he lacked. A poise, a certain assurance that was almost swagger. Shoes on their feet. The way they wore their clothes.

He had never worn shoes in his life, but once. Once, when he was about seventeen, his gran'pa had bought him a pair of yellow boots to wear Sundays. They were grand boots. They must have cost a pile of money. He wore them once to church. And that was enough. His feet inside boots didn't feel like his at all. He lost possession of them, and they behaved as though they knew it.

He let them go cheap to a boy he knew from the neighbouring district, about his size. The other fellow got a real bargain. They were grand boots. But he didn't care. He bought him a goat with the money. Now there were six goats the last time he heard from home and more coming along. He didn't care about the boots. Boots wore out and got old so you had to throw them away. But a goat gave you more and more goats. He liked goats. Now there was something he knew about.

One evening as he walked home with her – they were halfway through the dry gully course when he made bold enough to carry out the desperate scheme he had been turning over slowly, methodically in his mind all along – he suddenly blurted out.

'I seen you walking out with fellows.'

She looked up at him quickly.

Her eyes, he noticed, were bright like stars, her lips slightly parted, as though she were panting from walking too fast; but they had been coming along slowly, saying nothing, mostly; their bodies just touching, or almost touching, in the dark.

He said, stopping suddenly and looking down at her face.

'I would like for you to come out with me, once in a while. Eh?'

'How?' 'Where?'

'Movies?' It was a bold gesture. He had never been to a movie in his life ... now he was asking this girl to go with him. Just like that.

Unconsciously he was taking on to himself some of the easy swagger of the young men he'd seen Miranda with.

He said, coming closer to her: 'What say we go to a movie Sat'day night? You'n me. Eh?'

She looked up at his face ... and away ... and down at his feet.

Suddenly, unexpectedly, she burst out laughing. She just fell on the bank and squealed with laughter. She *was* a one for laughing!

But it did something to him. For one thing it made him lose all his recently acquired swagger; for another it made him all of a sudden fiercely resolved within his mind to make her take it all back. To make her look at him as she looked at her natty young men. Plus the special look she gave *him* – that said as plain as anything that she could like him – and more than a bit.

'All right,' he said in a terrible, calm voice. 'I know I'm not good enough for you. But all the same I love you, see.'

She stopped laughing immediately. She put the back of her hand to her mouth.

'Adrian,' she said. 'I – I'm not laughing – at what you think. I'm just laughing like – oh you don't understand about women, or you would know.'

He was silent for a while, chewing on this. Of course she was right. He didn't understand about women, either. Not her kind. She was miles above him. She would take *some* understanding. Of a sudden he felt great humility, standing before her ... great humility, and with it a great resolve.

The very next day he put the first part of his resolve into effect. He asked for time off in the afternoon and went into town to one of the big stores where they sold shoes and things.

'How much for the yellow ones in the window?' he asked, after the man at the store had showed him half-a-dozen pairs from the shelves.

'Now there's a pair of shoes for you! Genuine vici kid. You can't do better than that at any price, anywhere. It's marked twenty-five shillings. We sold the lot before this at twenty-seven and six. But I tell you what. Now I'm doing the best I can for you. It isn't like I'd do this for everyone. But I'll put them in for you – special – for twenty-two and elevenpence.'

'I'll take them,' said Adrian, without hesitation.

All that money for a pair of shoes. But he didn't mind that a bit. They were genuine vici kid. Goat skin leather, he knew that too. You could buy two goats, let alone the skins, for twenty-two and eleven. But he didn't mind that a bit. She put powder on all over her. He seen it himself. He knew!

Came Saturday night; and to Adrian it seemed none too soon, either.

He put on his best Sunday clothes of blue serge, and his yellow shoes. He looked down at his feet and admired the gleaming shine of them.

He went round by the back of the tennis court from the garage, through the little enclosed vegetable garden, to the back porch, where he knew he would find her, his shoes creaking faintly across the grass. His feet felt as though they were taking him places. This was different to just walking. Just walking you set your feet down, one before the other, without thinking about it. He'd heard about a man walking on a clothes line wire high above the ground. He'd often thought about it, wondering how it felt. He didn't any more after that night. He knew.

The family had dined, and had gone out in the car. He knew just where she would be, what doing, and that she would be alone.

When she saw him, she just stood looking at him for a time. Then she suddenly burst out laughing, as though she wouldn't stop.

She said: 'Where you all dressed up going to, Adrian?' Like that.

He said, coming up close to her: 'We're steppin' out.'

'My! Who an' you?'

'You an' me. Remember? You said if I got myself some shoes ... remember? Well, I got them. They cost a heap of money too. But I don't give it a thought.'

He swelled out his chest. He was almost as big as a barrel around. For a moment she looked at him with slightly troubled eyes. His body looked so strong and fine, beneath all the marks of the country lad on him. The awkwardness. You could see at a glance his flesh was good and strong. Her eyes sort of misted over a bit. For a moment though. And then they dropped to his feet again.

'What's the matter, don't they look all right?'

'Sure. They're swell. They must have cost a pile of money, I bet.'

And she burst out laughing.

At first he didn't understand, and he started laughing too, with his hearty country lad's guffaw. And then he saw her face; saw how she looked at his feet, and looked up and laughed again. And suddenly the laughter died out of him. Leaving him, as it were, standing there foolishly, with his mouth open, staring at her.

She said, curiously enough: 'Don't make me laugh!' gasping.

'But what – why – what's the matter with them?'

'Nothing, big boy. The shoes are fine. But they're not yours, that's all. They don't fit you, see?'

'They're a bit tight. But my feet'll get used to them after a spell.'

'That's where you are wrong. They never will. They'll always look just what they are – a pair of shoes carrying your feet around. All your life you've never worn shoes. You know that's true.'

He nodded.

'You can't educate them feet to shoes, big boy. Not as long as you live. You'll always *feel* as though you wearing shoes, and you'll *look* just the way you feel. Always. No, it's no good. Better take them off now. Perhaps if you clean the soles a bit they might even take them back from you at the store where you bought them.'

'But I don't want them to take them back. They're mine. You know why I got them,' he said, looking at them self-consciously. 'It was all for you.'

At that she burst out laughing again.

'Do you think I'm going out with you, in *them*?' she demanded scornfully. It was no use. No use at all thinking about sparing his feelings. He just didn't have sense enough for a child. Nothing short of this could make him understand. It was a pity, but none of her cooking, she was sure.

'I get you,' he said, slowly. 'I'm not good enough for you. Oh I know it. Still, you said if I got myself some shoes, like ... '

'Don't take it hard, big boy.' She laid a hand on his arm. But for a moment only, then she took it away. 'I tell you what,' she said in a low, husky voice. Perversely the firm, strong, clean touch of his flesh stung her like nettles; went driving with sharp pangs through her, stirring something in her blood. 'Tomorrow night we'll go for a walk. I know a place we can go where nobody'll be around.' A pause. 'That's a promise, now.'

But he remained for a space, looking away, saying nothing. Then he turned slowly, painfully away, with the unaccustomed pain of walking in tight shoes. But he was resolved upon this thing. He was going to walk them in ... going to walk those darned feet of his in. He'd do it if it broke his heart, if it killed him.

After walking about a mile, he came to a lonely spot on the road. He didn't even know where he was, but he didn't care.

He sat down on the side of the road and pulled off his shoes. He took each foot between his hands and chafed it gently, wriggling his toes until they felt like his own again.

She was just leading him on, she was. Playing him for a sucker ... all the time laughing at him, and carrying on with other fellows ... and laughing at him behind his back.

He felt in his pocket for his clasp knife and opened and tested the blade passing it along the ball of his thumb. There was a cold, still, sullen look in his eyes. Deadly like anger burned down to glowing coals of a still white heat.

What she wanted to make of him a blooming Cinderella for? Just so she could laugh at him!

He lifted his head and stared blankly up at the cold stars. There was nothing there. Beyond them the sombre mountains. They reminded him of his own mountains that seemed so far away, almost unreal – veiled as with a mist – and the mist was in his own eyes – trying to see byond the St Andrew hills, beyond the stars, horizon; space limitless like that.

He tested the edge of the blade against the ball of his thumb. And it was right. What she wanted to make of him a blooming Cinderella for?

He took the shoes, one at a time, and cut them into thin strips – all but the soles, which, because of their toughness he just cut any way.

Back there he belonged, where there was red dirt everywhere, and people didn't go around wearing shoes. Red dirt everywhere, on the tilled land as far as the eyes could see, and on the faces and bare arms and legs of men and women. Good, clean red dirt that he loved, that was the symbol of home to him, and more. Clean, happy faces that he loved, that were all frankness and homeliness. All that went for cleanness and wholeness. It was clean, the red dirt of his land, the place of his birth.

He looked down at the jagged strips of leather in his hand and his face became wonderfully luminous. He even smiled.

They were good shoes. Genuine vici kid. He paid twenty-two and elevenpence for them at the store.

In 'Look Out', the un-named girl who spends her time
'leaning against the gate, looking out doing nothing …
thinking about nothing', is Mais's representation of that
disillusionment after the march to the city that appears
in Martin Carter's great poem, *The University of
Hunger*.

Both these stories are well-shaped and tightly struc-
tured, each moving by clear progression towards a
moment of truth, each driving to the heart of a crisis for
the characters. Especially interesting are Mais's sugges-
tive dialogue, the conveying of author's attitudes without any jarring intrusion of the author's voice, and,
obviously of a piece with these, an ability to enter
delightedly into the thoughts and feelings of individual
characters and impersonate them. The exploitation of
short sentences in 'Look Out', the play with the word
'nothing', and the use of the moon help to convey the
intensity of the girl's consciousness, illustrating Mais's
deliberate craft at its most discreet.

Kenneth Ramchand

LOOK OUT

She was at the gate, resting her arms on the top rail, her chin on her
arms, looking out. Out being just any place that wasn't In. The
moon rode high in the sky above great banks of clouds. Last night
the moon was in eclipse. It was like someone had pulled a red curtain
down over the face of the moon. But it was the moon all the same. Come
clouds, come eclipse, it was all the same moon.

Somebody was calling to her from the house. That would be her
sister-in-law. Her dear brother's wife. But she didn't pay no attention to
her. She was a little cracked in the head. It was the moon, the moon
made her come out from inside herself where she was locked away; inside
her head, behind a smile that was like the double-blank in the box of
dominoes. The moon made her come out from behind that dead smile
and talk her head off. And shout her head off. But nobody paid no
attention to her at all. Her brother's half-crazy wife.

She heard the sound of boots. Someone was coming slowly up the
road. She didn't bother to turn her head to look. Just someone coming up
the road. No matter.

She said out loud. Just thinking: 'Couldn't be gone ten yet.'

He stopped as though she had spoken to him. He was wearing khaki
pants and a blue sport shirt. There was something about him that was

lean and hard and clean. Clean like he'd just come out of the tub. He stopped right under the street lamp that was before the gate and looked at his wrist watch.

'Ten past,' he said.

She made a little sound with her tongue against her teeth.

But he was still there. Hesitating in his mind. Whether to stop and chat with her, or go on. She didn't give him any encouragement, or otherwise. She just kept on looking out, her chin resting upon her arms, her arms resting on the top rail of the gate.

'You waiting for someone,' he said. But he wasn't asking. He stood there still hesitating in his mind whether to stop and chat, or to go on along his way.

Under the lamp post there was a diamond shaped sign that said 'Bus Stop'.

'The bus stops here,' he said. But he wasn't asking. He said it like he was reading the sign aloud, but to himself.

'It's going to rain,' he said. Lifting his face to the moon. 'Did you see the eclipse of the moon last night?' As you might say 'read any good books lately?'

'Uh-huh,' she said.

Somebody was calling her from the house. Calling in a loud queer voice. He moved just one step. That took him one step nearer to the bus sign, so that he now stood on neutral ground. He might be waiting for the bus at the stop sign, or he might be talking to a girl at her gate, if the bus should come along and he didn't want to take it.

'That's just my sister-in-law,' she said. 'I don't pay no mind to her.' Lifting a foot to the lowest rail of the gate, but without otherwise changing her position.

He lit a cigarette carelessly and looked up at the moon. He stood for a while like that, not saying anything, just looking up.

The clouds were banked up high against the moon, so that she looked wild and stormy tonight, and as though filled with a great unrest.

But cho! it was only the moon. Always the moon. The rest was trimmings. They didn't mean anything.

The man said: 'It's going to rain.' Blowing out a cloud of smoke. To him the trimmings meant something.

She wanted to laugh.

'What you are? A weather-prophet?'

'Them clouds,' he said. 'See them dark ones underneath like? They say rain!'

'Ain't you smart,' she mocked.

'That's right,' he said, without his face changing.

The man was a fool. She would snub him. She would wait for him to say something to her, and she would take pains to snub him.

Besides it wasn't right she should be here chatting with him. At any moment her brother might ride up on his bicycle. He would scold her, inside. Though who could say she was in fact chatting with anyone? Wasn't her fault there was a bus stop just outside their gate. Wasn't she put it there.

She said: 'Weren't you going for a walk?'

He said without looking at her: 'I was.'

'I changed my mind now,' he said. 'I'm waiting for the bus.'

Her foot on the rail started of itself bouncing her knee up and down. Like she might have been hushing a baby to bye-bye. She was doing that without thinking about it.

But he saw it out of the corner of his eye. Without looking around. Saw her bare knee bouncing. It was a pretty knee – to pass up just like that. She might be waiting for someone, sure. But all the same where he was standing was public thoroughfare. He might be going some place, or not. Wasn't anybody's business. She didn't have to answer back if she didn't want. He could say, it's going to rain, without him talking to anyone. Just saying it looked like it was going to rain.

The three children had been put to bed long ago. Her brother's children. Couldn't be anything she could do that her sister-in-law kept calling, calling at her. She just wouldn't pay any mind to her. Let her call. It was the moon. The moon was full tonight. Last night there had been an eclipse, and it looked just like someone had drawn a red blind down over the face of the moon. And bit by bit the blind had lifted. Until the last time she had looked at it, it was just like someone had broken a piece out of the moon somewhere near the top.

A few people passed in the street. She heard them come and go without looking at them. Except when they passed her line of vision looking straight out before her, she didn't see them. Two, three bicycles went by, but nothing to make her take her mind off what she was thinking about – nothing.

She wasn't thinking about anything tonight. She wasn't waiting for anyone either. Leastways she didn't know anyone she could be waiting for. Except it was that she was waiting for her brother to come home? And why should she be waiting for her brother to come home? She was just tired of staying indoors doing nothing. With a crazy woman for company. She was just leaning against the gate, looking out, doing nothing. Thinking about nothing.

Sometimes it got so bad sitting indoors with only her sister-in-law for company, that she wanted to put her hands up to her head and scream!

But she wasn't going to do that. She wasn't going to let it get her that way. The loneliness. The emptiness of everything. Ever since she had left home and come to live with her brother in the city. Because his wife was that way again, bringing them into the world faster than she could look after them.

If she let it get her, someday she would be getting like her sister-in-law. All shut inside her head. Her face blank. Her eyes. That fixed dead smile. All like the double-blank in the box of dominoes.

She hadn't known it was going to be like this in the city. Else she wouldn't have left home in the first place. Short of them hog-tying her and dragging her here. She hadn't known her brother meant to lock her inside a house and not want her to see anyone from outside, and not want her to have any friends or go anywhere. If she had known!

Maybe he was just one of those fresh guys. The city, she was warned, was full of them. Or maybe he was a married man himself with a family of three squalling children, and his wife that way again. But cho! That didn't bother her. She wasn't even giving him a thought. That way.

'Ever seen a man climb right up one of them electric line poles?' he said, looking at her.

'No,' she said. Was he trying to be funny?

Ever seen a man climbing a pole! What was he coming with now. What did he take her for? A fool? What was his line? What was he getting at? Ever seen a man climbing a pole indeed! What sort of fast one did he think he was pulling out from up his sleeve now. What was he getting around to? What was he coming with now?

Cho! It must be one of those jokes he was trying to tell her. Just one of these fresh guys. Trying to get fresh with her.

'What you talking about, a man climbing a pole?' she said.

'That's me,' he said 'Linesman'.

'Linesman?' she said.

'Linesman. That's what they call us. Wire-monkeys. We look after the lines.'

So. That was it. He was telling her about himself.

'So what?' she said. Doing her stuff. Pretending she was indifferent.

'You ought to see me going up one of them poles,' he said.

'Why?' she said. Like that.

'With my steel spurs on,' he said.

Steel spurs! What next. What did he take her for, anyway?

'Steel spurs,' he said again. Looking at her.

At the sides of his boots, he said, for gripping the pole. How else could you climb a pole, he said, if you come to think about it.

But she didn't say anything. Just kept on as she was, leaning against the gate looking out. Her bare knee kept on bouncing like all the time she didn't know she was doing it.

So he was a wire-monkey. He climbed poles! He did that for a living. She could see him in her mind's eye climbing up that pole across the way hand over hand – like a monkey – without thinking about it. Wondering how soon her brother might be happening along.

He too was silent. Thinking his own thoughts.

Why didn't he say something? She was suddenly and unaccountably annoyed with him. What did he think he was doing just standing there pulling at his cigarette in a self-satisfied way, like the world and everything in it belonged to him tonight, not saying anything. Just taking it in. Just letting things come to him, and taking it all in. He had nerve!

She wanted to hear more about him. About this queer occupation of his anyway. Fancy doing that for a living! Or was he just taking her along? Trying to get fresh with her?

'What you do when you climb the pole?' she said.

'Oh, things. Fix the lines. Put in new ones. Tend them in general?'

That made sense at least. The lines would need fixing. Somehow she had never thought of it before. What a lot of queer occupations there must be in the world. So many queer jobs to be done. Somebody had to do them. It was the same all over the world. Her job for instance. Taking care of her sister-in-law, her brother's children. That was one of them. Somebody had to do it. That was why her brother didn't want her to have any friends. Because he wanted her to do that job. He had a long head to his body; her brother.

It was dangerous work too. He might easily get killed fooling with them wires. They were charged with electricity. She knew that. She could see him, without thinking about it, atop one of them poles, caught somehow in amongst the wires, burning up.

'Isn't it dangerous?' she said.

'Not worth speaking of,' he said. 'That is, if you know what your doing. Them wires carry a powerful lot of volts. If I was to tell you how much you wouldn't believe me. Some of them. Could kill you quicker than thinking. If you don't mind your step.

She said: 'I should think so!' And he looked at her quickly, and smiled.

So then: 'That don't seem to me much of a way for a man to make his living,' she said.

He laughed at that. Just laughed. As though he was saying to himself, well she didn't know anything. A girl like that!

The bus came up to the stop then. Somebody got off. Two people. A girl first, and a man after her. They went on down the road. She saw them without looking at them. The bus went on again.

'Weren't you waiting for the bus?' she said.

'Did I say I was?' he said.

She made no answer.

'Maybe I changed my mind,' he said. Without looking at her.

'You live here,' he said. But he wasn't asking. He had a way of saying things like that. Like he was just thinking out aloud.

She said nothing.

'Maybe you would care to go for a walk,' he said. Looking at her. 'Not tonight,' he said, before she could say anything. 'Some other night.' And left it like that.

'No! No!' she said quickly, shaking her head.

'Why?' he said.

'Don't ask me why. It can't be, that's why.'

He just laughed.

'Maybe you'll change your mind,' he said.

'No! No!' she said.

'All right, he said 'I was just saying. Anyone can change their mind.'

A bicycle came round the bend up the road. She knew, without knowing, that it was her brother coming home.

'You must go now,' she said, quickly. 'Please go now.'

He looked at her. His face started to laugh, but dropped it. It was as though he understood everything without her saying it.

'Your husband eh?'

'No, my brother. You must go now. Please!'

In those few words he understood everything. More than enough to go on. Things she hadn't meant to let out to him. Had let out without knowing.

You must go now! Please! That made it right with him. That told him something besides. That already there was something between them. Something tacit, and implicit. He wasn't slow in these things.

'Goodnight, then. Be seeing you', he said, without looking at her.

With his hands in his pockets he sauntered off carelessly. A young man taking the air.

'What you doing here? Who you waiting for?' her brother questioned suspiciously as he came up.

'Nothing. Nobody,' she answered.

'You should be inside,' he said. 'No sense to stand at the gate looking out, for nothing.'

The wind died down. Suddenly there was no wind at all. Not so much as would stir a leaf. A great drop of rain fell plop against her cheek. She put her hand up to her cheek and took it away wet.

'It's going to rain!' she said, looking at her hand, as though she had made a wonderful discovery.

'Get inside,' he said, harshly. 'Get inside now. You have no business standing out here like that, for nothing.'

She moved slowly to do his bidding. As though it was his will not hers that moved the muscles in her body. That moved her legs along. But her mind. That was not his. She looked up at the face of the moon. Last night it was in eclipse. Tonight it was restless and driven, with great black clouds driving across the face of it.

And suddenly she wanted to cry. But not here, where he could see her. Inside in her own little room. Where no one could see her. She would just put her hand down and cry. And not because she was sad. And not because she was happy. She only knew she wanted to put her head down and cry her eyes out. And all for nothing.

JAN WILLIAMS

Jan Williams was born in England of Trinidadian
parents and now lives in Guyana.

ARISE, MY LOVE

Grappling every day with the sea has dulled for Frank
the adventure of peering into its close green depths or of
diving into rocky caverns after lurking lobsters, and
conches that cling. In addition, the repetitive toil of
extracting from the dry and reluctant earth a sad crop of
cotton, corn and peas has wearied him into accepting
that his own life can grow no more.

In the huddle of thatched huts that was once a
prosperous village, nothing happens. Only from time to
time there comes a little sloop from another island.
Frank is determined that his young cousin, Fibi, should
rise above what he sees as a coarse and coarsening island
life. His life is spoilt, but Fibi is a golden creature whom
he, dark and uncouth though he is, will one day rescue
from a way of life into which an unkind fate has flung
her.

Jan Williams allows us to see and deplore the self-
contempt and the yearning for transformation and
otherness in Frank's obstinate idealisation of Fibi. At the
same time, however, we recognise the nobility of his
wish to save her from the wretched conditions of island
life. When he is confirmed in his suspicion that Fibi is
pregnant (a passing sloop), and that she is no different
from the other girls on the island, Frank batters her to
death and wedges her body in a cleft in the rocks.
Williams makes us recognise Frank's sickness as sickness.

But the myth wins. In the final paragraph, a blinding
force of love overwhelms Frank. He must return to Fibi
and to his own re-birth by drowning. His touch releases
her from the rock and the liberated spirit arises gracefully out of the water, overcoming at last in death the
suffocating conditions that had denied her highest self.

Kenneth Ramchand

ARISE, MY LOVE

E ver since Frank could remember, he had lived on the island. There was the high blue smudge of St Vincent to the north on clear days and nearer and clearly marked, if you turned your head, the sharp, saw-toothed hills of Union Island, with Carriacou as a blue backdrop beyond. He knew all the islands by name – all rocky, dry and reluctantly giving up during the short rainy season a pathetic little crop of cotton, corn and peas.

'Ain' nothin' ever happen,' Frank had been saying since he was small, although big enough to lend a hand in the boat and pull on an oar as he went out with Grandmere into the clear green waters within the reef to tend the fishpots and dive for lobsters and conches.

'Ain' nothin' ever happen nowheres 'cept birth an' death an' livin' in between,' Grandmere would say, pursing her thick lips and resting on her oar as she wiped the sweat off her face. And then she would go on rowing in short, swift jerks from the wrist, stopping every so often to peer into the clear green depths or to slip over the side to dive towards some rocky cavern in which her sharp eyes could see a lurking lobster or a bed of rock where the conches clung thickly.

Sometimes at low tide they would row within the waters of the reef out to Shell Island, a sandy shell-strewn spit on which in the old days a few coconut-palms had fought their losing battles against the sea. Nothing was left of them now but a few stumps, soggy and shell-covered, in a desert of whitened shells and coral, brightened at times by a yellow sea fan, a pink conch, a large, dappled brown cowrie hurled up by the rising tide and left to fade under the merciless sun and to whiten like old bones.

Frank loved Shell Island. So did Fibi, his little cousin. Fibi's mother, Frank's Tante Mallie, had died when she was born; of a broken heart, some folk said, when the young Bajan from St Vincent had stopped coming to the island in his sloop, leaving Mallie to fend for herself, as men so often did. Frank remembered when she had died; remembered the muffled crying of Grandmere as she followed the coffin down through the valley and along the narrow hillside path to the little cemetery. He remembered, too, the shock of realisation that Mallie's voice was forever muted, leaving in its turn the weak wailing of Fibi, that was so easily silenced by a rag dipped in sweet water or by gentle rocking.

When she was a baby he used to sit for hours on the step of their thatched hut, holding her in his arms, marvelling at her pale-gold skin, the soft fine hair like the down of a baby chick, and her blue eyes flecked with brown like little freckles. His small black hands looked so dark and out of place as they held her and in his mind he early set her apart.

When she was big enough to go out in the boat with Grandmere and himself, he plaited her a hat from wild cane to protect her hair and face from the sun. But in time the sun had its way and Fibi at fifteen was a warm golden brown, her hair bleached yellow by salt water and sun.

Frank's heart would twist within him at the sight of her thin body in the sea-stained and tattered dress which was practically the only garment she possessed, her golden legs powdered grey by the dry dust or glistening a deeper gold when she scrambled back into the boat with a lobster or a conch.

'Fibi hadn't oughta look like dat,' he told himself, seeing in his mind's eye a picture of Fibi dressed like the girls in the magazines the padre sometimes gave him. He saw her in a clean white dress, her hair combed smooth, with perhaps a ribbon in it, instead of tangled and flying in the wind, or plaited pickny fashion by Grandmere on a Sunday, until the smooth strands escaped and grew tousled again in the wind. She would look good, too, he told himself, with lipstick and a dab of powder on her straight little nose with the gold freckles sprinkled across its bridge.

'One a dese days,' he told himself, 'I gettin' 'way from dis island. I going to Aruba or Trinidad or some place an' earnin' plenty plenty money for Fibi.' But he knew that as long as Grandmere lived he would have to stay, since there was no one to work their little plot of land or to catch fish to eke out their crop of dried peas and cornmeal.

His dark eyes would grow broody as he remembered the time when going out in the boat with Grandmere had been an adventure.

But that had quickly dulled with the passing years and had become, as Fibi and he had grown older, a grim, everyday search for food, as it was for Grandmere and most of the other people on the island. But the dream of earning money persisted, tinged though it was with hopelessness when he thought of Fibi and all he wanted to do for her. Her casual acceptance of things as they were crushed him into despair. His love she accepted too, without being aware of his growing fear of the day when the quiet backwater of her childhood would burst the dam and fling her into the stormy waters for which her comeliness had destined her. To Frank, Fibi was the one lovely thing in a life which held out no hope for the future; but behind the loveliness was fear.

Then one night it came upon him with full force like a blow between the eyes: he had to do something positive to prove his love for Fibi. He was returning to the village after hours spent on the rocks, catching crabs for bait by the light of a flambeau. He was going to catch fish from the rocks the next day, for they needed more mullet and chub than they could catch to make a meal, now their corn was all gone, and there was no money to buy any from the shop. He was going to try for something bigger — a red snapper or two, perhaps, or a cavalli. Then he might manage to sell one or two, to the agricultural officer who had just arrived at the government rest house. There were so few visitors to the island, this was an opportunity he dare not miss.

Picking his way carefully along the stony track that wound round the hill towards the village, he saw the slender mast of a sloop at anchor in the bay, silhouetted against a sky studded with stars and in which hung the silver thread of the new moon. Then he heard voices – the deep rumbling of a man's and the shrill laughter of a girl. It was Fibi. On an island where everybody knows everybody else, Frank knew that the man was a stranger. He stood still and listened. All he could hear was a faint rustling among the sea grape bushes bordering the beach.

'Dat yo, Fibi?' he called.

He waited and thought he caught a faint 'Ah' followed by a giggle.

'It late, Fibi,' he persisted. 'It time yo' in bed long long time.' The only answer was the sound of the sea lapping the white sand with deep sighs. He walked to the village slowly.

He lay in his corner in an agony of misery. Grandmere was snoring. A rooster crowed and another answered it. And somewhere a dog howled. The sound was mournful and eerie in the night. Until now he had seen Fibi as a child – a gay, uncomplaining companion of days in the boat or out hoeing in the hot sun – a golden creature whom he, dark and uncouth though he was, would one day rescue from a way of life into which an unkind fate had flung her. His mind stumbled numbly over the fact that Fibi, for all her golden skin and blue eyes, was as coarse as her environment and moulded her; that she was no different from the other girls on the island. Fibi in a temper could curse like the rest, pull out hair and throw stones. Fibi noisily sucking up fish tea from a tin pot, sucking and gnawing a fish head and spitting out the bones, belching loudly and wiping her mouth clean with the back of her hand, might look different from the darker girls, but she was no different really.

The realisation of this was like the stubbing of a toe against a sharp stone. It hurt.

Frank carried the hurt around for weeks, helplessly casting about for the right to speak to her, to make her understand; but finding he had no right. Who was he, he asked, to tell Fibi that he loved her?

After a few days, the sloop sailed, and Fibi's nocturnal disappearances ended, though Frank, watchful, saw a subtle change in her as the weeks merged into months. Always thin, she grew thinner, and the fine modelling of her face grew even finer, giving her a look of transparency which the blue veins at her temples accentuated.

She no longer sang as they rowed the boat. And once or twice he heard her crying in the night. He longed to take her in his arms, as he had done so often when she had been small; but he knew that his desire for the feel of her thin body against his own was for his own comfort as much as for hers. But she would only say, as she had been accustomed to saying, recently, whenever he touched her tousled head, 'Tak yo' han's offen me,' in a sharp, bitter voice so unlike her own. He retreated with his misery, just as Fibi did with her own.

One morning Grandmere did not get up. She lay on the torn canvas cot against the wall of the hut, her legs drawn up to her lean belly, shivering and mumbling to herself. Without the white cloth she usually wore twisted around her head, she looked very old, Frank thought, binding the leads along the edge of his cast-net while Fibi bent over the coal-pot by the door. His belly growled as he watched Fibi stirring sugar in the milk-can of hot water and then pouring it into the three tin pots.

'Ain' got no bakes this morning. Ain' got no more flour,' Fibi told him as she handed him the pot of sweet water.

'Dat a'right, Fibi. I ain't pertickler hungry dis mornin',' he replied.

He wanted to make an early start because the agricultural officer had said he would like some lobster and a big string of mullet to take back to St Vincent with him on the launch that afternoon. With luck they might catch enough to buy a little cornmeal and flour. Fibi could go into the shop. The sight of the tins of sardines, corned beef and salmon, the barrel of biscuits, the rum on the shelves, was torment to Frank. And the shopkeeper liked Fibi. Sometimes she managed to wheedle a penny loaf or a handful of broken biscuits from him.

Grandmere turned her head to the wall when Fibi took her the 'tea'. She left it on the floor beside her as they went out, Fibi carrying the net and gaff and Frank the oars and row-locks.

Rowing in silence, Frank kept his eyes on the church and the huddle of thatched huts that had once been a prosperous village in Grandmere's youth, when most of the island had been one estate. Frank wanted to look at the little gold tendrils of Fibi's hair and to imagine the lay of muscles under the bedraggled loose dress with the patch across the back – a patch that in its turn was soon going to need yet another patch. He wanted, too, to grip her arms until he hurt her, to shake her and say: 'Listen, Fibi, you gotta listen. Yo' gotta be different to de other girls, see, yo' just gotta.'

Then as they left the bay and were out round the point in the shallow green water within the reef, he became grimly intent on the day's work; years of habit, years of grappling with the sea to give up its life for food, translating from thought to instinct. And, as if by unspoken agreement, they both began to pull more slowly, their eyes searching the green depths for what they sought.

Twice he shipped his oar, slipped silently over the side, dived, came up for air, dived again, his grimy sea-and-work-stained shorts and shirt which were a miracle of patching, clinging to his lean body. Then he pulled himself into the boat, throwing Fibi a smile as he threw a lobster, tail thrashing, into the bilge. Time and again he and Fibi slipped over the side into the clear depths, until they reached Shell Island, for it was on the ledge of rock that ran like a spear out into the deeper water towards the reef that he would stand waiting to cast his net, while Fibi cruised around in the shallower water on the look out for lobsters and conches.

Just before they reached the ledge, Fibi suddenly shipped her oar and leaned over the gunwhale, retching miserably. Frank, appalled that what he had feared was now a fact, was filled with a blinding rage, not only against Fibi and himself, but against the island itself that had bred her. It crashed over him like a gigantic wave and the blood pounded in his head.

The instinct to destroy blotted out all else. Fibi was suddenly no longer to be rescued but to be destroyed, to banish his own anger and shame. Hardly knowing what he did, he suddenly brought his fist down on her golden head, bent miserably over the boat's side, with a violence that jarred his whole body.

Then, because the crumpled figure, with head lolling in the bilge where she had fallen, urged in him the stirring of fear and pity he could no longer bear to feel, and with a wild, searching glance at the shimmering white sand of the beach and the impertinent blue of the sea beyond, he lifted her and dropped her over the side of the boat. He leaned over and watched her, a wavy-edged, distorted figure in the clear water, as he had watched her many times before.

Then before he knew it, he dived towards her and she was no longer distorted like a figure in a fantasy but close and near to him. He tried to take hold of her but time after time she eluded him, carried this way and that by shifting currents. Again and again he rose to the surface, filled his lungs with great gulps of air and dived. When at last he managed to hold her and felt her body limp in his arms as he brought her to the surface, he suddenly became panic-stricken at what he had done. Thought, and with it terror, seeped into him again slowly.

Taking a deep breath, he dived again, down into the familiar depths they both had known so intimately in the past. Fighting the pressure of the water until little explosions went off inside his head, he pushed her body with all his remaining strength into a cleft in the rocks; went up for air and dived again to seize a huge chunk of coral to wedge her body more securely in the cleft.

Exhausted he dragged himself to the hot white sand and coral of the island, staring dully at the sky and the white scudding clouds racing across it, not sure if the thunder he heard was his own blood pounding in his head or the thunder of the surf on the reef. Love for Fibi burst like a great white light over him, wave after wave of timeless white light until, blinded by it, he slid into the water to escape its searing brightness. He had to see her once more. He could never go back now, back to Grandmere and life, any more than Fibi could. He saw one golden-brown arm waving in the water like a reed, and touched it, dislodging the rock. Opening his mouth, he tried to speak, and that was the last he saw of her as her slim brown body rose gracefully to the surface.

WILSON HARRIS

Wilson Harris was born in Guyana in 1921 and edu-
cated there. His first novel *The Palace of the Peacock*
was published in 1960 and this was followed by *The Far
Journey of Oudin* (1961), *The Whole Armour* (1962),
The Secret Ladder (1963), *Heartland* (1964), *The Eye of
the Scarecrow* (1965), *Tumatumari* (1968), *Sleepers of
Roraima* (1970), *Ascent to Omai* (1970), *Age of the
Rainmakers* (1971), *Black Marsden* (1972), *Compan-
ions of the Day and Night* (1975), *Da Silva Da Silva's
Cultivated Wilderness* (1977), *The Tree of the Sun*
(1978).

He now lives in London.

Banim Creek is from an unpublished novel which was
written in 1951 or 1952. It was my first experiment in
the novel-form. The manuscript was destroyed. An
extract survives because of its appearance in the
Guyanese magazine Kyk-Over-Al.

It may prove of interest perhaps to note that one or
two characters were translated into later novels. Paula
becomes Catalena, Jerry becomes Weng in *The Secret
Ladder* (1963) which is also set in the Canje River of
which Banim is a tributary. Van returns much later as
Hope in *Genesis Of The Clowns* (1977).

It is difficult to cast one's mind back to a vanished
book but I recall, in re-reading *Banim Creek*, my desire
to present a groping and uneasy awareness – in the
narrating and largely *naive* consciousness of Charles –
of an abyss that lay beneath the political, largely
Marxist, masquerade of the day. One sensed the seeds of
deep-seated malaise secreted in individual personalities.

Charles is cast as a rather earnest Catholic with an eye
upon heaven, purgatory and hell.

My intuitive concern was to demonstrate a diseased
masculine/feminine balance of selves that lay within the
persona Guyana presented to the world. This was a
legitimate and necessary, imaginative, obsession in
Guyana (it was then British Guiana), a largely unpopu-
lated territory with great stretches of profoundly beautiful yet dangerous riverain, complex rainforest, savannah, landscapes; a territory still plagued by legacies of
conquest and by an imbalance of sexes it had endured
until the 1920s because of unimaginative immigration
policies.

It was, still is, true that a certain density of population
could be found on the coastlands but even there signi-
ficant gaps occurred. In any case the wilderness or
hinterland that stretched into South America was an
inescapable factor in the psyche of community.

As a consequence the individual person exhibited
more startlingly perhaps, in his or her cell or degree of
isolation, traits and tendencies that would have seemed
absurd, or would have merged into collective invisibility, in greatly populated areas.

Jerry, 'the ruthless free man', exhibited the seed of
nihilism that has become a uniform symptom in the late
twentieth century world. Nihilism structures feud, sets
man against man, it subsists unconsciously perhaps on a
conception of incorrigible bias at the heart of existence.

Van, the carnival trickster, genuinely suffered the
torments of purgatory or hell. His sufferings were real
since they were rooted in a desire to please everybody, to
seduce all men and women, to possess the 'community'.
As such he was extremely vulnerable to those who
stalked him and made him pay for the deeds he per-

formed or secretly wished to perform. In him lay the seed of fascism.

It was Paula, the abused woman, who became the catalyst of a version of conscience. In her lay the dormant seed of passion, of complexity and of metamorphosis.

She is, it is true, a far cry from metamorphosis as I was to pursue it in later works. But it was a start anyway in that direction that remains a ceaselessly tormenting quest for *coniunctio* or true union, for profound and rich dialogue beyond the banalities of despair.

Wilson Harris

BANIM CREEK

I t was as a boarder occupying a room in the same house that I had learnt so much about Marie, Champ and Jerry. As fate would have it Champ, Jerry and I met again, so many years after, working on our present job. Van was apparently the complete stranger in our midst. But somehow from the outset he too seemed to belong to an exciting pattern of things like an integral link in a chain. The trend of my thoughts during the past hour had taken such a phenomenal grip on my mind that I felt a whole school of ideas seeking to be marshalled properly or related properly in perspective. I stirred uneasily and raised myself slightly on my elbow to see if there were signs of someone coming yet. The river was as calm as a lake. I felt suddenly stiff and arose to a sitting posture. I got up entirely after a while and sauntered slowly to the cokerite tree in the clearing. There was a better view of the river here, and I sat on the ground and leaned against the trunk of the cokerite palm.

There was a remarkable sameness about the river. The same jet-black water, the same green islands of grass. I asked myself – what was it that filled me with such a sense of foreboding? If I could answer this question I felt I would have the key to my present thoughts. Nothing had actually happened yet, to the best of my knowledge, but it was strange that I should feel as if something had happened or was actually happening, something terrible and tragic. The very sameness or apparent changelessness in the physical world in one's own experience suggested that things present had already existed, and things to come were already present. This gave me a core around which to order my thoughts. The drama of human life might be the visible form of event that had already occurred in the spiritual sense.

Herein lay the source of prophecy and even perhaps of every decision, conscious or unconscious, in that it was an awareness of the spiritual origin, and the material actual thing might even possibly offer a freedom to alter the fateful course of things! One's decision could be the veritable grace of God for someone else, who knows? or someone else's decision might be the miraculous stroke of fortune that influenced still someone else away from doom into an act of repentance. Heaven, hell and purgatory were surely the stages already present and active in human destiny: that is reward for the good, reward for the bad, and the grace that lies halfway in between, to be eternally chosen or eternally rejected ...

Banim Creek was the name of the place where the tide-readers' camp ground lay. We had travelled up the main river for many hours to get there. There were sixteen of us to be encamped in parties of four, several miles apart along the river banks. The officer in charge of operations had utilised the time travelling in discussion of the dry, statistical side of our job. Eventually he dumped four of us at Banim and steamed away in the big survey launch.

Van, the stranger amongst us, was a tall, handsome Negro. He was quite distinguished-looking with a strong face and a straight nose. His lips were his worst feature. They revealed a peculiar sore-looking scar like a burn when he opened his mouth to laugh or speak. There was something slightly repellent about that scar. But this flaw was lost in an earnest and serious quality that gave his whole expression an indefinable charm. It was a great disappointment to find as the weeks and months rolled by that Van very often was striking a pose. And yet to say precisely what that pose was, or to try to track him down in his trickery was to find oneself more and more deeply involved in a maze.

I used to watch Jerry staring at Van like a hunter at a new indefatigable animal. Jerry became more and more determined to expose Van once and for all.

As for Van he never lost sight of his objective, which was to captivate all with whom he came into contact and to worm himself into the hearts of men. He realised he might fail with Jerry but he kept a sharp eye on the remainder of us.

The first great battle of wits between Jerry and Van occurred in connection with a woman living six miles down-stream of Banim. She came to the camp for the first time selling greens and paw-paw fruit. She was Portuguese, fair-skinned, with light, waving brown hair that clung to her brow in moist places. She was very frail-looking in a sexy, appealing manner. I felt instantaneously drawn to her and yet repelled by a sort of bulging largeness beneath her eyes. There were also cruel weals across her face and arms. She appeared quite shamelessly prepared to expose these weals and seemed to derive satisfaction in explaining that her husband had brutally beaten her. It happened whenever he had no money to spend and became crazy for liquor, she said.

Her tale aroused in Jerry his high-pitched, bitter laugh.

'You look like you like getting beaten up!' he said. But Champ cried, selecting beans and fruit from the woman's basket at the same time, 'Don't worry with Jerry, madam. He's always like that, always disagreeable!'

'Disagreeable? And why not?' said Jerry. 'I always say some people always looking for trouble. They only happy when they getting tricked and they in trouble! I don't trust nobody. When I fall in with anybody I do it 'cause I got to. I watch every step after that!' He too selected greens from the basket on the stelling, exclaiming, 'You agree with what I say lady?' The woman replied vaguely – 'I don't know!' Van who had made no remark so far squatted near the woman and helped himself liberally to greens and fruit.

'Ah hope you will always trust me lady!' he said cheerfully. 'You ain't no man-hater, I can see that!' Champ had been counting some loose coins in his pocket. He drew the woman aside while paying her and whispered something. She nodded. Jerry gave his ironical laugh like a hunter who scents his game. Van too looked very thoughtful. Suddenly he had an idea and his countenance lit up.

'I got some washing,' he addressed the woman. 'It would put a bit in your way.'

The woman gave no answer but gently tidied her hair. Her hands were remarkably slender. I found myself observing them with fascination. They seemed entirely foreign, far too aristocratic for the circumstances in spite of several callouses. They had a miraculously blue, frail outline of veins.

'You always lived here in the river?' I asked her. She turned her bulging eyes on me and they seemed to grow even larger as she replied – 'I ran away from home when I was nineteen. My father is one of the wealthiest merchants in town.' She smiled when she saw my surprise, and continued before anyone could speak –

'I was educated at the best schools!'

'And your husband . . .?'

'He was my father's chauffeur.'

Jerry gave a grunting incredulous sound: 'You little liar! I bet you don't even know who your father is! You think we are fools, eh?'

The woman looked hurt and annoyed. Her face flushed. I saw a batting look come into Jerry's eyes.

'Well just tell us his name, this wealthy father of yours! I suppose he has cut you off without a cent, eh? Maybe you can never go back!'

'I am ashamed to go back,' the woman replied simply, the anger draining out of her countenance. 'And I don't care what you think or say since you do not understand. Have you ever found,' she said looking at us appealingly out of those sickening eyes of hers, 'that to go back, before you realised what caused you ever to leave, is sometimes to die? I prefer to learn to live wherever I am.'

'How do you mean to go back is to die?' Champ asked in bewilderment. 'And you say you got a wealthy old man to look after yuh?'

The woman caressed the weals on her skin, lost in thought. At last – 'I said I was ashamed to go back. I was wrong. It is my father who is ashamed of me and my husband. He does not wish us to remain together if I go back!'

'And you prefer to stay in this bush, and get bite by fly, mosquito? Get mark up and beat up by that precious husband of yours? You is a funny woman!'

'Don't you understand there is no place for me to go? It would have to be me and someone else, I can't go alone!' 'I understand just how you feel', said Van coming to her assistance with that earnest look of his. 'It's life, that's what it is. It's not you is funny. It's life is funny.'

The woman turned and stared at Van for the first time as if she hadn't seen him before. She felt that here was someone to whom she could talk. Champ was still bewildered. The lady did not fit into any scheme of things he had known in the past. And yet for some reason or other he felt an acute disgust with himself as though the whole matter should have been a simple one for him to understand, or any man for that matter. He wondered to himself whether the woman was lying, or whether the whole thing was not a kind of dream she had had, and that everybody has at some time or another and then after forgets! A dream of companionship you may call it perhaps.

Jerry had been following the conversation closely. He had been keeping a shrewd eye on Champ and Van.

'I feel so sorry for you lady! When I listen to you talk I feel you need a lot of good commonsense pumped into that head of yours.'

Jerry wagged a finger in the direction of Van and grimaced –

'Not a lot of easy romantic stuff. Believe me there's a trick in that for you!'

Champ silently agreed whole-heartedly with Jerry's remarks. Something like satisfaction with himself returned. The woman was obviously unwell! How could she so patiently endure the brutality in her present mode of living when a million dollars waited around the corner! Either she was a liar or a very sick woman to abandon everything for nothing. And she seemed to find something painfully pleasant in Jerry's words. She replied as if with melancholy relish 'Oh you're sorry for me? I do need your sympathy!'

Jerry laughed. It was his plan to play off Champ and Van against each other. He felt he had helped to restore Champ's belief in himself. The knight of compassion had been rudely shaken a short while ago, when the woman with the greens and paw-paw fruit, who stirred his interest and desire, appeared to move so strangely out of his grasp and comprehension like a phenomenon of nature! At the same time Jerry knew he had baited a trap for Van.

The great battle of wits had started in earnest. Champ took a corial and disappeared down river after sunset. Jerry jokingly remarked that Champ had gone on his mission of love. I too, remembered how Champ had whispered to the woman while paying for his share of the greens and fruit. It was a beautiful evening. Deep in the west a great glow still lingered, a blue pool charged by an expanding sensuous purity of light. But this expansion was only an illusion. The scene rapidly darkened and the stars had to come out rapidly on duty at last in every inch of the sky.

I booked the tide readings with the help of a torchlight hour after hour. It is strange how one's eyes become accustomed to the darkness, that inky-blue tropical darkness that floods the whole world. Then how innumerable and complex are the heavenly stars, and how sharp and clear are their earthly reflections in the mirror of waters! There came a ripple of disturbance as I watched and a corial shot up to the stelling, turning up the cold reflected watery stars into churning streaks of light. Champ had returned. He clambered up the ladder on the stelling and came over to me where I stood.

'Hi Charles,' he said. 'No go at all with that woman!' There was a note of bewilderment and exasperation in his voice. He stood for a long time pensive and then as if in explanation–

'The husband's away down river. I say to myself she hate him how she talk today! But don't know for sure now. She say adultery is not in her line!' Champ shook his head –

'The woman's crazy I tell you, Charles. But I like she all the same. Ah really like the kid and Ah going to look her up again!'

It was nearly midnight. I shone my torch on the gauge and booked the level of the river. The high tide was close at hand.

In spite of Champ's optimism fortune did not smile on him. The aristocratic woman of the fruit basket kept him at arm's length. Everyone in the camp sensed his disappointment, and Van constantly rebuked him.

'You still following up the little woman? Aw, have a heart. You can't see she ain't the kind of woman out for just a good time? You believe she come all the way in this jungle just for a good time? She is the sort of woman you got to love you before all you can come together and make one.'

'But she husband cruel to she!' Champ insisted.

'She still got pity for him,' Van declared. 'And who knows which is stronger – pity or love?'

'Love,' Champ cried.

'Well give her then,' Van laughed. 'If you've got it to give!'

Champ did not ever appear to lose hope that he had it to give. He looked forward constantly to the frequent visits the woman of the greens made to the camp. Most often Van was away hunting or collecting firewood. Jerry was often present, though sometimes he too was out hunting or fishing. Champ alone never missed her whenever she came. His approaches however, were all to no avail.

Jerry decided that the time had come for him to show his hand and spring the trap as every good hunter must eventually do. The afternoon came he had chosen for that purpose. He pattered out to meet the 'lady with the greens' when she arrived. It was a bright, glaring afternoon. The tide was falling and the inflowing stream had checked, the river was getting ready to turn. The floating patches of grass on the river seemed not to move at all as if time itself were dragging, waiting for a sudden impulse to give it direction.

'You look nice-nice lady!' Champ said.

'Nicer than usual when she comes here?' Jerry asked with a laugh.

'I dunno,' Champ said, wrinkling his brow. 'You know you treating me bad?' he whispered to the woman. She smiled in a nervous manner –

'I'm sorry Champ! Let's just be friends like that. What more can you really desire?'

Champ turned his hot gaze on her arms.

'You need someone to care you,' he muttered like a man repeating a timeworn lesson. Then uneasily realising that Jerry and I had overheard his remarks, he became silent and glum.

The woman completed her sales. She gathered the full white skirt of her dress closely around her, and gingerly lowered herself into her small craft by the stelling. A gentle twist and the craft entered the slow-moving stream. She waved her paddle, the blade flashed another day's farewell in the sun. Soon the craft turned the bend and could no longer be seen from the stelling.

No sooner had it disappeared than Jerry spun on us – 'A bitch! just a bitch. But that don't interest me anyway. She ain't my woman. And men are just as low anyway!' he laughed. 'That's why I trust nobody. No permanent woman for me and avoid trouble I say!' Then suddenly like a crouching panther, he spat out.

'She's been meeting Van when she leave hey at the plum tree past the bend. You doubt? Go now and see. I track them down a few times well! I tell you go and see him. You'll know what a low scheming crook the admirable Van is!' There was a blaze in his eyes as he continued almost to himself.

'Can you beat it? Men are all traitors I tell you! I've never forgotten that lesson. He has taken your place Champ. He's the fountainhead of compassion now.' Jerry laughed suddenly his high, ironical laugh, peering at Champ with a kind of frightful glee.

All Champ said was – 'Plum tree past the bend?' And he caught up a stick and was off. But even as he turned off the stelling to pass the camp, Van appeared coming from the very opposite direction, upriver. He had a bundle of firewood on his head, which he threw to the ground near the camp. We all stood dumbfounded watching him, and then Champ gave a shout —

'Look Van deh right here, Jerry! What in hell yuh bin trying to say?' Jerry gave a sulky grin. He cried to Van.

'How come you pass up the lady with the greens today Van? Like you miss her today! No kisses under the plums today?'

Van stared at Jerry coldly —

'You got a dirty mind, boy,' he said. 'What in hell are you talking about?'

'You know what I'm talking about,' said Jerry watchfully.

'You talking 'bout your own brutishness,' Champ cut in roughly. A terrible feeling of hate for Jerry suddenly possessed his entire heart and soul. 'You always know more than everybody. It's your hand always against every man's hand. You talk 'bout traitors. But you worse than a traitor. You ain't grow up yet man. You sick-sick-sick, man!' Champ choked on his own words. He felt empty and forsaken, ashamed in some tragic way.

Jerry said nothing. He remained extremely watchful. And then as if satisfied there was no real danger he relaxed. The decision for life or death always rests with the hunter, no, the hunted. He was quite sure of that.

Paula her name was: the aristocratic lady who sold greens, and had become such a centre of attraction. The surprising accusation that Jerry had levelled at Van made any reconciliation Van had hoped to accomplish with Jerry impossible. In one respect Van had emerged victorious in the battle of wits. For instance Champ now hated Jerry. But in another and hidden respect Van was involved in a deeper and more frightful struggle. His first adversary in the form of Jerry, the ruthlessly free man, retired behind a proud contemptuous barrier; and Van was left face to face with himself as in a mirror, and he did not like the image he saw there.

JOHN HEATH

JOHN HEARNE

John Hearne was born in Canada in 1926 and educated in Jamaica. He later attended Edinburgh and London universities and has published several novels including *Voices Under The Window* (1955), *Stranger At The Gate* (1956), *The Faces Of Love* (1957), *The Autumn Equinox* (1959), and *Land of the Living* (1961). His latest novel, *The Sure Salvation* was published by Faber in 1981.

He now lives in Jamaica where he works as a journalist and contributes regularly to *The Gleaner*.

In *At the Stelling*, John Hearne examines the rela-
tionships that exist between a group of men in the jungle
interior of a South American colony.

Mr Hamilton, the government officer, has been
moved out of the sight of his men to a post in the capital.
In his place comes Mr Cockburn, a brash, green city-boy
whose attitude to the men, especially John, the Amerin-
dian scout, deteriorates until the final catastrophe.

John Hearne gives a vivid account of the strains upon
the men, Cockburn's insensitivity, John's pride and
Hamilton's understanding all as seen through the eyes of
Dunnie, a young member of the gang.

Kenneth Ramchand

AT THE STELLING

'**D**is one is no boss fe' we, Dunnie,' Son-Son say. 'I don' like how
him stay. Dis one is boss fe' messenger an' women in department office, but not fe' we.'

'Shut your mout', I tell him. 'Since when a stupid, black nigger can like
and don't like a boss in New Holland? What you goin' do? Retire an' live
'pon your estate?' But I know say that Son-Son is right.

The two of we talk so at the back of the line; Son-Son carrying the
chain, me with the level on the tripod. The grass stay high and the ground
hard with sun. It is three mile to where the Catacuma run black past the
stelling, and even the long light down the sky can't strike a shine from
Catacuma water. You can smell Rooi Swamp, dark and sweet and
wicked like a woman in a bad house back in Zuyder Town. Nothing live
in Rooi Swamp except snake; like nothing live in a bad woman. In all
South America there is no swamp like the Rooi; not even in Brazil; not
even in Cayenne. The new boss, Mister Cockburn, walk far ahead with
the little assistant man, Mister Bailey. Nobody count the assistant. Him
only come down to the Catacuma to learn. John stay close behind them,
near to the rifle. The other rest of the gang file out upon the trail between
them three and me and Son-Son. Mister Cockburn is brand-new from

head to foot. New hat, new bush-shirt, new denim pant, new boot. Him walk new.

'Mister Cockburn!' John call, quick and sharp. 'Look!' I follow the point of John's finger and see the deer. It fat and promise tender and it turn on the hoof-tip like deer always do, with the four tip standing in a nickel and leaving enough bare to make a cent change, before the spring into high grass. Mister Cockburn unship the rifle, and *pow*, if we was all cow then him shoot plenty grass for us to eat.

'Why him don't give John de rifle?' Son-Son say.

'Because de rifle is Government,' I tell him, 'And Mister Cockburn is Government. So it is him have a right to de rifle.'

Mr Cockburn turn and walk back. He is a tall, high mulatto man, young and full in body, with eyes not blue and not green, but coloured like the glass of a beer bottle. The big hat make him look like a soldier in the moving pictures.

'Blast this sun,' he say, loud, to John. 'I can't see a damn' thing in the glare; it's right in my eyes.'

The sun is falling down the sky behind us but maybe him think we can't see that too.

John don't answer but only nod once, and Mister Cockburn turn and walk on, and I know say that if I could see John's face it would be all Carib buck. Sometimes you can see where the Indian lap with it, but other times it is all Indian and closed like a prison gate; and I knew say, too, that it was this face Mister Cockburn did just see.

'Trouble dere, soon,' Son-Son say, and him chin point to John and then to Mister Cockburn. 'Why Mister Hamilton did have to get sick, eh, Dunnie? Dat was a boss to have.'

'Whatever trouble to happen is John's trouble,' I tell him.

'John's trouble and Mister Cockburn's. Leave it. You is a poor naygur wid no schooling, five pickney and a sick woman. Dat is trouble enough for you.'

But in my heart I find agreement for what stupid Son-Son have to say. If I have only known what trouble . . .

No. Life don't come so. It only come one day at a time. Like it had come every day since we lose Mister Hamilton and Mister Cockburn take we up to survey the Catacuma drainage area in Mister Hamilton's stead.

The first day we go on the savannah beyond the stelling, I know say that Mister Cockburn is frighten. Frighten, and hiding his frighten from himself. The worst kind of frighten. You hear frighten in him when he shout at we to keep the chain straight and plant the markers where him tell us. You see frighten when him try to work us, and himself, one hour after midday, when even the alligators hide in the water. And you understand frighten when him try to run the camp at the *stelling* as if we was soldier and him was a general. But all that is because he is new and it would pass but for John. Because of John everything remain bad. From the first day when John try to treat him as he treat Mister Hamilton.

You see, John and Mister Hamilton was like one thing except that Mister Hamilton have schooling and come from a big family in Zuyder Town. But they each suck from a Carib woman and from the first both their spirit take. When we have Mister Hamilton as boss whatever John say we do as if it was Mister Hamilton say it, and at night when Mister Hamilton lie off in the big Berbice chair on the verandah and him and John talk it sound like one mind with two tongue. That's how it sound to the rest of we when we sit down the steps and listen to them talk. Only when Mister Cockburn come back up the river with we, after Mister Hamilton take sick, we know say all that is change. For Mister Cockburn is frighten and must reduce John's pride, and from that day John don't touch the rifle and don't come to the verandah except to take orders and for Mister Cockburn to show that gang foreman is gang foreman and that boss is always boss.

Son-Son say true, I think. Trouble is to come between John and Mister Cockburn. Poor John. Here, in the bush, him is a king, but in New Zuyder him is just another poor half-buck without a job and Mister Cockburn is boss and some he cast down and some he raiseth up.

Ahead of we, I see Mister Cockburn trying to step easy and smooth, as if we didn't just spend seven hours on the savannah. Him is trying hard but very often the new boot kick black dirt from the trail. That is all right I think. Him will learn. Him don't know say that even John hold respect for the sun on the Catacuma. The sun down here on the savannah is like the centurion in the Bible who say to one man, Come, and he cometh and to another, Go, and he goeth. Like it say go, to Mister Hamilton. For it was a man sick bad we take down to the mouth of the river that day after he fall down on the wharf at the stelling. And it was nearly a dead man we drive up the coast road one hundred mile to Zuyder Town. We did want to stop in Hendrikstadt with him that night, but he think him was dying – we think so too – and him would not stop for fear he die away from his wife. And afterwards the Government doctor tell Survey that he must stay in the office forevermore and even Mister Hamilton who think him love the bush and the swamp and the forest more than life itself was grateful to the doctor for those words.

So it was it did happen with Mister Hamilton, and so it was Mister Cockburn come to we.

Three weeks we is on the Catacuma with Mister Cockburn, and every new day things stay worse than the last.

In the morning, when him come out with the rifle, him shout: 'Dunnie! Take the corial across the river and put up these bottles.' And he fling the empty rum and beer bottle down the slope to me and I get into the corial and paddle across the river, and put the necks over seven sticks on the other bank. Then him and the little assistant, Mister Bailey, stay on the verandah and fire across the river, each spelling each, until the bottle is all broken.

And John, down by the river, in the soft morning light, standing in the corial we have half-buried in the water, half-drawn upon the bank, washing himself all over careful like an Indian and not looking to the verandah.

'John!' Mister Cockburn shout, and laugh bad. 'Careful, eh, man. Mind a *perai* don't cut off your balls.'

We have to stand in the corial because *perai* is bad on the Catacuma and will take off your heel and your toe if you stand in the river six inches from the bank. We always joke each other about it, but not the way Mister Cockburn joke John. That man know what him is doing and it is not nice to hear.

John say nothing. Him stand in the still water catch of the corial we half-sink and wash him whole body like an Indian and wash him mouth out and listen to Mister Cockburn fire at the bottle across the river. Only we know how John need to hold that rifle. When it come to rifle and gun him is all Indian, no African in it at all. Rifle to him is like woman to we. Him don't really hold a rifle, him make love with it. And I think how things go in Mister Hamilton's time when him and John stand on the verandah in the morning and take seven shots break seven bottle, and out in the bush they feel shame if four shot fire and only three piece of game come back. Although, I don't talk truth, if I don't say how sometimes Mister Hamilton miss a shot on the bottle. When that happen you know him is thinking. He is a man think hard all the time. And the question he ask! 'Dunnie,' he ask 'What do you see in your looking-glass?' or, 'Do you know, Dunnie, that this country has had its images broken on the wheels of false assumptions? Arrogance and servility. Twin criminals pleading for the mercy of an early death.' That is how Mister Hamilton talk late at night when him lie off in the big Berbice chair and share him mind with we.

After three weeks on the Catacuma, Mister Cockburn and most of we go down the river. Mister Cockburn to take him plans to the Department and the rest of we because nothing to do when him is gone. All the way down the river John don't say a word. Him sit in the boat bows and stare down the black water as if it is a book giving him secret to remember. Mister Cockburn is loud and happy, for him feel, we know say, now, who is boss and him begin to lose him frighten spirit. Him is better now the frighten gone and confidence begin to come.

'Remember, now,' him say in the Department yard at Zuyder Town. 'Eight o'clock sharp on Tuesday morning. If one of you is five minutes late, the truck leaves without you. Plenty of men between here and the Catacuma glad to get work.' We laugh and say, 'Sure, boss, sure,' because we know say that already him is not so new as him was and that him is only joking. Only John don't laugh but walk out of the yard and down the street.

Monday night, John come to my house; I is living in a little place between the coolie cinema and the dockyard.

'Dunnie,' he say, 'Dunnie, you have fifteen dollar?'

'Jesus,' I say, 'what you need fifteen dollar for, man? Dat is plenty, you know?'

'All right,' he say. 'You don't have it. I only ask.'

Him turn, as if it was the time him ask and I don't have no watch.

'Hold on, hold on,' I tell him. 'I never say I don't have fifteen dollar. I just say what you want it for?'

'Lend me. I don't have enough for what I want. As we pay off next month, you get it back. My word to God.'

I go into the house.

'Where de money?' I ask the woman.

'What you want it for?' she ask. 'You promise say we don't spend dat money until we marry and buy furnitures. What you want tek it now for?'

'Just tell me where it stay,' I tell her. 'Just tell me. Don't mek me have to find it, eh?'

'Thank you, Dunnie,' John say when I bring him the fifteen dollar. 'One day you will want something bad. Come to me then.'

And him gone up the street so quick you scarcely see him pass under the light.

The next morning, in the truck going down to the boat at the Catacuma mouth, we see what John did want fifteen dollar for.

'You have a licence for that?' Mister Cockburn ask him, hard and quick, when he see it.

'Yes,' John say and stow the new Ivor-Johnson repeater with his gear up in the boat bows.

'All right,' Mister Cockburn say. 'I hope you do. I don't want any unlicensed guns on my camp.'

Him and John was never born to get on.

We reach the stelling late afternoon. The bungalow stand on the bluff above the big tent where we sleep and Zacchy, who we did leave to look to the camp, wait on the wharf waving to us.

When we passing the gear from the boat, John grab his bundle by the string and swing it up. The string break and shirt, pant and handkerchief fly out to float on the water. Them float but the new carton of .32 ammunition fall out too and we see it for a second, green in the black water as it slide to the bottom and the mud and the *perai*.

Mister Bailey, the little assistant, look sorry, John look sick, and Mister Cockburn laugh a little up in the back of him nose.

'Is that all you had?' him ask.

'Yes,' John say. 'I don't need no more than that for three weeks.'

'Too bad,' Mister Cockburn reply. 'Too bad. Rotten luck. I might be able to spare you a few from stores.'

Funny how a man who can stay decent with everybody always find one other who turn him bad.

Is another three weeks we stay up on the survey. We triangulate all the stretch between the Rooi Swamp and the first forest. Things is better this time. Mister Cockburn don't feel so rampageous to show what a hard boss him is. Everything is better except him and John. Whenever him and John speak, one voice is sharp and empty and the other voice is dead, and empty too. Every few day him give John two-three cartridge, and John go out and come back with two-three piece of game. A deer and a *labba*, maybe. Or a bush pig and an agouti. Whatever ammunition John get him bring back meat to match. And, you know, I think that rowel Mister Cockburn's spirit worse than anything else John do. Mister Cockburn is shooting good, too, and we is eating plenty meat, but him don't walk with the gun like John. Who could ever. Not even Mister Hamilton.

The last Saturday before we leave, John come to Mister Cockburn. It is afternoon and work done till Monday. Son-Son and me is getting the gears ready for a little cricket on the flat piece under the *kookorit* palms. The cricket gears keep in the big room with the other rest of stores and we hear every word John and Mister Cockburn say.

'No, John,' Mister Cockburn tell him. 'We don't need any meat. We're leaving Tuesday morning. We have more than enough now.'

Him voice sleepy and deep from the Berbice chair.

'Sell me a few rounds, Mister Cockburn,' John say, 'I will give you store price for a few rounds of .32.'

'They're not mine to sell,' Mister Cockburn say, and him is liking the whole business so damn' much his voice don't even hold malice as it always do for John. 'You know every round of ammunition here belongs to Survey. I have to indent and account for every shot fired.'

Him know, like we know, that Survey don't give a lime how much shot fire up in the bush so long as the men stay happy and get meat.

'You can't give three shot, Mister Cockburn?' John say. You know how bad John want to use the new repeater when you hear him beg.

'Sorry, John,' Mister Cockburn say. 'Have you checked the caulking on the boat? I don't want us shipping any water when we're going down on Tuesday.'

A little later all of us except John go out to play cricket. Mister Cockburn and Mister Bailey come too and each take captain of a side. We play till the parrots come talking across the river to the *kookorits* and the sky turn to green and fire out on the savannah. When we come back to the camp John is gone. Him take the corial and gone.

'That damn' buck,' Mister Cockburn say to Mister Bailey. 'Gone up the river to his cousin, I suppose. We won't see him until Monday morning now. You can take an Indian out of the bush, but God Almighty himself can't take the bush out of the Indian.'

Monday morning, we get up and John is there. Him is seated on the stelling and all you can see of him face is the teeth as him grin and the cheeks swell up and shiny with pleasure. Lay out on the stelling before him is seven piece of game. Three deer, a *labba* and three bush pig. None of we ever see John look so. Him tired till him thin and grey, but happy and proud till him can't speak.

'Seven,' him say at last and hold up him finger. 'Seven shots, Dunnie. That's all I take. One day and seven shot.'

Who can stay like an Indian with him game and no shot gone wide?

'What's this?' a voice call from up the verandah and we look and see Mister Cockburn in the soft, white-man pyjamas lean over to look at we on the stelling. 'Is that you, John? Where the devil have you been?'

'I make a little trip, Mister Cockburn,' John say. Him is so proud and feel so damn' sweet him like even Mister Cockburn. 'I make a little trip. I bring back something for you to take back to town. Come and make your choice, sir.'

Mister Cockburn is off the verandah before the eye can blink, and we hear the fine red slipper go slap-slap on the patch down the bluff. Him come to the wharf and stop short when him see the game. Then him look at John for a long time and turn away slow and make water over the stelling edge and come back, slow and steady.

'All right,' him say, and him voice soft and feel bad in your ears, like you did stumble in the dark and put your hand into something you would walk round. 'All right, John. Where did you get the ammunition? Who gave it you, eh?'

Him voice go up and break like a boy's voice when the first hairs begin to grow low down on him belly.

'Mister Cockburn,' John say, so crazy proud that even now him want to like the man and share pride with him. 'I did take the rounds, sir. From your room. Seven shot I take, Mister Cockburn, and look what I bring you back. Take that deer, sir, for yourself and your family. Town people never taste meat like that.'

'You son of a bitch,' Mister Cockburn reply. 'You damned impertinent, thieving son of a bitch. Bailey!' and him voice scream until Mister Bailey come out to the verandah. 'Bailey! Listen to this. We have a thief in the camp. This beauty here feels that the government owes him his ammunition. What else did you take?'

Him voice sound as if a rope tie round him throat.

'What else I take?' John look as if him try to kiss a woman and she slap him face. 'How I could take anything, Mister Cockburn? As if I am a thief. Seven little shot I take from the carton. You don't even remember how many rounds you did have left. How many you did have leave, eh? Tell me that.'

'Don't back chat me, you bloody thief!' Mister Cockburn yell. 'This is your last job with Survey, you hear me? I'm going to fire your arse as soon as we get to the river mouth. And don't think this game is yours to give away. You shot it with government ammunition, with stolen government ammunition. Here! Dunnie! Son-Son! Zacchy! Get that stuff up to the house. Zacchy, gut them and hang 'em. I'll decide what to do with them later.'

John stay as still as if him was dead. Only when we gather up the game and a kid deer drop one splash of dark stomach blood onto the boards him draw one long breath and shiver.

'Now,' Mister Cockburn say, 'Get to hell out of here! Up to the tent. You don't work for me anymore. I'll take you down river on Tuesday and that's all. And if I find one dollar missing from my wallet I'm going to see you behind bars.'

It is that day I know say how nothing so bad before but corruption and rottenness come worse after. None of we could forget John's face when we pick up him game. For we Negro, and for the white man, and for the mulatto man, game is to eat sometimes, or it is play to shoot. But for the Indian, oh God, game that him kill true is life everlasting. It is manhood.

When we come back early in the afternoon, with work done, we don't see John. But the corial still there, and the engine boat, and we know that him not far. Little later, when Zacchy cook, I fill a billy pot and go out to the *kookorits*. I find him there, in the grass.

'John,' I say. 'Don't tek it so. Mister Cockburn young and foolish and don't mean harm. Eat, John. By the time we reach river mouth tomorrow everyt'ing will be well again. Do, John. Eat dis.'

John look at me and it is one black Indian Carib face stare like statue into mine. All of him still, except the hands that hold the new rifle and polish, polish, polish with a rag until the barrel shine blue like a chinee whore hair.

I come back to the stelling. Mister Cockburn and Mister Bailey lie into two deck chair under the tarpaulin, enjoying the afternoon breeze off the river. Work done and they hold celebration with a bottle. The rest of the gang sit on the boards and drink too. Nothing sweeter than rum and river water.

'Mister Cockburn,' I tell him, 'I don't like how John stay. Him is hit hard, sah.'

'Oh, sit down, Dunnie,' him say. 'Have a drink. That damned buck needs a lesson. I'll take him back when we reach Zuyder Town. It won't do him any harm to miss two days' pay.'

So I sit, although I know say I shouldn't. I sit and I have one drink, and then two, and then one more. And the Catacuma run soft music round the piles of the stelling. All anybody can feel is that work done and we have one week in Zuyder Town before money need call we to the bush again.

Then as I go to the stelling edge to dip water in the mug I look up and see John. He is coming down from the house, gliding on the path like Jesus across the Sea of Galilee, and I say, 'Oh God, Mister Cockburn! Where you leave the ammunition, eh?'

But already it is too late to say that.

The first shot catch Mister Cockburn in the forehead and him drop back in the deck chair, peaceful and easy, like a man call gently from sleep who only half wake. And I shout, 'Dive-oh, Mister Bailey!' and as I drop from the stelling into black Catacuma water, I feel something like a marabunta wasp sting between my legs and know say I must be the first thing John ever shoot to kill that him only wound.

I sink far down in that river and already, before it happen, I can feel *perai* chew at my fly button and tear off my cod, or alligator grab my leg to drag me to drowning. But God is good. When I come up the sun is still there and I strike out for the little island in the river opposite the stelling. The river is full of death that pass you by, but the stelling holds a walking death like the destruction of Apocalypse.

I make ground at the island and draw myself into the mud and the bush and blood draw after me from between my legs. And when I look back at the stelling, I see Mister Cockburn lie down in him deck chair, as if fast asleep, and Mister Bailey lying on him face upon the boards, with him hands under him stomach and Zacchy on him back with him arms flung wide like a baby, and three more of the gang, Will, Benjie and Sim, all sprawl off on the boards, too, and a man more, the one we call 'Venezuela' fallen into the grass, and a last one, Christopher, walking like a chicken without a head until him drop close to Mister Bailey and cry out once before death hold him. The other seven gone. Them vanish. All except Son-Son, poor foolish Son-Son, who make across the flat where we play cricket, under the *kookorits* and straight to Rooi Swamp.

'Oh Jesus, John!' him bawl as him run. 'Don't kill me, John! Don't kill me, John!'

And John standing on the path, with the repeater still as the finger of God in him hands, aim once at Son-Son, and I know say how, even at that distance, him could break Son-Son's back clean in the middle. But him lower the gun, and shrug and watch Son-Son into the long grass of the savannah and into the swamp. Then him come down the path and look at the eight dead men. 'Dunnie!' him call. 'I know you is over there. How you stay?'

I dig a grave for the living into the mud.

'Dunnie!' him call again. 'You hurt bad? Answer me, man, I see you, you know? Look!'

A bullet bury itself one inch from my face and mud smack into my eye. 'Don't shoot me, John,' I beg. 'I lend you fifteen dollar, remember?'

'I finish shooting, Dunnie,' him say. 'You hurt bad?'

'No,' I tell him the lie. 'I all right.'

'Good,' him say from the stelling. 'I will bring the corial come fetch you.'

'No, John!' I plead with him. 'Stay where you is. Stay there! You don't want kill me now.' But I know say how demon guide a Carib hand sometimes and make that hand cut throats.

'Stay there, John!'

Him shrug again and squat beside Mister Cockburn's chair, and lift the fallen head and look at it and let the head fall again. And I wait. I wait and bleed and suffer, and think how plenty women will cry and plenty children bawl for them daddy when John's work is known in Zuyder Town. I think these things and watch John the way I would watch a bushmaster snake and bleed in suffering until dark fall. All night I lie there until God take pity and close my eye and mind.

When my mind come back to me, it is full day. John gone from the stelling and I can see him sit on the steps up at the house, watching the river. The dead stay same place where he drop them. Fever burn in me, but the leg stop bleed and I dip water from the river and drink.

The day turn above my head until I hear a boat engine on the far side of the bend, and in a little bit a police launch come up mid-stream and make for the stelling. When they draw near, one man step to the bows with a boat hook, and then the rifle talk from the steps and the man yell, hold him wrist and drop to the deck. Him twist and wriggle behind the cabin quicker than a lizard. I hear an Englishman's voice yell in the cabin and the man at the wheel find reverse before the yell come back from the savannah. The boat go down-stream a little then nose into the overhang of the bank where John's rifle can't find them. I call out once and they come across to the island and take me off on the other side, away from the house. And is when I come on board that I see how police know so quick about what happen. For Son-Son, poor foolish old Son-Son, who I think still hide out in the swamp is there. Him have on clothes not him own, and him is scratched and torn as if him had try to wrestle with a jaguar.

'Man,' the police sergeant tell me. 'You should have seen him when they did bring to us. Swamp tear off him clothes clean. Nearly tear off him skin.'

As is so I learn that Son-Son did run straight as a peccary pig, all night, twenty mile across Rooi Swamp where never any man had even put him foot before. Him did run until him drop down in the camp of a coolie rancher bringing cattle down to the coast, and they did take him from there down to the nearest police post. When him tell police the story, they put him in the jeep and drive like hell for the river mouth and the main station.

'Lord witness, Son-Son,' I say, 'You was born to hang. How you didn't meet death in Rooi Swamp eh?'

Him just look frighten and tremble, and the sergeant laugh.

'Him didn't want to come up river with me,' he say, 'Superintendent nearly have to tie him before him would step on the boat.'

'Sergeant,' the Superintendent say (him was the Englishman I hear call out when John wound the policeman). 'Sergeant, you take three men and move in on him from behind the house. Spread out well. I'll take the front approach with the rest. Keep low, you understand. Take your time.'

'Don't do it, Super,' I beg him. 'Look how John stay in that house up there. River behind him and clear view before. Him will see you as you move one step. Don't do it.'

Him look at me angry and the white eyebrow draw together in him red face.

'Do you think I'm going to leave him up there?' he say. 'He's killed eight and already tried to kill one of my men.'

Him is bad angry for the constable who sit on the bunk and holding him wrist in the red bandage.

'No, Super,' I tell him. 'John don't try to kill you. If him did try then you would have take one dead man out of the river. Him only want to show you that him can sting.'

But what use a poor black man talk to police. The sergeant and him three stand on the cabin roof, hold onto the bank and drag themself over. Then the Super with him five do the same. I can hear them through the grass like snakes on them stomach. John let them come a little way to the house, and then, with him first shot, him knock the Super's black cap off, and with him second, him plug the sergeant in the shoulder. The police rifles talk back for a while, and Son-Son look at me.

When the police come back, I take care to say no word. The sergeant curse when the Super pour Dettol on the wound and beg the Super to let him go back and bring John down.

'We'll get him', the Super say. 'He knows it. He knows he doesn't stand a chance.'

But him voice can't reach John to tell him that, and when them try again one man come back with him big toe flat and bloody in the police boot. When I go out, though, and walk along the bank to the stelling and lay out the bodies decent and cover them with canvas from the launch, it could have been an empty house up there on the bluff.

Another hour pass and the police begin to fret, and I know say that them is going to try once more. I want to tell them don't go, but them is police and police don't like hear other men talk.

And is then, as we wait, that we hear a next engine, an outboard, and round the bend come a Survey boat, and long before it draw up beside the overhang, my eye know Mister Hamilton as him sit straight and calm in the bows.

'Dunnie, you old fool,' him say and hold me by the shoulders. 'Why didn't you stop it? D'you mean to say you couldn't see it coming?'

Him smile to show me that the words is to hide sorrow. Him is the same Mister Hamilton. Dress off in the white shirt and white stocking him always wear, with the big linen handkerchief spread upon him head under the hat and hanging down the neck back to guard him from sun.

'I came as soon as I could,' him say to the Super. 'As soon as the police in Zuyder rang Survey and told us what you had 'phoned through.'

You can see the Super is glad to have one of him own sort to talk with. More glad, though, because it is Mister Hamilton and Mister Hamilton's spirit make all trouble seem less.

'We might have to bomb him out,' Super say. 'I've never seen a man to shoot like that. He must be a devil. Do you think he's sane, Hamilton?'

Mister Hamilton give a little smile that is not a smile.

'He's sane now,' he say. 'If he wasn't he'd have blown your head off.'

'What's he going to do?' Super ask.

Mister Hamilton lift him shoulder and shake him head. Then him go up to the cabin top and jump on the bank and walk to the stelling. Not a sign from the house.

I follow him and move the canvas from all the staring dead faces and him look and look and pass him hand, tired and slow, across him face.

'How did it go, Dunnie?' him ask.

I tell him.

'You couldn't have stopped him?'

'No,' I say. 'Him did have pride to restore. Who could have stop that? You, maybe, Mister Hamilton. But I doubt me if even you.'

'All right,' him say. 'All right.'

Him turn and start to walk to the house.

'Come back, man,' Super shout from where him lie in the grass on the bank. Mister Hamilton just walk on regular and gentle.

John's first bullet open a white wound in the boards by Mister Hamilton's left foot. The next one do the same by the right. Him never look or pause; even him back, as I watch, don't stiffen. The third shot strike earth before him and kick dirt onto him shoe.

'John!' him call, and Mister Hamilton have a voice like a howler monkey when him want. 'John, if you make a ricochet and kill me, I'm going to come up there and break your ——ing neck.'

Then I know say how this Mister Hamilton is the same Mister Hamilton that left we.

Him walk on, easy and slow, up the path, up the steps, and into the house.

I sit by the dead and wait.

Little bit pass and Mister Hamilton come back. Him is alone, with a basket in him hand. Him face still. Like the face of a mountain lake, back in the Interior, where you feel but can't see the current and the fullness of water below.

'Shirley,' him call to the Super, 'Bring the launch up to the stelling. You'll be more comfortable here than where you are. Its quite safe. He won't shoot if you don't rush him.'

I look into the basket him bring down from the house. It full of well-cooked *labba*. Enough there to feed five times the men that begin to gather on the stelling.

The super look into the basket also, and I see a great bewilderment come into his face.

'Good God!' him say. 'What's all this? What's he doing?'

'Dunnie,' Mister Hamilton say to me. 'There's a bottle of rum in my boat. And some bread and a packet of butter. Bring them over for me, will you? Go on,' him tell Super. 'Have some. John thought you might be getting hungry.' Him draw up the deck-chair in which Mister Cockburn did die. I go to the Survey boat and fetch out the rum and the bread and butter. The butter wrap into grease paper and sink in a closed billy pot of water to keep it from the sun. I bring knife, also, and a plate and a mug for Mister Hamilton, and a billyful of river water for put into the rum. When everything come, him cut bread and butter it and pour rum for Super and himself, and take a leg of *labba*. When him chew the food, him eat like John. The jaws of him mouth move sideways and not a crumb drop to waste. The rest of we watch him and Super, and then we cut into the *labba* too, and pour liquor from the bottle. The tarpaulin stretch above we and the tall day is beginning to die over the western savannah.

'Why did he do it?' Super say and look at the eight dead lay out under the canvas. 'I don't understand it, Hamilton. Christ! He *must* be mad.'

Him lean over beside Mister Hamilton and cut another piece of *labba* from the basket.

'What does he think he can do?' him ask again. 'If he doesn't come down I'm going to send down river for grenades. We'll have to get him out somehow.'

Mister Hamilton sit and eat and say nothing. Him signal to me and I pass him the bottle. Not much left into it, for we all take a drink. Mister Hamilton tilt out the last drop and I take the billy and go to the stelling edge and draw a little water for Mister Hamilton and bring it back. Him draw the drink and put the mug beside him. Then him step under the tarpaulin and fling the empty bottle high over the Catacuma water. And as the bottle turn and flash against the dying sun, I see it fall apart in the middle and broken glass falling like raindrops as John's bullet strike.

We all watch and wait, for now the whole world stand still and wait with we. Only the water make soft music round the stelling.

Then from up the house there is the sound of one shot. It come to us sudden and short and distant, as if something close it round.

'All right,' Mister Hamilton say to the Super. 'You better go and bring him down now.'

WAYNE BROWN

Wayne Brown was born in Trinidad in 1944 and was educated at the University of the West Indies at Mona in Jamaica. He was for some years literary critic of the *Trinidad Guardian* and also Gregory Fellow in Poetry at the University of Leeds. His first collection of poems, *On the Coast* was published in 1972, was a Poetry Book Society Recommendation and was awarded the Commonwealth Prize for Poetry. His other publications include *Selected Poetry of Derek Walcott* and *Edna Manley: The Private Years*. He now lives and writes in Jamaica.

The story that follows bears no resemblance whatever to the setting in which it was written: a spacious, soulless detached house in flat but pleasant Surrey with a vaguely alarming address: Whitehill End, Green Lane, Ockham ('How come?'). It was begun in March '74. Winter that year had been mild but nonetheless numbing to this small-islander: I remember pestering my wife with vigilant notations of the temperature and of the contraction of the light, saying things like 'You realise it was dark by twenty to four today?' with a kind of bitter fascination.

In February there was a false spring. Buds appeared on the plantstalks and trees, and the grass grabbed the chance and grew. I suspect it was in compensation for this (when winter, returning, clamped back down, freezing each hastily growing thing hopelessly at attention once more) that memory, unsummoned, arrived and transported the present writer into altogether another time and place . . .

. . . Dawn in the Savannah in Port of Spain, in the early 'sixties: horses cantering on the sand track; spectators in clusters, like bleary-eyed lab technicians with stop-watches and binoculars and shooting sticks; the earth fragrant, the grass pale, the beams of the blocked sun high in the sky . . . and all of it, all of it, experienced from that nondescript house in suburban Surrey with the elation of total recall!

Such a simple scene, such narrow nostalgia, could never have sustained a novel. Yet the story grew and grew. And in a puzzling departure for someone whose previous excursions into prose fiction had all been hit-and-run affairs, I found myself writing slowly and rewriting, piecemeal, endlessly. When it was finished I discovered I had committed some 20,000 words – and had landed cleanly between the stools of competing themes.

Back in Trinidad in 1976 I rewrote the whole thing, bringing to centerstage a bucolic narrator – one or two of whose quips survive parenthetically here – rendering the characters frankly as figments of his imagination, and turning the language baroque. The result was a completely different story – with the same formal fault.

So in the end I hacked away everything from the storyline, keeping only the racetrack, the race and its essential witnesses; and that is what appears here, along with the not quite exorcised ghosts of certain other scenes and siblings. (I notice that in the process a vaguely emblematic character – a laconic *parimutuel* seller, her red blouse 'darkened by sweat in the usual places' – got edited out of existence; that of some enigmatic 'Yankee executive' – all that remain are his disembodied white hands lying immobile on some desk in the sky; and that a certain shadowy girl, one doomed and lovely 'Lydia' – whose appearance, if the truth be known, like a silent orbiting moon first tugged the settling story out of shape – is mentioned here only by name.)

Bring on the Trumpeters appeared first, in this form, in *Tapia* of 2 January, 1977. Minds trained to leach philosophy from fiction will have no difficulty in discerning in it such themes as the trials and tribulations of nationalism or the intolerable opposition between Beauty and Truth, or in discoursing upon Comedy as the Mode of Exile.

If in addition to all this (or in lieu of it) the reader finds certain scenes or sayings staying with him beyond the story's end, we may yet have the last laugh on the author of that false spring in '74.

Wayne Brown

BRING ON THE TRUMPETERS

'**B**et on The Wrag then,' the short one (Rupert to you) was saying. 'Bet on anything.' He got up from the depopulated bank halfway along the backstretch and looked around him vaguely. Then, either because there was nothing to see or because the physical act had absorbed its emotional imperative, he promptly sat down again. 'Bet on The Wrag then,' he muttered.

The taller boy – henceforth Johnathan – drew inward his brows, perhaps to deflect the other's words (since verbal anger finds its mark, like a sharpshooter's bullet, right between the eyes) but he did not otherwise respond. Instead he plucked a spear of grass from the vicinity of his hip and tore it carefully lengthwise along the spine before losing interest and letting the halves drop. They lay where they fell. Rupert tried again.

'Look' he said exasperatedly, 'Stargazer never lose yet. Nine outa nine he beat them.'

'Nine outa nine!' he repeated, one clawed and lifted hand alerting the sombre heavens to bear witness.

'But now' – sotto voce, slant-eyed – 'suddenly you say he cyar win.'

'I never say he cyar win. I say I don't *think* he could win.'

Rupert looked uncertain. Then: 'Words,' he decided bitterly, 'Just words.' He squinted up at the sky and the other boy might be excused for thinking he was about to comment on the weather, but sad Rupert only crossed his elbows between his thighs and, jack-knifing slowly, forward, applied his shining forehead to his knees.

Out of sight of the track, discrete, but near, like a parent – and, like a

parent, never wholly to be ignored – lies the Allotment: a rhomboid of
ruined pastureland across whose weedy surface generations of beeline
walkers have impressed a pattern of dirt tracks like spokes. Mysteriously,
it has escaped development, and the mystery is heightened by the fact
that it has never been far from the minds of an alert populace, members
of whom have periodically written in to the press suggesting how it
should be put to use. *Concerned Patriarch* – an enduring eyesore –
invited the Government to remember the tourists; *Pedagogue* begged
leave to postulate for it, a regional conference centre; and *Housewife*
suggested, timidly, a park, 'with statues and fountains and trees.' *NASP*
demanded a national stadium; *Comrades in Christ*, a shrine. Committees
rose up, recommended, and subsided. There was even an ode by an old
and much read poet which began 'Thou alone, O desert hoar/Shalt the
sands of Time deride', and for which the opening rhymes were 'gnaw'
and 'pride'. The Chamber of Commerce ('a gross waste of resources')
asked the Government for a statement of intent; whereupon the Children
of Africa warned the people's Government not to 'let the Chamber of
Commerce get its – here followed a tantalising trickle of dots the
handiwork no doubt of a prudent but scrupulous editor – hands on it.'
When word spread that an American hotelier, one Ludendorf (a shady
character) had approached the Government to buy it everyone wrote at
once, and the ode-writer swept off his metrical steed by the reverbera-
tions of the fray, adding a scalding cascade of *vers libre*. But nothing was
ever actually done. Beneath the crossfire of recommendation and report
the Allotment, dourly oblivious, remained what by default it had long
become: a playground for the children of the poor.

But today it was a carpark for the race meeting and when, a couple of
hours ago, our young friends walked past it on their way to the track it
had already been filled. 'Boy,' quipped lanky Johnathan (a compulsive
quipper), 'Look at the desert whore today!' 'More like a tank factory to
me,' retorted stubby Rupert. And in truth there was a sinister air about
the cars – as though, standing shoulder to shoulder, rank on rank, they
concealed a collective and malignant will of their own, the more potent
for their having been left unattended. (Some of their windshields blazed
in the sun).

In the distance now a loud speaker said something which ended in a
brief scream, and Johnathan looking up from the bank, saw that the
betting booths has set up a mild magnetic field and were drawing people
gently towards them from all along the homestretch rail. The betting
booths were low green-painted structures built predominantly of corru-
gated zinc. They had been created a month ago, they would be abolished
in a month's time, but now they squatted, tremulous in the afternoon
heat, looking passably like a pair of poorly camouflaged pillboxes
(grim Rupert's remark) facing the stands with the winning post showing

between them. Johnathan eased his binoculars from their case and focused them to the offside of the betting booths where the parade ring would be and, yes, was. There was nothing happening there and he lowered the glasses, telling himself that there was still plenty of time. He reversed the binoculars – extracting process (left cap, right cap, fold the wings, slide, change hands, buckle the case), and, having deposited that precious possession tenderly flat on the grass, glanced wearily at his companion.

Rupert sat with his back to the stands, glaring at the inocuous mountains. It was hotter now that the sun had gone in and the mountains, blue and vague, gave off a directionless haze. Above them the sky was high and silvery, like the light which announces the sea. Looking at it hurt the eyes. Johnathan returning his gaze to his friend's immobile face, with its stubbled beard and slighting bulging eyes, thought: The boy could be a statue, or dead. 'Boy,' he attempted, 'You sitting there like a statue. Wapnin' Einstein?'

The statue of Einstein blinked. 'I just want to know,' it said gloomily, 'how you could be so mulish. Every tipster in town say Stargazer but you there with The kiss-me-ass Wrag. I just don't unnerstand you.'

Arguments like this one, when indulged in by the young, are apt to ramble on into the dusk, since the young are both more adamant and more generous than us, their brittle-spirited elders. What follows is therefore a ruthlessly telescoped version of the ensuing conversation.

Stargazer, like most local horses, had been bred to sprint (Johnathan), though he'd won a mile race (Rupert). That had been a slowly run mile (Johnathan) and Stargazer had been pushed to win it (Johnathan), but these were both big lies (Rupert). The race today was two furlongs longer (Johnathan), which hadn't seemed to worry the tipsters (Rupert), who were being sentimental (Johnathan) like everyone else (Johnathan) though 'everyone' obviously did not include him, Johnathan (Rupert, scathingly). A man had to know what he knew (Johnathan) and a man had to know what he felt (Rupert) though feelings couldn't change facts (Johnathan) and Johnathan knew everything, right? (Rupert).

'Awright!' declared violently irritated Johnathan, 'Tell me this. When last, *when last*, a creole win the Governor's Cup?'

'Governor-General's Cup,' corrected Rupert acidly. 'Try to remember, the name change.'

'Same race,' muttered Johnathan.

'Well,' said Rupert bitterly, 'I glad you say it . . .' Hugging his knees he had begun to rock back and forth.

'Say what?'

'What you just say. That a local horse could never beat a English horse. That a English horse mus' always beat a local horse. I glad you put it like that. At leas' now we know where you stand.'

A petrified instant fled by before Johnathan understood. 'We?' he demanded threateningly. 'Who we?'

'We, the people of this country.'

A mirror-multiplication of Petrified Instances marched stiffly out of sight. Johnathan stared at Rupert.

'Look you!' he yelled suddenly, 'Just go to hell, you hear?'

Rupert stiffened but did not reply. Abruptly he got up, dusting his trousers, and set off in the direction of the betting booths.

'Where you going?' called Johnathan (Poor Johnathan!)

'Hell.'

Johnathan sat and watched until the other boy, grown anonymously small, disappeared into the crowd around the betting booths. Then he got up, shouldered the binoculars, stuck his hands in his pockets, and set off miserably in that direction himself.

Now Johnathan loved racing. It was a true love, in that it lifted him out of himself, and it might have saved him (indeed, may yet have done so, for who is to say that in some simultaneous, purified Universe – all essences, not, like ours, hopelessly mired in dross – some negative of that melancholic boy does not sit in eternal, self-forgetting animation at the right hand of the Track Steward?). Many mornings rising early, he would cycle up to the track to watch the horses exercise before getting back on his bicycle to pedal the rest of the way to school. In this way he had learnt many things. He knew the tipsters by their first names now, and the man who rode the snow-cone cart across the park on his way to the city, appearing promptly every morning at 6.50 around the edge of the foothills. He had come to look forward to watching the mountains change, altering from black to grey, from grey to blue, from blue to green and black as the sun climbed; to look forward to the smell and creak of leather, and the stable boys' cries, which carried emptily, without resonance, across the early-morning fields; and to hearing the horses hooves thud when it was dry and splash when it had rained. He could recreate at will now the scent of wet grass, the great beams of light which the sun threw across the sky, like the headlamps of a conquering army, in the minutes before it cleared the mountain, and its sudden warmth on his face when it did. You could tell the time, he knew, by the way in which the cars trickled, and then poured, into sight around the bend from which, earlier, the snow-cone man had come; and if the Indian coconut vendor had done well the night before you knew by the chippings swept beneath the bench near the spot where he parked his cart each evening. Kaiser, the tipster, had a habit of enthusing when a horse he was sure would not win put in a good gallop, as such horses sometimes did – and of falling furtively silent whenever one went by whom he did think would do well; so you knew that too, and you watched him, and hoped, beside, that one day you would know as much about racehorses as was contained behind that bucolic expression, with its slack mouth and chronically bleary eyes. Likewise, you watched the trainers: Tall, black, austere Tom Charles, and the others, like red-faced, foul-mouthed DeVere and his polar opposite, Chin-Yen; or you tried to edge near enough to overhear what little, quick-talking Boodoo had to say to his trainer when he came back on Morgan's Folly from a mile run which began cunningly at the four-furlong post and ended abruptly in the backstretch, leaving you with your stopwatch ticking foolishly on; and, in between all this, you watched the girls. You watched with frank interest the daughters of the owners, standing around in jeans and boys' shirts and chatting, like girls who are not being watched; and you watched, with 16-year-old shyness, the wives: handsome, mature, brown-skinned women for whom a husband seemed always at hand when needed for something, such as to explain the significance of a gallop, or help with the adjusting of a shooting stick, or confirm what their stopwatches said.

But mostly you watched the horses: stocky, barrel-chested bays that swished their tails and bowed and seemed to feel the ground often with their forehooves, until released into a gallop; long-legged chestnuts, matt or gloss, cantering like dogs with their heads down; long-striding, mottle-silk-coated greys; the occasional high-stepping black – month in, month out you watched them, learning their habits and matching proportions with names until you could tell a horse at a distance, and which had acquired or shed bandages since when, who had the leg up on whom in whose place, and which would go left better than right. Then in your first free period at school, you wrote it all down in a red-covered notebook, shielding what you wrote with your left hand and glancing up often at the presiding priest; and in the evening, sitting in the lounge with the TV on, or in the pencil-biting silence of your sister's room, you tried to work out what it all meant.

They sat on the bank shelling and eating the peanuts. Rupert ate with concentration, decanting the shelled nuts into one hand and raising his cupped palm to his lips as if to drink. After several minutes: 'Hey, guess what?' he said.

Johnathan tossed a nut into the air and moved his face about under it so that it fell into his mouth. 'What?'

'Hosang find a next way to get rich.'

'A-gain?'

Hosang was a boy at school they disliked.

'He invent a non-sticky icetray.'

Johnathan snorted. 'You tell him about the new frigedaire from America with the automatic ice-maker attach?'

'Is that what I tell him. Exactly! I say, "Hosang, lemme ask you something. It already have fridge with automatic icemaker attach. You ever think of that?" I know because I see one already. Johnson father have one in the den.'

'I seen it, is a damn good den. So, what he say?'

Rupert shrugged. 'What he could say? I catch him there!'

'Hosang is a ass.'

'Boy, you could say that again.'

There was a short silence.

Johnathan squinted up at the skyline where now clouds lay heavily piled. It was getting very dark.

'One hell of a rain coming,' he said – and he thought at once of Stargazer, and that the race was still to come. I wish to God it would rain like hell, he thought, let them cancel the damn race. But he did not think that would happen, and looking for some other way out, he wondered next if he might indeed be wrong and if Stargazer might hang on to win. Then it came back to him, the mile Stargazer had won, and he felt sure that he was not wrong.

He remembered that race too well. Morales had ridden cleverly and won by a length, but Johnathan had only just bought the binoculars, he had kept them trained on the big chestnut the whole way, even after they had passed the post, and he had seen, what the tipsters had not or not wished to, how the horse's ears had gone back in the last strides, and how quickly he had come to a stop, shaking his head and changing down into a loose-jointed, slowing-up trot while the chasing pack swarmed around and past him; and Johnathan had known then with a thrill of surprise that Stargazer had been dead on his feet.

If only, he thought, old man Dixon had not been so wilful. If only, for the creole's first race among the imported horses, he had sent him in the sprint.

Johnathan could see it now: the long, bunched, driving run up the backstretch, with Stargazer outsprinting the fastest of them; Stargazer laying out on the corner, clear; Stargazer stretching forward his great golden neck and coming pounding down the homestretch rail ... They would have come at him in the straight, to be sure, especially a strong brute like The Wrecker, and probably there would have been Andromeda too, finishing fast and wide under the stands; but Stargazer would have held them he was certain of it, he would have hit the straight so full of running, and there would have been the roar of the crowd and he would have been one of them, leaping in the air and shouting, like everyone else ... Johnathan saw it all, as if it were really happening, saw it from start to finish; and when it was over he found himself grieving for the race that would not now be run, and cursing the greed and stupidity of old man Dixon that he should send his great horse out to meet defeat for the first time like this.

'Listen,' he said gently to Rupert, 'They making a mistake, you know.'

'Who?'

'The Stargazer people.'

Rupert grew wary. 'How come?'

'They shoulda send him in the sprint. He'd a'bound to win that.'

Rupert looked as though any moment he might frown.

'What I don't understand,' persisted Johnathan (again, boy?) 'Is why is so important. I mean, okay, so he's a local horse, and it would be nice if he won. But why it should be a matter of life and death – that is what I don't understand.'

'Sometimes,' Rupert muttered, 'I think you don't understand anything.'

'Listen man,' Rupert went on turning to look squarely at the other boy. 'You don't see what happening here today? You don't see how this horse bring everybody together? Black, white, rich, poor, everybody unite in this horse. When last you see this place like that, with everybody laughing and talking with everybody else?'

'Don't know,' admitted Johnathan.

'Not since Independence. Not since Independence! You don't see is not just a race? Everybody feeling this thing! Look around. Everybody have their money on the creole to win. Everybody excepting you.'

'Me and somebody else,' said Johnathan. And he told Rupert about the odds shortening like that on The Wrag, and about the image that had come into his mind.

Rupert listened attentively and, when he had finished, noted.

'Exactly, Exactly. Some white man. Some Yankee executive, come down to bleed the people. You see it yourself. Man, Johnathan I don't know. Sometimes I just wonder. How you could gang up with a man like that?'

'Is not ganging up.'

'Old man, people have to back up their own! You don't see it?'

'People have to know what they know.'

'Oh shit! You always know what you know. You is God.'

'Well,' said Johnathan churlishly 'This good united feeling you say everybody feeling. I only hope they still feeling it after the race. After Stargazer lose.'

It was happening and he did not want it to happen. A fear, greater it seemed than any the occasion could have warranted, was closing in on him, and now he was afraid, afraid. He said quickly, 'I wonder where they are,' meaning Lydia, meaning: I wish she were here; if she were here everything would be okay.

'Probably over by the stands,' Rupert said, sullen, but accepting the offer. He stood up, peering, and Johnathan thought that he had seen her and was going to wave. But when Rupert spoke it was only to say, in a voice to which all the deadness had returned, 'The horses out.'

Now the start of a race was something our Johnathan tried never to watch. The shattering wail of the bell, the instantly answering roar of the crowd as if it were some monstrous animal, which the bell, a spear, had found out as the startled horses leapt from their stalls – these were things he shied away from. He too would be pierced by the bell if he watched; he too would want to cry out as in pain.

Nor, he amended, was there any sense in trying to pick them up too early. They would break from the ten-furlong gates, he knew, only to disappear almost at once into the corridor between the stands and the home-stretch crowd, and there would be the baulked, heart-beating seconds with only the caps of the jockeys going along above the crowd as behind a hedge and flickering in and out behind the betting booths and the tote board before they poured into sight at the far end and ran down, in clear view now, to the seven-furlong pole and the long banked turn at the bottom end of the course. So now he raised the binoculars and found that marker and worked the cogs to bring it into clearest focus – and when the red light began to flash, when the bell wailed and the crowd answered, when Rupert said softly, once 'O God!' and a man nearby began immediately to leap in the air and shout 'The Gazer! The Gazer!' in a voice which seemed to start below his collarbone and to rattle with saliva as it emerged, Johnathan raised his binoculars and fixed them on the crowd-free place near the seven furlong pole and tried to keep his hands from shaking.

They were a long time in coming. The roar of the stands' crowds reached crescendo, passed, and he thought 'They coming now,' then, 'Now!' and still they did not appear. Then they came, one horse by itself and then the rest all at once, and he swung the binoculars to find the leading horse again and it was in truth the red and black of Stargazer, and he was two lengths clear.

'Who?' demanded Rupert, 'Who?' And when he said 'Stargazer,' Rupert shouted once, 'The creole!' before demanding 'Who next? Who next?' Johnathan did not answer at once. He was raking the field for the green and gold of The Wrag and not finding him. Then he saw him, lying seventh or eighth on the rails, and Johnathan kept the binoculars on him for several strides until he was sure that Maraj was doing nothing, just crouching over the horse's neck with his hands still, and that The Wrag was neither dawdling nor pulling but running strongly and steadily in his place, and then, answering Rupert, he said 'Oleander,' and eased the binoculars to the right to find Stargazer again.

'How he look?' asked Rupert, suddenly anxious.

'Okay. He look okay.'

They were streaming around the bottom turn now to come up into the backstretch and Stargazer had gone three lengths clear. He's going too fast, Johnathan thought, but he did not say it, only wondered whether this was old man Dixon's idea of tactics. Maybe he would rest him going up the hill, but it was still bloody stupid – except that Oleander was already being broken, slipping back through the field, and now Great Vulcan had come up and was second. The horses swung into the back-stretch, seeming to concertina as they came, and Rupert was shouting again. 'Come on, Stargazer!' and now Johnathan said it.

'He's going too fast.'

'Bullshit!'

'Watch and see.'

'You watch and see!'

They were coming up the long slope now, and even with them heading straight for you you could tell that Stargazer was in front and running all by himself. In the binoculars he was very near, and Johnathan was struck by a kind of light, a kind of energy that played off him as he raced, and he thought, *But in truth that is some horse*! He could see Morales sitting high and looking grim and pinch-faced behind his goggles, and Johnathan felt a knot starting in his throat and his eyes were beginning to swim. The binoculars were dragging his eyes out and he lowered them against his chest and watched the race coming, the horses spread out across the track but with the chestnut drumming strictly along in front. He could see the depth of his chest now, and the exultation in his swift earthpounding stride and in the way the horse kept swinging its head from side to side against the restraining of the reins, as if seeking a way to break free of them and into the pure joy of running and Johnathan felt his insides turn over, and he whispered, 'Oh, Christ, but he's beautiful!'

But travelling too fast: the thought came slamming back as from some iron arctic in his mind, and a great weight of doom passed over him and left him trembling slightly with anger and with fear. 'Such a horse,' he thought angrily, 'should not be doomed. Everything's wrong in this world.' But then, as the horses stormed up to where he stood, as the thunder of their hooves rose up to overwhelm the returning cries of the spectators, the beauty and the doom seemed to fall together within him and mix, his body blazed, the earth shook terribly under his feet and they were gone, going away, already gone, leaving falling at his feet a brief shower of sods, the lone note of a jockey's desolate, cautionary cry, and the tail of the last horse swishing helplessly.

Someone, far off, then nearer, was screaming, one word he could not understand.

'Stargazer!' Rupert screamed, 'Stargazer!' He ran stiff-legged a few paces after the receding horses; stopped; ran back; turned. There was a rigid, convulsed quality about all he did and Johnathan, watching him, incomprehension giving way to recognition, came slowly, dismayingly back to himself and looked around.

The crowd had entered ecstasy. Men, their heads back, fists held to the sky, stood rigid as lightning conductors, but roaring; women grabbed each other and screamed; and one man (whom Johnathan recognised as the man who had started bawling 'The Gazer!' from the word go) now abandoned his place on the backstretch rail and ran thunderingly across the field towards the winning pole, stopping suddenly to peer over, like a startled animal, at the hurrying horses and to bellow once 'The Gazer' before dashing off again.

Johnathan remembered the horses. Reluctantly he raised the binoculars. A slow dread was staining through him and he did not want to look at them. But something made him look.

They were pouring around the home turn now and the creole was still three lengths clear. Behind him, Johnathan knew, the jockeys would be shouting and jostling. Those who felt they had a winning chance would be hustling to get into position; some, boxed in, would be pleading to be let through. Some, sensing their mounts had had enough, would pull out and drop back as Great Vulcan was doing now; others, unsure of their chances, would be sitting stubbornly in their places, uncertain but riding hard and waiting to see what the homestretch would bring. Johnathan found Stargazer in the glasses and saw that he was running on the bit still, and, startled, thought: *Jesus, suppose* ...

Then, abruptly, as he watched something gave, some rhythm, some harmony vanished, and there was no longer the effortless onward-sweeping of the horse, no longer the great neck motionlessly sailing, but Stargazer's head was going up and down, Morales' hands were scything on his neck, and the horses were bunching up behind him to swing for home. And Johnathan, with the returning sorrow of a man who has laughed himself empty, steadied the binoculars on the chasing pack and waited, knowing that what would happen would come from there.

They were in the straight now and he saw that The Wrag was through on the rails and going up to close with the leader. Helen's Armour was finding nothing, he could tell, and something in pastel colours, its jockey's whip hand flailing, was coming up fast on the outside, going past horse after horse but with a lot of ground to make up. Johnathan watched only long enough to see The Wrag go clear, and to make sure the pastel-coloured jockey had left it too late, and then he lowered his binoculars. They would be going into the crowd soon, he knew, and besides he would not need them for the rest. You did not need binoculars to tell who that far, toylike figure of a horse was, sinking, as you watched, so quickly through the field, no longer second, nor third, fourth now, no longer fourth, sixth, seventh, out of it; nor to see the pastel colours go clear in second. Nor did you need binoculars to see your friend, Lydia's boyfriend, standing dream-like with his hands by his sides, slowly opening and closing his fists. A man might curse and throw his tickets away but you did not need binoculars for that, nor to know that all the shouting had ended and that people were standing numbly in their places.

Nor to watch Rupert's hands.

Johnathan looked at his friend's hands, obliviously, rhythmically clenching and unclenching, and thought suddenly of those other, white hands lying immobile on the desk in the sky, and he felt a great surge of pity for the hands before him here, seeing how helpless, how childlike they seemed. Watching them, he forgot everything else. Then Rupert turned and looked at him and he knew that the race was over, and that it was time to speak.

JEAN RHYS

Jean Rhys was born in Dominica in 1894. She spent her childhood there and although she left the West Indies when a girl of sixteen, the Caribbean theme is discernible throughout her work and for this reason she is regarded as a West Indian writer.

She lived an eventful life in Paris during the 1920's and 1930's and was encouraged to write by the English novelist Ford Madox Ford. Her first book was a collection of short stories *The Left Bank* (1928) which was followed by novels such as *Postures* (1928), *After Leaving Mr McKenzie* (1931), *Voyage in the Dark* (1934), and *Good Morning, Midnight* (1939).

Jean Rhys disappeared during the 1950's to reappear in Cornwall in 1966 when *Wide Sargasso Sea* (her story of the early life of the first Mrs Rochester in Charlotte Brontë's *Jane Eyre*, and arguably her most famous book) was published. It was followed by *Tigers are Better Looking* (1968), *Sleep It Off, Lady* (1974) and *Smile Please* (1979), her autobiography. She died in England in 1979.

In *Let Them Call It Jazz*, Jean Rhys demonstrates once again that the success of a writer is always, in the first place, a triumph of language. The story may be classified as an exile story – many of the issues it points to are treated in works like *To Sir, With Love*, *The Lonely Londoners*, and *The Emigrants*.

Selina Davis's encounters with landlords, neighbours, policemen, prison and an alien landscape are described in her own words. Selina comes over as a very clearly defined character in her own right, more objectified, distanced from her creator (on the surface) than most of Jean Rhys's other female protagonists. This achievement springs from the language Jean Rhys invents for Selina.

Jean Rhys left Dominica (the island of her birth) early in this century when she was a young girl. Her contact with dialect and dialect-speaking characters subsequently can only have been minimal. Yet remarkably in this story of the late 1970's her dialect strikes us as modern and realistic. Miss Rhys's native feeling for the dialect tone is so tenacious, and her inwardness with its essential rhythms and principles of grammar and syntax, so intuitive and intelligent that in all her work she can generate a convincing modified dialect and dialect-speaking character almost at will.

Kenneth Ramchand

LET THEM CALL IT JAZZ

One bright Sunday morning in July I have trouble with my Notting Hill landlord because he ask for a month's rent in advance. He tell me this after I live there since winter, settling up every week without fail. I have no job at the time, and if I give the money he want there's not much left. So I refuse. The man drunk already at that early hour, and he abuse me – all talk, he can't frighten me. But his wife is a bad one – now she walk in my room and say she must have cash. When I tell her no, she give my suitcase one kick and it burst open. My best dress fall out, then she laugh and give another kick. She say month in advance is usual, and if I can't pay find somewhere else.

Don't talk to me about London. Plenty people there have heart like stone. Any complaint – the answer is 'prove it'. But if nobody see and bear witness for me, how to prove anything? So I pack up and leave. I think better not have dealings with that woman. She too cunning, and Satan don't lie worse.

I walk about till a place nearby is open where I can have coffee and a sandwich. There I start talking to a man at my table. He talk to me already, I know him, but I don't know his name. After a while he ask, 'What's the matter? Anything wrong?' and when I tell him my trouble he say I can use an empty flat he own till I have time to look around.

This man is not at all like most English people. He see very quick, and he decide very quick. English people take long time to decide – you three-quarters dead before they make up their mind about you. Too besides, he speak very matter of fact, as if it's nothing. He speak as if he realise well what it is to live like I do – that's why I accept and go.

He tell me somebody occupy the flat till last week, so I find everything all right, and he tell me how to get there – three-quarters of an hour from Victoria Station, up a steep hill, turn left, and I can't mistake the house. He give me the keys and an envelope with a telephone number on the back. Underneath is written 'After 6 p.m. ask for Mr Sims'.

In the train that evening I think myself lucky, for to walk about London on a Sunday with nowhere to go – that take the heart out of you.

I find the place and the bedroom of the downstairs flat is nicely furnished – two looking glass, wardrobe, chest of drawers, sheets, everything. It smell of jasmine scent, but it smell strong of damp too.

I open the door opposite and there's a table, a couple chairs, a gas stove and a cupboard, but this room so big it look empty. When I pull the blind up I notice the paper peeling off and mushrooms growing on the walls – you never see such a thing.

The bathroom the same, all the taps rusty. I leave the two other rooms and make up the bed. Then I listen, but I can't hear one sound. Nobody come in, nobody go out of that house. I lie awake for a long time, then I decide not to stay and in the morning I start to get ready quickly before I change my mind. I want to wear my best dress, but it's a funny thing – when I take up that dress and remember how my landlady kick it I cry. I cry and I can't stop. When I stop I feel tired to my bones, tired like old woman. I don't want to move again – I have to force myself. But in the end I get out in the passage and there's a postcard for me. 'Stay as long as you like. I'll be seeing you soon – Friday probably. Not to worry.' It isn't signed, but I don't feel so sad and I think, 'All right, I wait here till he come. Perhaps he know of a job for me.'

Nobody else live in the house but a couple on the top floor – quiet people and they don't trouble me. I have no word to say against them.

First time I meet the lady she's opening the front door and she give me a very inquisitive look. But next time she smile a bit and I smile back – once she talk to me. She tell me the house very old, hundred and fifty year old, and she and her husband live there since long time. 'Valuable property,' she says, 'it could have been saved, but nothing done of course.' Then she tells me that as to the present owner – if he is the owner – well he have to deal with local authorities and she believe they make difficulties. 'These people are determined to pull down all the lovely old houses – it's shameful.'

So I agree that many things shameful. But what to do? What to do? I say it have an elegant shape, it make the other houses in the street look cheap trash, and she seem pleased. That's true too. The house sad and out of place, especially at night. But it have style. The second floor shut up, and as for my flat I go in the two empty rooms once, but never again.

Underneath was the cellar, full of old boards and broken-up furniture – I see a big rat there one day. It was no place to be alone in I tell you, and I get the habit of buying a bottle of wine most evenings, for I don't like whisky and the rum here no good. It don't even *taste* like rum. You wonder what they do to it.

After I drink a glass or two I can sing and when I sing all the misery goes from my heart. Sometimes I make up songs but next morning I forget them, so other times I sing the old ones like *Tantalizin'* or *Don't Trouble Me Now.*

I think I go but I don't go. Instead I wait for the evening and the wine and that's all. Everywhere else I live – well, it doesn't matter to me, but this house is different – empty and no noise and full of shadows, so that sometimes you ask yourself what make all those shadows in an empty room.

I eat in the kitchen, then I clean up everything and have a bath for coolness. Afterwards I lean my elbows on the windowsill and look at the garden. Red and blue flowers mix up with the weeds and there are five-six apple trees. But the fruit drop and lie in the grass, so sour nobody want it. At the back, near the wall, is a bigger tree – this garden certainly take up a lot of room, perhaps that's why they want to pull the place down.

Not much rain all the summer, but not much sunshine either. More of a glare. The grass get brown and dry, the weeds grow tall, the leaves on the trees hang down. Only the red flowers – the poppies – stand up to that light, everything else look weary.

I don't trouble about money, but what with wine and shillings for the slot-meters, it go quickly; so I don't waste much on food. In the evening I walk outside – not by the apple trees but near the street – it's not so lonely.

There's no wall here and I can see the woman next door looking at me over the hedge. At first I say good evening, but she turn away her head, so afterwards I don't speak. A man is often with her, he wear a straw hat with a black ribbon and goldrim spectacles. His suit hang on him like it's too big. He's the husband it seems and he stare at me worse than his wife – he stare as if I'm wild animal let loose. Once I laugh in his face because why these people have to be like that? I don't bother them. In the end I get that I don't even given them one single glance. I have plenty other things to worry about.

To show you how I felt. I don't remember exactly. But I believe it's the second Saturday after I come that when I'm at the window just before I go for my wine I feel somebody's hand on my shoulder and it's Mr Sims. He must walk very quiet because I don't know a thing till he touch me.

He says hullo, then he tells me I've got terrible thin, do I ever eat. I say of course I eat but he goes on that it doesn't suit me at all to be so thin and he'll buy some food in the village. (That's the way he talk. There's no village here. You don't get away from London so quick.)

It don't seem to me he look very well himself, but I just say bring a drink instead, as I am not hungry.

He come back with three bottles – vermouth, gin and red wine. Then he ask if the little devil who was here last smash all the glasses and I tell him she smash some, I find the pieces. But not all. 'You fight with her, eh?'

He laugh, and he don't answer. He pour out the drinks then he says, 'Now, you eat up those sandwiches.'

Some men when they are there you don't worry so much. These sort of men you do all they tell you blindfold because they can take the trouble from your heart and make you think you're safe. It's nothing they say or do. It's a feeling they can give you. So I don't talk with him seriously – I don't want to spoil that evening. But I ask about the house and why it's so empty and he says:

'Has the old trout upstairs been gossiping?'

I tell him, 'She suppose they make difficulties for you.'

'It was a damn bad buy,' he says and talks about selling the lease or something. I don't listen much.

We were standing by the window then and the sun low. No more glare. He puts his hand over my eyes. 'Too big – much too big for your face,' he says and kisses me like you kiss a baby. When he takes his hand away I see he's looking out at the garden and he says this – 'It gets you. My God it does.'

I know very well it's not me he means, so I ask him, 'Why sell it then? If you like it, keep it.'

'Sell what?' he says. 'I'm not talking about this damned house.'

I ask what he's talking about. 'Money,' he says. 'Money. That's what I'm talking about. Ways of making it.'

'I don't think so much of money. It don't like me and what do I care?' I was joking, but he turns around, his face quite pale and he tells me I'm a fool. He tells me I'll get pushed around all my life and die like a dog, only worse because they'd finish off a dog, but they'll let me live till I'm a caricature of myself. That's what he say, 'Caricature of yourself.' He say

I'll curse the day I was born and everything and everybody in this bloody world before I'm done.

I tell him, 'No I'll never feel like that,' and he smiles, if you can call it a smile, and says he's glad I'm content with my lot. 'I'm disappointed in you, Selina. I thought you had more spirit.'

'If I contented that's all right,' I answer him. 'I don't see very many looking contented over here.' We're standing glaring at each other when the doorbell rings. 'That's a friend of mine,' he says. 'I'll let him in.'

As to the friend, he's all dressed up in stripe pants and a black jacket and he's carrying a brief-case. Very ordinary looking but with a soft kind of voice.

'Maurice, this is Selina Davis,' says Mr Sims, and Maurice smiles very kind but it don't mean much, then he looks at his watch and says they ought to be getting along.

At the door Mr Sims tells me he'll see me next week and I answer straight out, 'I won't be here next week because I want a job and I won't get one in this place.'

'Just what I'm going to talk about. Give it a week longer, Selina.'

I say, 'Perhaps I stay a few more days. Then I go. Perhaps I go before.'

'Oh no you won't go,' he says.

They walk to the gates quickly and drive off in a yellow car. Then I feel eyes on me and it's the woman and her husband in the next door garden watching. The man make some remark and she look at me so hateful, so hating I shut the front door quick.

I don't want more wine. I want to go to bed early because I must think. I must think about money. It's true I don't care for it. Even when somebody steal my savings – this happen soon after I get to the Notting Hill house – I forget it soon. About thirty pounds they steal. I keep it roll up in a pair of stockings, but I go to the drawer one day, and no money. In the end I have to tell the police. They ask me exact sum and I say I don't count it lately, about thirty pounds. 'You don't know how much?' they say. 'When did you count it last? Do you remember? Was it before you move or after?'

I get confuse, and I keep saying, 'I don't remember,' though I remember well I see it two days before. They don't believe me and when a policeman come to the house I hear the landlady tell him, 'She certainly had no money when she came here. She wasn't able to pay a month's rent in advance for her room though it's a rule in this house. 'These people terrible liars,' she say and I think 'It's you a terrible liar, because when I come you tell me weekly or monthly as you like.' It's from that time she don't speak to me and perhaps it's she take it. All I know is I never see one penny of my savings again, all I know is they pretend I never have any, but as it's gone, no use to cry about it. Then my mind goes to my father, for my father is a white man and I think a lot about him. If I could see him only once, for I too small to remember when he was there. My mother is fair coloured woman, fairer than I am they say, and she don't stay long with me either. She have a chance to go to Venezuela when I three-four year old and she never come back. She send money instead. It's my grandmother take care of me. She's quite dark and what we call 'country-cookie' but she's the best I know.

She save up all the money my mother send, she don't keep one penny for herself – that's how I get to England. I was a bit late in going to school regular, getting on for twelve years, but I can sew very beautiful, excellent – so I think I get a good job – in London perhaps.

However, here they tell me all this fine handsewing take too long. Waste of time – too slow. They want somebody to work quick and to hell with the small stitches. Altogether it don't look so good for me, I must say, and I wish I could see my father. I have his name – Davis. But my grandmother tell me, 'Every word that comes out of that man's mouth is a damn lie. He is certainly first class liar, though no class otherwise.' So perhaps I have not even his real name.

Last thing I see before I put the light out is the postcard on the dressing table. 'Not to worry.'

Not to worry! Next day is Sunday, and it's on the Monday the people next door complain about me to the police. That evening the woman is by the hedge, and when I pass her she says in very sweet quiet voice, '*Must* you stay? *Can't* you go?' I don't answer. I walk out in the street to get rid of her. But she run inside her house to the window, she can still see me. Then I start to sing, so she can understand I'm not afraid of her. The husband call out: 'If you don't stop that noise I'll send for the police.' I answer them quite short. I say, 'You go to hell and take your wife with you.' And I sing louder.

The police come pretty quick – two of them. Maybe they just round the corner. All I can say about police, and how they behave is I think it all depends who they dealing with. Of my own free will I don't want to mix up with police. No.

One man says, you can't cause this disturbance here. But the other asks a lot of questions. What is my name? Am I tenant of a flat in No 17? How long have I lived there? Last address and so on. I get vexed the way he speak and I tell him, 'I come here because somebody steal my savings. Why don't you look for my money instead of bawling at me? I work hard for my money. All-you don't do one single thing to find it.'

'What's she talking about?' the first one says, and the other one tells me, 'You can't make that noise here. Get along home. You've been drinking.'

I see that woman looking at me and smiling, and other people at their windows, and I'm so angry I bawl at them too. I say, 'I have absolute and perfect right to be in the street same as anybody else, and I have absolute and perfect right to ask the police why they don't even look for my money when it disappear. It's because a dam' English thief take it you don't look,' I say. The end of all this is that I have to go before a magistrate, and he fine me five pounds for drunk and disorderly, and he give me two weeks to pay.

When I get back from the court I walk up and down the kitchen, up and down, waiting for six o'clock because I have no five pounds left, and I don't know what to do. I telephone at six and a woman answers me very short and sharp, then Mr Sims comes along and he don't sound too pleased either when I tell him what happen. 'Oh Lord!' he says, and I say I'm sorry. 'Well don't panic,' he says, 'I'll pay the fine. But look, I don't think ...' Then he breaks off and talk to some other person in the room. He goes on, 'Perhaps better not to stay at No 17. I think I can arrange something else. I'll call for you Wednesday – Saturday latest. Now behave till then.' And he hang up before I can answer that I don't want to wait till Wednesday, much less Saturday. I want to get out of that house double quick and with no delay. First I think I ring back, then I think better not as he sound so vex.

I get ready, but Wednesday he don't come, and Saturday he don't come. All the week I stay in the flat. Only once I go out and arrange for bread, milk and eggs to be left at the door, and seems to me I meet up with a lot of policemen. They don't look at me, but they see me all right. I don't want to drink – I'm all the time listening, listening and thinking, how can I leave before I know if my fine is paid? I tell myself the police let me know, that's certain. But I don't trust them. What they care? The answer is Nothing. Nobody care. One afternoon I knock at the old lady's flat upstairs, because I get the idea she give me good advice. I can hear her moving about and talking, but she don't answer and I never try again.

Nearly two weeks pass like that, then I telephone. It's the woman speaking and she say, 'Mr Sims is not in London at present.' I ask, 'When will he be back – it's urgent,' and she hang up. I'm not surprised. Not at all. I knew that would happen. All the same I feel heavy like lead. Near the phone box is a chemist's shop, so I ask him for something to make me sleep, the day is bad enough, but to lie awake all night – Ah no! He gives me a little bottle marked '*One or two tablets only*' and I take three when I go to bed because more and more I think that sleeping is better than no matter what else. However, I lie there, eyes wide open as usual, so I take three more. Next thing I know the room is full of sunlight, so it must be late afternoon, but the lamp is still on. My head turn around and I can't think well at all. At first I ask myself how I get to the place. Then it comes to me, but in pictures – like the landlady kicking my dress, and when I take my ticket at Victoria Station, and Mr Sims telling me to eat the sandwiches, but I can't remember everything clear, and I feel very giddy and sick. I take in the milk and eggs at the door, go in the kitchen and try to eat but the food hard to swallow.

It's when I'm putting the things way that I see the bottles – pushed back on the lowest shelf in the cupboard.

There's a lot of drink left, and I'm glad I tell you. Because I can't bear the way I feel. Not any more. I mix gin and vermouth and I drink it quick, then I mix another and drink it slow by the window. The garden looks different, like I never see it before. I know quite well what I must do, but it's late now – tomorrow I have one more drink, of wine this time, and then a song comes in my head, I sing it and I dance it, and more I sing, more I am sure this is the best tune that has ever come to me in all my life.

The sunset light from the window is gold colour. My shoes sound loud on the boards. So I take them off, my stockings too and go on dancing but the room feel shut in, I can't breathe, and I go outside still singing. Maybe I dance a bit too. I forget all about that woman till I hear her saying, 'Henry, look at this.' I turn around and I see her at the window. 'Oh yes, I wanted to speak with you,' I say, 'Why bring the police and get me in bad trouble? Tell me that.'

'And you tell me what you're doing here at all,' she says. 'This is a respectable neighbourhood.'

Then the man come along. 'Now young woman, take yourself off. You ought to be ashamed of this behaviour.'

'It's disgraceful,' he says, talking to his wife, but loud so I can hear, and she speaks loud too – for once. 'At least the other tarts that crook installed here were *white* girls,' she says.

'You a dam' fouti liar,' I say. 'Plenty of those girls in your country already. Numberless as the sands on the shore. You don't need me for that.'

'You're not a howling success at it certainly.' Her voice sweet sugar again. 'And you won't be seeing much more of your friend Mr Sims. He's in trouble too. Try somewhere else. Find somebody else. If you can, of course.' When she say that my arm moves of itself. I pick up a stone and bam! through the window. Not the one they are standing at but the next, which is of coloured glass, green and purple and yellow.

I never see a woman look so surprise. Her mouth fall open she so full of surprise. I start to laugh, louder and louder – I laugh like my grandmother, with my hands on my hips and my head back. (When she laugh like that you can hear her to the end of our street.) At last I say, 'Well, I'm sorry. An accident. I get it fixed tomorrow early.' 'That glass is irreplaceable,' the man says. 'Irreplaceable.' 'Good thing,' I say, 'those colours look like they sea-sick to me. I buy you a better windowglass.'

He shake his fist at me. 'You won't be let off with a fine this time,' he says. Then they draw the curtains, I call out at them. 'You run away.

Always you run away. Ever since I come here you hunt me down because I don't answer back. It's you shameless.' I try to sing *Don't trouble me now*.

> *Don't trouble me now*
> *You without honour.*
> *Don't walk in my footstep*
> *You without shame.*

But my voice don't sound right, so I get back indoors and drink one more glass of wine – still wanting to laugh, and still thinking of my grandmother for that is one of her songs.

It's about a man whose *doudou* give him the go-by when she find somebody rich and he sail away to Panama. Plenty people die there of fever when they make that Panama canal so long ago. But he don't die. He come back with dollars and the girl meet him on the jetty, all dressed up and smiling. Then he sing to her, 'You without honour, you without shame'. It sound good in Martinique patois too: 'Sans honte'.

Afterwards I ask myself, 'Why I do that? It's not like me. But if they treat you wrong over and over again the hour strike when you burst out that's what.'

Too besides, Mr Sims can't tell me now I have no spirit. I don't care, I sleep quickly and I'm glad I break the woman's ugly window. But as to my own song it go *right* away and it never come back. A pity.

Next morning the doorbell ringing wake me up. The people upstairs don't come down, and the bell keeps on like fury self. So I go to look, and there is a policeman and a policewoman outside. As soon as I open the door the woman put her foot in it. She wear sandals and thick stockings and I never see a foot so big or so bad. It look like it want to mash up the whole world. Then she come in after the foot, and her face not so pretty either. The policeman tell me my fine is not paid and people make serious complaints about me, so they're taking me back to the magistrate. He show me a paper and I look at it, but I don't read it. The woman push me in the bedroom, and tell me to get dress quickly, but I just stare at her, because I think perhaps I wake up soon. Then I ask her what I must wear. She say she suppose I had some clothes on yesterday. Or not? 'What's it matter, wear anything,' she says. But I find clean underclothes and stocking and my shoes with high heels and I comb my hair. I start to file my nails, because I think they too long for magistrate's court but she get angry. 'Are you coming quietly or aren't you?' she says. So I go with them and we get in a car outside.

I wait for a long time in a room full of policemen. They come in, they go out, they telephone, they talk in low voices. Then it's my turn, and first thing I notice in the court room is a man with frowning black eyebrows. He sit below the magistrate, he dressed in black and he so handsome I can't take my eyes off him. When he see that he frowns worse than before.

First comes a policeman to testify I cause disturbance, and then comes the old gentleman from next door. He repeat that bit about nothing but the truth so help me God. Then he says I make dreadful noise at night and use abominable language, and dance in obscene fashion. He says when they try to shut the curtains because his wife so terrify of me, I throw stones and break a valuable stain-glass window. He say his wife get serious injury if she'd been hit, and as it is she in terrible nervous condition and the doctor is with her. I think, 'Believe me, if I aim at your wife I hit your wife – that's certain.' 'There was no provocation,' he says. 'None at all.' Then another lady from across the street says this is true. She heard no provocation whatsoever, and she swear that they shut the curtains but I go on insulting them and using filthy language and she saw all this and heard it.

The magistrate is a little gentleman with a quiet voice, but I'm very suspicious of these quiet voices now. He ask me why I don't pay my fine, and I say because I haven't the money. I get the idea they want to find out all about Mr Sims – they listen so very attentive. But they'll find out nothing from me. He ask how long I have the flat and I say I don't remember. I know they want to trip me up like they trip me up about my savings so I won't answer. At last he ask if I have anything to say as I can't be allowed to go on being a nuisance. I think, 'I'm a nuisance to you because I have no money that's all.' I want to speak up and tell him how they steal all my savings, so when my landlord ask for month's rent I haven't got it to give. I want to tell him the woman next door provoke me since long time and call me bad names but she have a soft sugar voice and nobody hear – that's why I broke her window, but I'm ready to buy another after all.

I want to say all I do is sing in that old garden, and I want to say this in decent quiet voice. But I hear myself talking loud and I see my hands waving in the air. Too besides it's no use, they won't believe me, so I don't finish. I stop, and I feel the tears on my face. 'Prove it.' That's all they will say. They whisper, they whisper, They nod, they nod.

Next thing I'm in a car again with a different policewoman, dressed very smart. Not in uniform. I ask her where she's taking me and she says 'Holloway' just that 'Holloway'.

I catch hold of her hand because I'm afraid. But she takes it away. Cold and smooth her hand slide away and her face is china face – smooth like a doll and I think, 'This is the last time I ask anything from anybody. So help me God.'

The car came up to a black castle and little mean streets are all round it. A lorry was blocking up the castle gates. When it get by we pass through and I am in jail. First I stand in a line with others who are waiting to give up handbags and all belongings to a woman behind bars like in a post office. The girl in front bring out a nice compact, look like gold to me, lipstick to match and a wallet full of notes. The woman keep the money, but she give back the powder and lipstick and she half-smile. I have two pounds seven shillings and sixpence in pennies. She take my purse then she throw me my compact (which is cheap) my comb and my handkerchief like everything in my bag is dirty. So I think, 'Here too, here too.' But I tell myself, 'Girl, what you expect, eh? They all like that. All.'

Some of what happen afterwards I forget, or perhaps better not remember. Seems to me they start by trying to frighten you. But they don't succeed with me for I don't care for nothing now, it's as if my heart hard like a rock and I can't feel.

Then I'm standing at the top of a staircase with a lot of women and girls. As we are going down I notice the railing very low on one side, very easy to jump, and a long way below there's the grey stone passage like it's waiting for you.

As I'm thinking this a uniform woman step up alongside and grab my arm. She say, 'Oh no you don't.'

I was just noticing the railing very low that's all – but what's the use of saying so.

Another long line waits for the doctor. It move forward slowly and my legs terrible tired. The girl in front is very young and she cry and cry. 'I'm scared,' she keeps saying. She's lucky in a way – as for me I never will cry again. It all dry up and hard in me now. That, and a lot besides. In the end I tell her to stop, because she doing just what these people want her to do.

She stop crying and start a long story, but while she is speaking her voice get very far away, and I find I can't see her face clear at all.

Then I'm in a chair, and one of those uniform women is pushing my head down between my knees, but let her push – everything go away from me just the same.

They put me in the hospital because the doctor say I'm sick. I have cell by myself and it's all right except I don't sleep. The things they say you mind I don't mind.

When they clang the door on me I think, 'You shut me in, but you shut all those other dam' devils *out*. They can't reach me now.'

At first if bothers me when they keep on looking at me all through the night. They open a little window in the doorway to do this. But I get used to it and get used to the night chemise they give me. It very thick, and to my mind not very clean either – but what's that matter to me? Only the food I can't swallow – especially the porridge. The woman ask me sarcastic, 'Hunger striking?' But afterwards I can leave most of it, and she don't say nothing.

One day a nice girl come around with books and she give me two, but I don't want to read so much. Beside one is about a murder, and the other is about a ghost and I don't think it's at all like those books tell you.

There is nothing I want now. It's no use. If they leave me in peace and quiet that's all I ask. The window is barred but not small, so I can see a little thin tree through the bars, and I like watching it.

After a week they tell me I'm better and I can go out with the others for exercise. We walk round and round one of the yards in that castle – it is fine weather and the sky is a kind of pale blue, but the yard is a terrible sad place. The sunlight fall down and die there. I get tired walking in high heels and I'm glad when that's over. We can talk, and one day an old woman come up and ask me for dog-ends. I don't understand, and she start muttering at me like she very vexed. Another woman tell me she mean cigarette ends, so I say I don't smoke. But the old woman still look angry, and when we're going in she give me one push and I nearly fall down. I am glad to get away from these people, and hear the door clang and take my shoes off.

Sometimes I think, 'I'm here because I wanted to sing' and I have to laugh. But there's a small looking glass in my cell and I see myself and I'm like somebody else. Like some strange new person. Mr Sims tell me I too thin, but what he say now to this person in the looking glass? So I don't laugh again.

Usually I don't think at all. Everything and everybody seem small and far away, that is the only trouble.

Twice the doctor come to see me. He don't say much and I don't say anything, because a uniform woman is always there. She looks like she thinking, 'Now the lies start'. So I prefer not to speak. Then I'm sure they can't trip me up. Perhaps I there still, or in a worse place. But one day this happen.

We were walking round and round in the yard and I hear a woman singing – the voice come from high up, from one of the small barred windows. At first I don't believe it. Why should anybody sing here? Nobody want to sing in jail, nobody want to do anything. There's no reason, and you have no hope. I think I must be asleep, dreaming, but I'm awake all right and I see all the others are listening too. A nurse is with us that afternoon, not a policewoman. She stop and look up at the window.

It's a smoky kind of voice, and a bit rough sometimes, as if those old dark walls theyselves are complaining, because they see too much misery – too much. But it don't fall down and die in the courtyard; seems to me it could jump the gates of the jail easy and travel far, and nobody says one word. But as we go in I ask the woman in front who was singing. 'That's the Holloway song,' she says. 'Don't you know it yet? She was singing from the punishment cells, and she tell the girls cheerio and never say die.' Then I have to go one way to the hospital block and she goes another so we don't speak again.

When I'm back in my cell I can't just wait for bed. I walk up and down and I think. 'One day I hear that song on trumpets and these walls will fall and rest.' I want to get out so bad I could hammer on the door, for I know now that anything can happen, and I don't want to stay lock up here and miss it.

Then I'm hungry. I eat everything they bring and in the morning I'm still so hungry I eat the porridge. Next time the doctor come he tells me I seem much better. Then I say a little of what really happen in that house. Not much. Very careful.

He look at me hard and kind of surprised. At the door he shake his finger and says, 'Now don't let me see you here again.'

That evening the woman tells me I'm going, but she's so upset about it I don't ask questions. Very early, before it's light she bangs the door open and shouts at me to hurry up. As we're going along the passages I see the girl who gave me the books. She's in a row with the others doing exercises. Up Down, Up Down, Up. We pass quite close and I notice she's looking very pale and tired. It's crazy, it's all crazy. This up down business and everything else too. When they give me my money I remember I leave my compact in the cell, so I ask if I can go back for it. You should see that policewoman's face as she shoo me on.

There's no car, there's a van and you can't see through the windows. The third time it stop I get out with one other, a young girl, and it's the same magistrates' court as before.

The two of us wait in a small room, nobody else there, and after a while the girl say, 'What the hell are they doing? I don't want to spend all day here.' She go to the bell and she keep her finger press on it. When I look at her she say, 'Well, what are they *for*?' That girl's face is hard like a board – she could change faces with many and you wouldn't know the difference. But she gets results certainly. A policeman comes in, all smiling, and we go in the court. The same magistrate, the same frowning man sits below, and when I hear my fine is paid I want to ask who paid it, but he yells at me, 'Silence'.

I think I will never understand the half of what happen, but they tell me I can go, and I understand that. The magistrate ask if I'm leaving the neighbourhood and I say yes, then I'm out in the streets again, and it's the same fine weather, same feeling I'm dreaming.

When I get to the house I see two men talking in the garden. The front door and the door of the flat are both open. I go in, and the bedroom is empty, nothing but the glare streaming inside because they take the Venetian blinds away. As I'm wondering where my suitcase is, and the clothes I leave in the wardrobe, there's a knock and it's the old lady from upstairs carrying my case packed, and my coat is over her arm. She says she sees me come in. 'I kept your things for you.' I start to thank her but she turn her back and walk away. They like that here, and better not expect too much. Too besides, I bet they tell her I'm terrible person.

I go in the kitchen, but when I see they are cutting down the big tree at the back I don't stay to watch.

At the station I'm waiting for the train and a woman asks if I feel well. 'You look so tired,' she says. 'Have you come a long way?' I want to answer, 'I come so far I lose myself on that journey.' But I tell her, 'Yes, I am quite well. But I can't stand the heat.' She says she can't stand it either, and we talk about the weather till the train come in.

I'm not frightened of them any more – after all what else can they do? I know what to say and everything go like a clock works.

I get a room near Victoria where the landlady accept one pound in advance, and next day I find a job in the kitchen of a private hotel close by. But I don't stay there long. I hear of another job going in a big store – altering ladies' dresses and I get that. I lie and tell them I work in very expensive New York shop. I speak bold and smooth faced, and they never check up on me. I make a friend there – Clarice – very light coloured, very smart, she have a lot to do with the customers and she laugh at some of them behind their backs. But I say it's not their fault if the dress don't fit. Special dress for one person only – that's very expensive in London. So it's take in, or let out all the time. Clarice have two rooms not far from the store. She furnish herself gradual and she gives parties sometimes Saturday nights. It's there I start whistling the Holloway song. A man come up to me and says, 'Let's hear that again.' So I whistle it again (I never sing now) and he tells me 'Not bad'. Clarice have an old piano somebody gave her to store and he plays the tune, jazzing it up. I say, 'No, not like that,' but everybody else say the way he do it is first class. Well I think no more of this till I get a letter from him telling me he has sold the song and as I was quite a help he encloses five pounds with thanks.

I read the letter and I could cry. For after all, that song was all I had. I don't belong nowhere really, and I haven't money to buy my way to belonging. I don't want to either.

But when that girl sing, she sing to me and she sing for me. I was there because I was *meant* to be there. It was *meant* I should hear it – this I *know*.

Now I've let them play it wrong, and it will go from like all the other songs – like everything. Nothing left for me at all.

But then I tell myself all this is foolishness. Even if they played it on trumpets, even if they played it just right, like I wanted – no walls would fall so soon. 'So let them call it jazz,' I think, and let them play it wrong. That won't make no difference to the song I heard.

I buy myself a dusty pink dress with the money.

GEOFFREY DRAYTON

Geoffrey Drayton was born in Barbados in 1924 and educated there and at Cambridge University. He has written two novels: *Christopher* (1959), and *Zohara* (1961) and a book of poems, *Three Meridians* published in 1951. He now lives in London.

Although it is more frequently true of poetry, novels and short stories are sometimes born of a phrase or sentence that swims uninvited into the mind. I once wrote a novel on the sole inspiration of: 'For years Mr Peabody had looked forward to dying so that he could haunt his wife'. The novel has not been published, no doubt because the rest of it did not live up to the promise of the opening line!

This story had a similar origin – in the doggerel phrase 'Mr Dombey, the zombie'. It was 1952, and I was then trying to make my way as a freelance writer. To this end I was living in a London suburb of great cheapness but depressing conformity, human and architectural. Much of my time was spent in the reading room of the British Museum, where I was studying the origins of *obeah* and *voodoo* in the belief that it would be possible to discover from what part of Africa the populations of various West Indian islands had come, by relating the religions and beliefs of the continent to their vestiges in the islands. Nothing came of the idea, since my freelancing gave me the time but not the money to pursue it. So the freelancing had to end: I joined the lines of morning faces that waited at the station (the same blank faces at the same hour every day) for the train to London and a nine to five job. 'Mr Dombey' was the result of this conjunction of circumstances.

Geoffrey Drayton

MR DOMBEY

Mr Dombey, the zombie, took the 8.10 train every morning of the working week. On the way to London he read a newspaper, carefully digesting the long spates of words so that their essence might be spewed up again, in a form acceptable to his *hounsi*. She, as a priestess of voodoo, was chiefly interested in the latest murders, rapes, etc., but her interest was insufficient to make her read through whole columns for the sake of a few sharp thrills they offered. Anyhow, it was to save herself such useless bother that she had gone to the trouble of acquiring a zombie. Mr Dombey not only read the newspapers and books – Crime Club for the most part – but he kept her garden tidy, mowed the lawn, washed the dishes. He could not of course earn very much money, because, being a zombie and capable only of habitual action, he was forced to work at mechanical tasks, under orders from a superior. At times this annoyed her and she berated him for it; but since it was not really his fault – and, in any case, he could not argue back – she was restricted in her displeasure. Usually she vented it by imposing on him some especially disagreeable task – like cleaning out the chicken-coops or scrubbing the kitchen-floor. The chickens were a most unfriendly lot, perhaps because they knew that they were only kept to provide sacrifices at the right times of year; they never appeared to lay eggs – or so Mr Dombey would have been led to presume if he had been capable of presuming anything. They pecked him when he came near; but by his nature he was oblivious to the pecking of hens. No doubt if he had been human he would have been less oblivious, perhaps even fearful. As it was, his only fear was of the woman who had charmed his spirit out and obtained control of his body. He had been dying at the time, otherwise her spells would not have succeeded; the spirit was now imprisoned in a large, curiously carved and decorated gourd which reposed on the mantlepiece in the sitting-room. Until the gourd was broken, and the spirit rejoined the body, Mr Dombey would be incapable of dying, would have to continue in servile obedience.

This state of affairs had continued for more than thirty years, when suddenly one day the *hounsi* fell ill. She tried various herbs and remedies of her own concoction, even certain spells that she had inherited from the *mamaloi* of her faith; but all to no avail. Eventually she was forced to take to her bed; and since she could not trust anyone else in the house, Mr Dombey no longer caught the 8.10 train to his daily task in the city. He remained by her bedside, fetching and carrying. She grew worse. At last she decided to summon a doctor. Obviously Damballa was angry with her. She had gone through the rites necessary for his godly placation, but all had failed; she could now do herself no further harm by trying the sorceries of science.

But the *hounsi* had waited too late. The doctor discovered her in the final grimaces of life. In the post-mortem he diagnosed death by arsenic-poisoning.

It was all, of course, a ghastly mistake. The *hounsi* had been in the habit of taking a stomach-powder – for some strange disease of her kind known as flatulence. On the latest occasion of his being sent to purchase this commodity, Mr Dombey had been ordered to buy arsenic as well – for killing rats. A malignant hand of Providence – Damballa's no doubt – had substituted the stomach-powder for the arsenic. As a result the *hounsi* had been attempting to cure her flatulence with arsenic.

The newspapers blamed Mr Dombey. They were, of course, quite mistaken; but neither the journalists concerned, nor, later, the police knew anything about voodoo and zombies; and Mr Dombey was incapable of informing them. The result was a gross miscarriage of justice. Mr Dombey was found guilty of murder and sentenced to death by hanging.

Had matters proceeded in an ordinary fashion – as they no doubt would have done if Mr Dombey had been an ordinary man – there would have been no merit in bringing up this old tale. But at this point what had seemed straightforward suddenly became bizarre. The newspapers screamed with delight. Mr Dombey was transformed, overnight, into a sort of hero. Some even found proof of his innocence – as with the mediaeval ordeals – in the fact that he could not be hanged. On the first occasion of his hanging, the trap-door had failed to open. The rope had broken on a second attempt. But – great climax of all – when the apparatus had finally worked and Mr Dombey had been seen to swing in orthodox fashion, the corpse showed a most unexpected co-operation in helping his executioners lift it down.

Mr Dombey's sentence was commuted to life imprisonment. He was said to be nearly sixty at this time, and, judging by his gauntness, the deathlike pallor of his face, and the fact that he had recently undergone unnerving experiences, everyone who thought about it decided that the state would not have to support him for long. At that point the newspapers turned their attentions elsewhere, though keeping the matter in mind, anticipating an obituary in which the sensational hanging might be again used to titillate the public.

But newspapermen die, and their dreams die with them. Mr Dombey, on the other hand, persisted in living. He was still alive seventy years later – growing parched and withered to be sure, but by no means an invalid. He had seen many prison wardens and convicts come and go. But he did nothing to bring himself to their attention, so that he was successfully forgotten and his age uncommented on.

Mr Dombey was, in fact, a hundred and thirty years old when his great-great nephews decided to springclean their attic.

After the death of Mrs Dombey and the imprisonment of her supposed murderer, relatives had taken over the ill-omened house, the chickens and the gourd. They had slaughtered the chickens; but, not knowing what to do with the strange sitting room ornament, they had put it into the attic along with several other of the inherited monstrosities. There the gourd had remained, for two generations, growing wizened and dusty, but with Mr Dombey's spirit safe in its bowels. Now, on this day of springcleaning, it was again brought forth. Quite unceremoniously – since who was to know that it had a value above a cremation-urn? – it was thrown on the bonfire. Without a murmur it dissolved into ashes.

And so Mr Dombey again cheated the newspapers and the seekers after truth – and to be exact, the police records. If a little pile of ashes in a prison courtyard had been able to speak it might have related that Mr Dombey had suddenly felt a raging fever. The next moment he was dust. Then the wind blew and Mr Dombey was dissipated among the other particles.

SAMUEL SELVON

Samuel Selvon was born in Trinidad in 1923 and educated there. He has written several novels: *A Brighter Sun* (1952), *An Island is a World* (1955), *The Lonely Londoners* (1956), *Turn Again Tiger* (1958), *I Hear Thunder* (1965), *The Housing Lark* (1965), *A Drink of Water* (1968), *Those Who Eat The Cascadura* (1972), *Moses Ascending* (1975), and a collection of short stories *Ways of Sunlight* published in 1958.

He has written extensively on the subject of West Indians who arrived in Britain in the 1950's and the problems they faced in settling there and coming to terms with a way of life very different from that which they had been used to in the Caribbean.

He now lives in Canada.

These two stories are widely separated by time, style and location, among other things. *Cane is Bitter* was written in Trinidad in 1949, when I was still living in the island and writing was for me more of a vehicle for self-expression than the promise of a future career. It was one of my earliest attempts at 'conscious' writing – deliberately working on the story to incorporate social commentary, in this case the economic circumstances which necessitated the use of child labour among East Indians on the sugarcane estates, and the caution with which they approached education as it threatened their way of life.

Samuel Selvon

CANE IS BITTER

In February they began to reap the cane in the undulating fields at Cross Crossing estate in the southern part of Trinidad. 'Crop time coming boy, plenty work for everybody,' men in the village told one another. They set about sharpening their cutlasses on grinding stones, ceasing only when they tested the blades with their thumb-nails and a faint ping! quivered in the air. Or they swung the cutlass at a drooping leaf and cleaved it. But the best test was when it could shave the hairs of your leg.

Everyone was happy in Cross Crossing as work loomed up in the way of their idleness, for after the planting of the cane there was hardly any work until the crop season. They laughed and talked more and the children were given more liberty than usual, so they ran about the barracks and played hide and seek in those canefields which had not yet been fired to make the reaping easier. In the evening, when the dry trash was burnt away from the stalks of sweet juice, they ran about clutching the black straw which rose on the wind: people miles away knew when crop season was on for the burnt trash was blown a great distance away. The children smeared one another on the face and laughed at the black streaks. It wouldn't matter now if their exertions made them hungry, there would be money to buy flour and rice when the men worked in the fields, cutting and carting the cane to the weighing-bridge.

In a muddy pond about two hundred yards east of the settlement, under the shade of spreading laginette trees, women washed clothes and men bathed mules and donkeys and hogcattle. The women beat the clothes with stones to get them clean, squatting by the banks, their skirts drawn tight against the back of their thighs, their saris retaining grace of arrangement on their shoulders even in that awkward position. Naked children splashed about in the pond, hitting the water with their hands and shouting when the water shot up in the air at different angles, and trying to make brief rainbows in the sunlight with the spray. Rays of the morning sun came slantways from halfway up in the sky, casting the shadow of trees on the pond, and playing on the brown bodies of the children.

Ramlal came to the pond and sat on the western bank, so that he squinted into the sunlight. He dipped his cutlass in the water and began to sharpen it on the end of a rock on which his wife Rookmin was beating clothes. He was a big man, and in earlier days was reckoned handsome. But work in the fields had not only tanned his skin to a deep brown but actually changed his features. His nose had a slight hump just above the nostrils, and the squint in his eyes was there even in the night, as if he were peering all the time, though his eyesight was remarkable. His teeth were stained brown with tobacco, so brown that when he laughed it blended with the colour of his face, and you only saw the lips stretched wide and heard the rumble in his throat.

Rookmin was frail but strong as most East Indian women. She was not beautiful, but it was difficult to take any one feature of her face and say it was ugly. Though she was only thirty-six, hard work and the bearing of five children had taken toll. Her eyes were black and deceptive, and perhaps she might have been unfaithful to Ramlal if the idea had ever occurred to her. But like most of the Indians in the country districts, half her desires and emotions were never given a chance to live, her life dedicated to wresting an existence for herself and her family. But as if she knew the light she threw from her eyes, she had a habit of shutting them whenever she was emotional. Her breasts sagged from years of suckling. Her hands were wrinkled and callous. The toes of her feet were spread wide from walking without any footwear whatsoever: she never had need for a pair of shoes because she never left the village.

She watched Ramlal out of the corner of her eye as he sharpened the cutlass, sliding the blade to and fro on the rock. She knew he had something on his mind, that was how he had come silently and sat near to her pretending that he could add to the keenness of his razor-sharp cutlass. She waited for him to speak, in an oriental respectfulness. But from the attitude of both of them, it wasn't possible to tell that they were about to converse, or even that they were man and wife. Rookmin went on washing clothes, turning the garments over and over as she pounded them on a flat stone, and Ramlal squinted his eyes and looked at the sun.

At last, after five minutes or so, Ramlal spoke.

'Well, that boy Romesh coming home tomorrow. Is six months since he last come home. This time, I make up my mind, he not going back.'

Rookmin went on scrubbing, she did not even look up.

'You see how city life change the boy. When he was here the last time, you see how he was talking about funny things?'

Rookmin held up a tattered white shirt and looked at the sun through it.

'But you think he will agree to what we are going to do?' she asked. 'He must be learning all sorts of new things, and this time might be worse than last time. Suppose he want to take creole wife?'

'But you mad or what? That could never happen. Ain't we make all arrangements with Sampath for Doolsie to married him? Anyway,' he went on, 'is all your damn fault in the first place, wanting to send him for education in the city. You see what it cause? The boy come like a stranger as soon as he start to learn all those funny things they teach you in school, talking about poetry and books and them funny things.'

'I did never want to send him for education, but it is you who make me do it.'

'Education is a good thing,' Rookmin said, without intonation. 'One day he might come lawyer or doctor, and all of we would live in a big house in the town, and have servants to look after we.'

'That is only foolish talk,' Ramlal said. 'You think he would remember we when he comes a big man? And besides, by that time you and me both dead. And besides, the wedding done plan and everything already.'

'Well, if he married Doolsie everything might work out.'

'How you mean if? I had enough of all this business. He have to do what I say, else I put him out and he never come here again. Doolsie father offering big dowry, and afterwards the both of them could settle on the estate and he could forget all that business.'

Rookmin was silent. Ramlal kept testing the blade with his nail, as if he were fascinated by the pinging sound, as if he were trying to pick out a tune.

But in fact he was thinking, thinking about the last time his son Romesh had come home ...

It was only his brothers and sisters, all younger than himself, who looked at Romesh with wonder, wanting to ask him questions about the world outside canefields and the village. Their eyes expressed their thoughts, but out of some curious embarrassment they said nothing. In a way, this brother was a stranger, someone who lived far away in the city, only coming home once or twice a year to visit them. They were noticing a change, a distant look in his eyes. Silently, they drew aside from him, united in their lack of understanding. Though Romesh never spoke of the great things he was learning, or tried to show off his knowledge, the very way he bore himself now, the way he watched the cane moving in the wind was alien to their feelings. When they opened the books he had brought, eager to see the pictures, there were only pages and pages of words, and they couldn't read. They watched him in the night, crouching in the corner, the book on the floor near to the candle, reading. That alone made him different, set him apart. They thought he was going to be a pundit, or a priest, or something extraordinary. Once his sister had asked: 'What do you read so much about, *bhai*?' and Romesh looked at her with a strange look and said. 'To tell you, you wouldn't understand. But have patience, a time will come soon, I hope, when all of you will learn to read and write.' Then Hari, his brother, said, 'Why do you feel we will not understand? What is wrong with our brains? Do you think because you go to school in the city that you are better than us? Because you get the best clothes to wear, and shoes to put on your feet, because you get favour from *bap* and *mai*?' Romesh said quickly, '*Bhai*, it is not that. It is only that I have left our village, and have learned about many things which you do not know about. The whole world goes ahead in all fields, in politics, in science, in art. Even now the governments in the West Indies are talking about federating the islands, and then what will happen to the Indians in this island? But we must not quarrel, soon all of us will have a chance.' But Hari was not impressed. He turned to his father and mother and said: 'See how he has changed. He don't want to play no games anymore, he don't want to work in the fields, he is too much of a bigshot to use a cutlass. His brothers and sisters are fools, he don't want to talk to them because they don't understand. He don't even want to eat we food again, this morning I see he ain't touch the *baghi*. No. We have to get chicken for him, and the cream from all the cows in the village. Yes, that is what. And who it is does sweat for him to get him pretty shirt to wear in Port of Spain?' He held up one of the girls' arms and spanned it with his fingers. 'Look how thin she is. All that is for you to be a big man, and now you scorning your own family?' Romesh got up from the floor and faced them. His eyes burned fiercely, and he looked like the pictures of Indian Gods the children had seen in the village hall. 'You are all wrong!' He cried in a ringing voice. 'Surely you, *bap*, and you, *mai*, the years must have taught you that you must make a different life for your children, that you must free them from ignorance and the wasting away of their lives? Do you want them to suffer as you have?' Rookmin looked like she was going to say something, but instead she shut her eyes tight. Ramlal said: 'Who tell you we suffer? We bring children in the world and we happy.' But Romesh went on, 'And what will the children do? Grow up in the village here, without learning to read and write? There are schools in San Fernando, surely you can send them there to learn about different things besides driving a mule and using a cutlass? Oh *bap*, we are such a backward people, all the others move forward to better lives, and we lag behind believing that what is to be, will be. All over Trinidad, in the country districts, our people toil on the land and reap the cane. For years it has been so, years in the same place, learning nothing new, accepting our fate like animals. Political men come from India and give speeches in the city. They speak of better things, they tell us to unite and strive for a greater goal. And what does it mean to you? Nothing. You are content to go hungry, to see your children run about naked, emaciated, grow up dull and stupid, slaves to your own indifference. You do not even pretend an interest in the Legislative Council. I remember why you voted for Pragsingh last year, it was because he gave you ten dollars – did I not see it for myself? It were better that we returned to India than stay in the West Indies and live such a low form of existence.' The family watched Romesh wide-eyed. Ramlal sucked his clay pipe noisily. Rookmin held her youngest daughter in her lap, picking her head for lice, and now and then shutting her eyes so the others wouldn't see what she was thinking. 'There is only one solution,' Romesh went on, 'We must educate the children, open up new worlds in their minds, stretch the horizon of their thoughts ...' Suddenly he stopped. He realised that for some time now they weren't listening, his words didn't make any sense to them. Perhaps he was going about this in the wrong way, he would have to find some other way of explaining how he felt. And was he sufficiently equipped in himself to propose vast changes in the lives of the people? It seemed to him then how small he was, how there were so many things he didn't know. All the books he'd read, the knowledge he'd lapped up so hungrily in the city, listening to the politicians making speeches in the square – all these he mustered to his assistance. But it was as if his brain were too small, it was like putting your mouth in the sea and trying to drink all the water. Wearily, like an old man who had tried to prove his point merely by repeating, 'I am old, I should know,' Romesh sat down on the floor, and there was a silence in the hut, a great silence, as if the words he'd spoken had fled to the place and gone outside with the wind and the cane.

And so after he had gone back to the city his parents discussed the boy, and concluded that the only thing to save his senses was to marry him off. 'You know he like Sampath daughter from long time, and she is a hard-working girl, she go make good wife for him.' Rookmin had said. Ramlal had seen Sampath and everything was fixed. Everybody in the village knew of the impending wedding ...

Romesh came home the next day. He had some magazines and books under his arm, and a suitcase in his hand. There was no reception for him; everyone who could work was out in the fields.

He was as tall as the canes on either side of the path on which he walked. He sniffed the smell of burning cane, but he wasn't overjoyed at coming home. He had prepared for this, prepared for the land on which he had toiled as a child, the thatched huts, the children running naked in the sun. He knew that these things were not easily forgotten which he had to forget. But he saw how waves of wind rippled over the seas of cane and he wondered vaguely about big things like happiness and love and poetry, and how they could fit into the poor, toiling lives the villagers led.

Romesh met his sisters at home. They greeted him shyly but he held them in his arms and cried, '*Beti*, do you not know your own brother?' And they laughed and hung their heads on his shoulder.

'Everybody gone to work,' one girl said, 'and we cooking food to carry. Pa and Ma was looking out since early this morning, they say to tell you if you can come in the fields.'

Romesh looked around the hut in which he had grown up. It seemed to him that if he had come home after ten years, there would still be the old table in the centre of the room, its feet sunken in the earthen floor, the black pots and pans hanging on nails near the window. Nothing would change. They would plant the cane, and when it grew and filled with sweet juice cut it down for the factory. The children would waste away their lives working with their parents. No schooling, no education, no widening of experience. It was the same thing the man had lectured about in the public library three nights before in the Port of Spain. The most they would learn would be to wield a cutlass expertly, or drive the mule cart to the railway line swiftly so that before the sun went down they would have worked sufficiently to earn more than their neighbours.

With a sigh like an aged man Romesh opened his suitcase and took out a pair of shorts and a polo shirt. He put these on and put the suitcase away in a corner. He wondered where would be a safe place to put his books. He opened the suitcase again and put them in.

It was as if, seeing the room in which he had argued and quarrelled with the family on his last visit, he lost any happiness he might have had on coming back this time. A feeling of depression overcame him.

It lasted as he talked with his sisters as they prepared food to take to the fields. Romesh listened how they stumbled with words, how they found it difficult to express themselves. He thought how regretful it was that they couldn't go to school. He widened the thought and embraced all the children in the village, growing up with such little care, running naked in the mud with a piece of *roti* in their hands, missing out on all the things that life should stand for.

But when the food was ready and they set off for the fields, with the sun in their eyes making them blind, he felt better. He would try to be happy with them, while he was here. No more preaching. No more voicing of opinion on this or that.

Other girls joined his sisters as they walked, all carrying food. When they saw Romesh they blushed and tittered, and he wondered what they were whispering about among themselves.

There were no effusive greetings. Sweating as they were, their clothes black with the soot of burnt canes, their bodies caught in the motions of their work, they just shouted out, and Romesh shouted back. Then Ramlal dropped the reins and jumped down from his cart. He curved his hand like a boomerang and swept it over his face. The soot from his sleeves smeared his face as he wiped away the sweat.

Rookmin came up and opened tired arms to Romesh. '*Beta*,' she cried as she felt his strong head on her breast. She would have liked to stay like that, drawing his strength and vitality into her weakened body, and closing her eyes so her emotion wouldn't show.

'*Beta*,' his father said, 'you getting big, you looking strong.' They sat down to eat on the grass. Romesh was the only one who appeared cool, the others were flushed, the veins standing out on their foreheads and arms.

Romesh asked if it was a good crop.

'Yes *Beta*,' Ramlal said, 'Is a good crop, and plenty of work for everybody. But this year harder than last year, because rain begin to fall early, and if we don't hurry up with the work, it will be too much trouble for all of us. The overseer come yesterday, and he say a big bonus for the man who do the most work. So everybody working hard for that bonus. Two of my mules sick, but I have to work them, I can't help. We trying to get the bonus.'

After eating Ramlal fished a cigarette out from his pocket and lit it carefully. First greetings over, he had nothing more to tell his son, for the time being anyway.

Romesh knew they were all remembering his last visit, and the things he had said then. This time he wasn't going to say anything, he was just going to have a holiday and enjoy it, and return to school in the city refreshed.

He said, 'Hari, I bet I could cut more canes than you.'

Hari laughed. 'Even though I work the whole morning already is a good bet. You must forget to use *poya*, your hands so soft and white now.'

That is the way life is, Ramlal thought as Romesh took his cutlass. Education, school, *chut*! It was only work put in a *roti* in your belly, only work that brought money. The marriage would soon change Romesh. And he felt a pride in his heart as his son spat on the blade.

The young men went to a patch of burnt canes. The girls came too, standing by to pile the fallen stalks of sweet juice into heaps, so that they could be loaded quickly and easily on to the carts and raced to the weighing bridge.

Cane fell as if a machine were at work. The blades swung in the air, glistened for a moment in the sunlight, and descended on the stalks near the roots. Though the work had been started as a test of speed, neither of them moved ahead of the other. Sometimes Romesh paused until Hari came abreast, and sometimes Hari waited a few canes for Romesh. Once they looked at each other and laughed, the sweat on their faces getting into their mouths. There was no more enmity on Hari's part: seeing his brother like this, working, was like the old days when they worked side by side at all the chores which filled the day.

Everybody turned to in the field striving to outwork the others, for each wanted the bonus as desperately as his neighbour. Sometimes the women and the girls laughed or made jokes to one another, but the men worked silently. And the crane on the weighing bridge creaked and took load after load. The labourer manipulating it grumbled: there was no bonus for him, though his wage was more than that of the cane-cutters.

When the sun set all stopped work as if by signal. And in Ramlal's hut that night there was laughter and song. Everything was all right, they thought. Romesh was his natural self again, the way he swung that cutlass! His younger sisters and brother had never really held anything against him, and now that Hari seemed pleased, they dropped all embarrassment and made fun. 'See *bhai*, I make *meetai* especially for you,' his sister said, offering the sweetmeat.

'He work hard, he deserve it,' Hari agreed, and he looked at his brother, almost with admiration.

Afterwards, when Ramlal was smoking and Rookmin was searching in the youngest girl's head for lice ('put pitch-oil, that will kill them,' Ramlal advised), Romesh said he was going to pay Doolsie a visit.

There was a sudden silence. Rookmin shut her eyes, the children stopped playing, and Ramlal coughed over his pipe.

'Well what is the matter?' Romesh asked, looking at their faces.

'Well, now,' Ramlal began, and stopped to clear his throat. 'Well now, you know that is our custom, that a man shouldn't go to pay a visit to the girl he getting married ...'

'What!' Romesh looked from face to face. The children shuffled their feet and began to get embarrassed at the stranger's presence once more.

Ramlal spoke angrily. 'Remember this is your father's house! Remember the smaller ones! Careful what you say, you must give respect! You not expect to get married one day, eh? Is a good match we make, boy, you will get good dowry, and you could live in village and forget them funny things you learning in the city.'

'So it has all been arranged,' Romesh said slowly. 'That is why everybody looked at me in such a strange way in the fields. My life already planned for me, my path pointed out – cane, labour, boy children, and the familiar village of Cross Crossing.' His voice had dropped lower, as if he had been speaking to himself, but it rose again as he addressed his mother: 'And you, *mai*, you have helped them to do this to me? You whose idea it was to give me an education?'

Rookmin shut her eyes and spoke. 'Is the way of our people, is we custom from long time. And you is Indian? The city fool your brains, but you will get back accustom after you married and have children.'

Ramlal got up from where he was squatting on the floor, and faced Romesh. 'You have to do what we say', he said loudly. 'Ever since you in the city, we notice how you change. You forgetting custom and how we Indian people does live. And too besides, money getting short. We want help on the estate. The garden want attention, and nobody here to see about cattle and them. And no work after crop, too besides.'

'Then I can go to school in San Fernando,' Romesh said desperately. 'If there is no money to pay the bus, I will walk. The government schools are free, you do not have to pay to learn.'

'You will be married and have boy children,' Ramlal said, 'and you will stop answering your *bap* . . .'

'*Hai*! *Hai*!' Drivers urged their carts in the morning sun, and whips cracked crisply on the air. Dew still clung to the grass as workers took to the fields to do as much as they could before the heat of the sun began to tell.

Romesh was still asleep when the others left. No one woke him; they moved about the hut in silence. No one spoke. The boys went to harness the mules, one of the girls to milk the cows and the other was busy in the kitchen.

When Romesh got up he opened his eyes in full awareness. He could have started the argument again as if no time had elapsed, the night had made no difference.

He went into the kitchen to wash his face. He gargled noisily scraped his tongue with his teeth. Then he remembered his toothbrush and toothpaste in his suitcase. As he cleaned his teeth his sister stood watching him. She never used a toothbrush: they broke a twig and chewed it to clean their mouths.

'You going away, *bhai*?' she asked him timidly.

He nodded, with froth in his mouth.

'If you stay, you could teach we what you know,' the girl said.

Romesh washed his mouth and said, '*Baihin*, there are many things I have yet to learn.'

'But what will happen to us?'

'Don't ask me questions little sister,' he said crossly.

After he had eaten he left the hut and sulked about the village, walking slowly with his hands in his pockets. He wasn't quite sure what he was going to do. He kept telling himself that he would go away and never return, but bonds he had refused to think about surrounded him. The smell of burnt cane was strong on the wind. He went to the pond, where he and Hari used to bath the mules. What to do? His mind was in a turmoil.

Suddenly he turned and went home. He got his cutlass – it was sharp and clean, even though unused for such a long time. Ramlal never allowed any of his tools to get rusty.

He went out into the fields, swinging the cutlass in the air, as if with each stroke he swept a problem away.

Hari said: 'Is time you come. Other people start work long time, we have to work extra to catch up with them.'

There was no friendliness in his voice now.

Romesh said nothing, but he hacked savagely at the canes, and in half an hour he was bathed in sweat and his skin scratched from contact with the cane.

Ramlal came up in the mule cart and called out, 'Work faster! We a whole cartload behind!' Then he saw Romesh and he came down from the cart and walked rapidly across. 'So you come! Is a good thing you make up your mind!'

Romesh wiped his face. 'I am not going to stay, *bap*.' It was funny how the decision came, he hadn't known himself what he was going to do. 'I will help with the crop, you shall get the bonus if I have to work alone in the night. But I am not going to get married. I am going away after the crop.'

'You are mad, you will do as I say.' Ramlal spoke loudly, and other workers in the field stopped to listen.

The decision was so clear in Romesh's mind that he did not say anything more. He swung the cutlass tirelessly at the cane and knew that when the crop was finished, it would be time to leave his family and the village. His mind got that far, and he didn't worry about after that ...

As the wind whispered in the cane, it carried the news of Romesh's revolt against his parents' wishes, against tradition and custom.

Doolsie, working a short distance away, turned her brown face from the wind. But women and girls working near to her whispered among themselves and laughed. Then one of the bolder women, already married, said, 'Well girl, is a good thing in a way. Some of these men too bad. They does beat their wife too much – look at Dulcie husband, he does be drunk all the time, and she does catch hell with him.'

But Doolsie bundled the canes together and kept silent.

'She too young yet,' another said. 'Look, she breasts not even form yet!'

Doolsie did not have any memories to share with Romesh, and her mind was young enough to bend under any weight. But the way her friends were laughing made her angry, and in her mind she too had revolted against the marriage.

'All-you too stupid!' she said, lifting her head with a childish pride so that her sari fell on her shoulder. 'You wouldn't say Romesh is the only boy in the village! And too besides, I wasn't going to married him if he think he too great for me.'

The wind rustled through the cane. Overhead, the sun burned like a furnace.

CLYDE HOSEIN

Clyde Hosein was born in Trinidad in 1940. After a
spell in London during the early sixties he returned
home to work as a producer/broadcaster with Radio
Trinidad. Since then he has worked in advertising, with
the Ministry of Education and as a journalist on the
Trinidad Guardian. For the last seven years he has been
in Canada, working with the CBC and studying film
direction. He is the author of the collection of stories,
The Killing of Nelson John (London Magazine Editions)
and hopes to return soon to Trinidad to finish a novel.

Woodford Square, in the centre of Port of Spain's commercial district, has been for generations the address of derelicts and dropouts, some of whom play at being philosophers, political thinkers and cousins of the Queen.

They are dour or humorous, dull or witty, obstreperous or easy-going and Trinidadians have come to see these vagrants as harmless 'characters' and let them be.

The more eccentric make deep impressions in the minds of the populace, as was the case with old Craig, who for decades cooked, ate, washed and slept under a tree in the Square. He also composed political and philosophical treatises and held up his handwritten gems for pedestrians to read through the piked fence. Some said he had once been a schoolmaster and 'had gone off his head'. Be that as it may, Craig was to many a model of detachment from the foolish world. So great was his impact upon the popular imagination that it was not unusual for a newsman to report Craig's reaction to some national or world issue.

However, not all the residents of Woodford Square are as flamboyant or outspoken. Gina of *Her House* is modelled on the many reticent old women, who like 'the old girl' in the song, *The Streets of London*, live on a bench, or in a box under a tree, or on a sidewalk below a shop's eave, their worldly possessions in a bag or two.

In Woodford Square there is suffering and despair and courage that touches you as you walk by.

Clyde Hosein

HER HOUSE

Please God, let them lawyers leave the house and go. I can't stand Woodford Square any longer. So long I sitting here under the kumquat tree on this concrete walk, one of eight like spokes in a wheel with the fountain right in the middle of the hub.

It's there my friend, the blind man, does stand behind his white kerchief darken with pennies people throw. The more they throw the harder he sing. Right now he humming quiet to himself, his one tune, *Throw out the life line, thow out the life line ...*

Mr Torrie, Mr Gangadeen, why you all don't go home? It turning night, your wife waiting for you. By now I could well be sitting in my bag in the gazebo where I belong.

Aha, the lights gone out. Soon they'll drive out in their cars and leave my house to me. Tell me, how they could take a fine house like that and make office?

I used to stand on the pavement and watch how they breaking down the fretwork gallery and the turret roof. 'What right you have?' I shout at the carpenters, but they laugh, imagine that. 'You making a big mistake spoiling this house.' People stop and stare at me as I walk up and down abusing the workmen. They throw away the louvre door, balusters, turret roof, even the baskets of fern, and leave them in a heap at the bottom of the garden near the back wall.

I reach the pretty wire gate and though it now dark like hell I watch all around before I pull back the catch and swing the gate in. Two-three steps on the front path and the sweet smell of the tuberoses hit me. If it wasn't for me picking up the roots and planting them after the workers mash them with their big foot, hmmm, I tell you.

From the back stairs one path go so, to the pond that dry up now; another one go so, to the gazebo. Like it waiting for me.

A cool wind rustle the dragon's bush; the ravenala clacking like a wheel of fortune. I walk off the path and up the three little steps.

I know exactly which floorboards rotten. Putting down my basket, I sit with my back against the curlicue iron wall.

I can't begin to tell you how much I glad to be here. I don't say that the servants' quarters wouldn't be better to spread my sugar bag. But what use crying over spill milk? They break them down, they break down the stables too, leaving bush to grow up all the way to the back wall.

I ent complaining, but still I can't help thinking if Mr de Gannes didn't go to Australia, who knows? They might not have kick me out and everything would be as it was when Mr Heathcliff was alive and I was living here, his loyal servant, and later he was so good to me. They can take away everything, but those happy times lock away forever in my heart.

Saturday nights, like pride self, I stand at the dining table I already set, linen sparkling white, and after Mr Heathcliff and Madam welcome everybody I send the children off to Imelda. Miss Patty so grown-up, offering to do this, do that, and getting Maillotte de Gannes to help too. Sonny Decle, Master Vern and all the other young men giving me jokes behind their parents' back. So much birthdays. When they light the cake candles and I switch off the lamps, the gallery light used to shine through the big louvre door and dance on everybody. Mr de Gannes, Mr Pampellone, all the Jennings and the MacLeans there in the drawing room and I telling the ladies how I season the roast or make the crab callaloo or boil the pastelles.

Time flying, time flying, but what to do?

First madam dead. Her friends say is because of a broken heart, but I know is the bottle she like so bad that kill her. Then Master Vern didn't come back, neither his friend Sonny Decle, who went over same time with the West India Regiment.

Miss Patty write and say that after finishing school, she staying on in the States; she getting a good job and she could manage. That too break Mr Heathcliff heart.

Poor man. He come so worried he used to sit in the gallery saying nothing at all, just smelling the tuberoses, drinking the strong black coffee I make and tapping the fretwork with his cane. All his friends give up on him, except Mr de Gannes.

And then one day I close the lids over his staring eyes and I know from then on is me and me alone.

Miss Patty come down and we bury her father as if in secret. Some people send wreaths but only Mr de Gannes come to the church and cemetery.

Only once Miss Patty walk over from Queen's Park Hotel and visit. I watch her sitting by the lily pond, a red hibiscus in her hand, and I wonder about all those years when I mind her and her brother as if they was my own flesh and blood.

She tell me she would see me again soon, she flying back to New York. She say nothing about the house and I just continue living in it.

Washing clothes on Oxford Street, bearing insults for a few shillings, waiting for Miss Patty. 'I only a caretaker,' I tell the government man who come and ask, 'Who own this house? Who will pay the taxes?'

I bend to pick the tomatoes I plant in the flower beds. 'Miss Patty coming from New York soon,' I tell him. I weed the pigeon peas and hope he will go away.

'We could sell it for the arrears,' he say.

You think I don't know I live in the public now? That's what everybody saying, that I don't know, I mad. Crazy Gina they call me and stone down my box-house under the kumquat tree against the railing inside Woodford Square.

Cool breeze. The wind must be blow away the rain clouds, the moon peeping out.

The light falling on the house, it shining just like the night I come over on the schooner. Like a castle the house was and everything in it strange and frightening to me a thirteen-year-old girl crying for Auntie and the shack in Mesopotamia Valley where I was born and live not knowing mother or father.

Mr Heathcliff was on the docks that evening and it look like he follow my voice to the corner, and when the people with the mattresses and bundles on their heads move back, he say 'What's wrong child?' And I say, 'Sir, my Auntie send me from St Vincent to live here.' Well, not as plain as that. He had to worm it out of me about how the woman who Auntie promise would meet me and help me get a job never show up on

Queen's Docks.

That night Hetty, the head maid, talk to me like a mother and I sleep with her in the big room in the servants' quarters.

Ah moon, all these years you sit there the same over dark-blue hills.

Time passing. Who could tell me what it mean?

I spread my sugar-bag and fold my cloth into a pillow.

I wake up to hear the scavengers scraping rubbish from the drain. As they drive off, their racatang truck rattle. I sit up in the bag, all my bones aching. A ci-ci zeb fly up and come back down on the wall, whistling and whistling for a girlfriend.

A few rays hitting the yard. I go near the back stairs and watch the purple hills. The smell of the dou-douce mango rise from the basket on my arm and mix with the cool smell of the morning. Dew shine on the hibiscus they spare when they build the garage. I pull out some more lovevine from the hedge; strange how something so fine like gold wire is a pest and a parasite.

The lawyers coming for eight. I ent 'fraid them, but better not let them find me here. Nobody on the street; I slip out and down to the Square.

This is the time I love best. The sun hitting the courthouse and the library with gold and the green grass shining. Kumquat wet and orange all over the ground. It so quiet I hear the old men snoring on the benches near the fountain. My box ent behind the frangipani.

I find it near the stinking lavatory. It look like if somebody kick it all the way here. They write some nastiness just below *Hotpoint 20.2 cu. ft.* But don't mind. I put up the box and anchor it with a stone. I get my coalpot and things from the hole near the root of the kumquat. I fill the tin with water from the standpipe and light the pitchpine under the coals. When Trinity clock strike seven I watching the eddoes boil.

They take a while to cool. The knife have no handle but it does still work. I scrape off the brown sticky skin. I eat and watch the few people crossing the Square, some going into stores and offices, others lining outside the Red House for birth certificates.

I put away my things, except my basket, in the hole, and start to walk to Lapeyrouse Cemetery. People shout at me from a car, 'Crazy Gina, crazy Gina, your sorefoot smelling!'

Soon I reach the gate. I go in and find the headstone:

Sacred to
the memory of
HEATHCLIFF
Montgomery
HENDERSON
b. Hampstead 1885
d. 24th May 1958

I read it over and over again and the tears come, not so much for him – his bread must be butter even if he get throw in hell – but for my little child I send away because of Madam. Norma, Norma, where is my Norma now?

'All I know is she never write one single word,' I tell the headstone.

The sun come out hard and I see the stars in the marble that cut rough. I say, 'You wanted to give her a good education, Mr Heathcliff, but education can't buy good manners.'

I tell the stone, 'One time I used to think that Norma come back. I used to walk about and hope that every red girl I see was she.'

Through the samaan trees the hills look near. I feel emptier and lonelier than Sundays.

When I get back to the Square, the corner by the library and town hall thick with shoppers, saga boys and the courthouse crowd. The heat haze dancing over melting tar on the road. I sit near the fountain and spread my cloth.

What all those people going by in a blur think when they look down on me? The mad old lady with white hair, in her rags, sitting on the concrete walk begging for her bread. When some of the men who dress nice in dark suits and shiny shoes drop a five or ten-cents piece on the cloth, I say, 'God bless.'

I see the taxi-driver coming and I collect most of the coins and put them in my basket. As usual, he bringing tourist people, a man and a woman this time. The driver say, 'This is Crazy Gina, she lives in that box over there.' The white man write in a book.

When the lady drop a dollar bill on the cloth, I smile and pose for the picture.

The sky cloud over and bring down the heat. From my bosom I take out my kerchief and put the dollar with the other bills, some tearing where they crease. I hear rain coming like people running over roofs all the way from Belmont. The crowd scatter, some holding *Evening News* over their heads like umbrella.

I fold the box, take my basket and run across the road into the library entrance hall where the *Guardian* pin up page by page. I look at all the pictures.

The rain stop but the sky still set up. A mist cover the hills.

I pass by the Syrian stores and in ten minutes I reach the market. It full with farmers' and shoppers' voices. One vendor sit in her stall crying, 'Nice pumpkin here! Only fifteen cents a pound!' The butcher standing behind a curtain of bloody meat call, 'Fresh beef, fresh pig foot, fresh black pudding!'

Somebody say, 'Why the market officer don't kick out this crazy woman, she dirty like sin!' Then I reach the man who give me the eddoes the other day.

'Take this.' He put some plantain in my basket. Pushing back my hand with the loose change I collect today, he say, 'Nobody will buy overripe plantain, it will only waste.'

Since the supermarkets build, mostly poor people coming to buy here; everything getting run-down. You could feel how everybody sad. I sit in a corner and wait for the market to close. As soon as a vendor pack up and go, I search the stall. Soon I collect a heap of coffee, pepper, some okra, a small moonshine fish. I wrap them in a piece of *Evening News*.

A woman with a breast hanging out of her bodice, feeding a baby, call me and give me a nice calabash mango. It smell so sweet I eat it right away.

The night cool, a fine drizzle falling, A whole lot of old talk, shouting and singing coming from the rum shops on Prince Street. The smell of rum and gutter water remind me of the day I walk to Shanty Town to see what I could pick up from the trucks that bring refuse from the nice houses in the valley. A truck come, scattering corbeaux as it drive through the dumping ground. The scavenger birds fly and sit high on heaps of rubbish. I see little boys running in all that stink and mud and when the truck stop, they start to bawl and fight for the things it bring. When I see that my mind turn, I feel to vomit.

But now I have plaintain, okra, fish in my basket. I feel good.

In the Square I put up the box under the kumquat, fetch water and light the coalpot. The frangipani smell high. The wind blow pink petals to my feet.

The sauce get slimy; as I stir white flesh fall off and show bones like the teeth of a comb. I pick up the tin to eat, forgetting that it have to cool first and nearly spill the food. My mouth working, a car passing, young men shout to each other about the pictures they going to see at Strand.

Not a soul in the Square after I wash up and put away. I come to Mr Heathcliff house. When I used to live here alone, moonlight always find me there by the lily pond. I can even hear the parang music and the voices at the rum punch parties under the lights Mr Heathcliff string from gazebo to ravenala, ravenala to dragon's bush. A memory of a memory.

When I reach gazebo I see silver heaps on the ground. A-a, at last they cut down all that bush. I could even see the wood and galvanize there by the wall.

Down the path to the shadows. The first thing I make out is the louvre door, it leaning on the wall.

I try to raise a set of slats but the paint swell. The long key in the big lock.

The key too stick, but after I play with it, play with it, it come out, rusty and wet.

Then I remember something, something Torrie and Gangadeen don't know. In the old houses one key used to fit all the locks. After Hetty dead and gone Mr Heathcliff give me the key she used to wear around her waist. I wear that key with pride knowing that he trust me with everything he had.

I walk up the back stairs. My hand tremble as I turn the key. My heart start to pound.

My shadow is like a jumbie with horns in the doorway. I stand listening.

Slow, slow, like a thief I go in. I know to walk down one step into the kitchen. But it ent a kitchen anymore.

Paper scatter all over. I smell dust. In this corner, the old sideboard covered with books. Over there, the safe that used to stand in tins of water to stop ants from getting at the food. I feel the rolled top, the fine wire tear up.

I want to turn on the light but somebody might come, or call police. How could I tell the constable that Mr Heathcliff leave me in charge; me, a white-head old woman who does live in a box in the Square?

The drawing room door open with a creak. I nearly jump out of my skin, the clock begin to chime, one, two ... ten. The same mahogany clock standing on the Indian rug. Moonlight streaming through the new glass window that take up nearly the whole wall.

I go from room to room. Look, the wide boards, the high frilly ceiling, the dark stain floor. Moonlight coming into the bedrooms too. The towerbolts still on the inside of the doors. Desk and filing cabinet where beds used to be.

I begin to dust. I just take out my cloth from the basket and is wipe I wiping. The clock, the mahogany bookcase, the foxhunt picture. In the dining room I dust the carved round table, the walnut chairs and sofa. The chandelier still here hanging from the ceiling and now they have photos of people and all kind of framed writing on the wood panels under the lattice.

I walk about all over again before I sit in the nice soft chair. It so warm and dry in here. I close my eyes. I hear, throw out the life line, throw out the life line ... I sit up and is foreday morning.

The courthouse standing out against the grey. My blind friend passing below, singing on his way to the Square. I never sleep so good in a long time.

Suppose somebody come now! But inside me saying, Relax Gina, is a long time till eight. I yawn and stretch and smile for tonight.

Ah, a ball of twine in a tray. I cut off a length and make a belt for the key.

NOEL WOODROFFE

Noel Woodroffe was born in Mt Pleasant, Tobago in December 1952, but grew up in the famous Pitch-Lake village of La Brea on the south-western peninsula of Trinidad. He attended the Brighton Anglican Primary School in La Brea, and then went on to secondary education in 1964 at Presentation College, the Roman Catholic High School in the town of San Fernando. After an abortive attempt at the study of Natural Sciences at the University of the West Indies at St Augustine, which he entered in 1970, he transferred to the Faculty of Arts in 1972 and graduated with a Bachelor's Degree in English and History in 1975. He entered the Ph.D programme in 1976 and was awarded the Doctorate in Philosophy in English early in 1981 for a thesis on the works of Chinua Achebe, the Nigerian novelist. Mr Woodroffe has been at various times, a vacation-school teacher, a clerk in the Government Service, a department store salesman, a university tour guide, a general dogsbody for an electrical contractor, a teaching assistant at the University, and is now a teacher at the San Juan Government Secondary School. He is married and has two daughters.

The story grew out of my experience of living in the village of La Brea during a major part of my youth. When my parents moved to St Augustine, I was boarded with relatives in the town of San Fernando, so that I could attend secondary school there. In writing this story, as I reflected on the years in La Brea, it seemed that village life was flavoured with a peculiar atmosphere of desolation. My parents' house in La Brea was situated just across a pasture from the sea and on the horizon across the Gulf of Paria could be seen the blue hills of Venezuela in South America. Most of my hours after school were spent on the beach and so it seemed to me that I existed in a fringe-life between land and sea. My village vision looks not inward into the centre of the island but seems to force its way to the sea and looks out upon the water.

The section of La Brea in which we lived was also slowly decaying. The village was developing inward, receeding away from the coast. The picture of a decaying village on an empty southern coast speaks to something deep within me with a particularly sharp pain. The Chinese shop was a feature of the village. It was where the boys met on their bikes and scooters, and we were constantly shuttling between the shop and our homes on small errands. The Chinese were a mystery to me, closeted in a dark, decaying shop, talking among themselves in Chinese, seeming so totally out of place, so incongruous. So alienated and cut off from a vast Oriental land which revealed its mystery and deep grandeur as I read of its history and culture later in life.. In such a land action could achieve heroic proportions. I attempted in the story to pierce the veil that covers the life of the shop Chinese. What was the quality of their alienation? How does Wing deal with the desperation of being condemned to a village prison which offers no sustenance to his life? I felt that behind the apparently stagnant life of the village Chinese there must be longing and perception and a sense of beauty born out of acute suffering. The story deals, of course, with the older generation of Chinese who travelled here to the island on the invitation of relatives who had come earlier, and who have a keen memory of a life back on the continent. In *Wing's Way* I peered into Wing's life and tried to show that however neuter or unnoticed we are, each human life is filled with grandeur.

Noel Woodroffe

WING'S WAY

The road from the city first ran down the coast, squeezed between the flooded mangroves to the left and the crumbling sea-wall to the right. On windy days at high tide when the sea was brown and the wild cry of the seagulls filled the air as they wheeled over the small pirogues careering madly across the waves to the little harbour locked in a fold of the coast, it seemed to passengers in taxis that plied the route out of the city southward that one had left hold of the permanence of the land, and a sense of danger and unease took powerful possession.

The road snaked through a massively built iron bridge, painted silver, constructed on piles driven into the mouth of a little river that twisted out of the mangroves, and then plunged inland into the depths of the island, through little villages with Arawak and Spanish names, through estates of cocoa with immortelle trees showering flowers onto the asphalt, over sunlit hills and then down into damp, dark little valleys, past the shacks of muscle-bound men who walked with the knotted gait of labourers back to their homes and women after a heavy day in the fields. And then the road burst out of the rubber plantation, in which the last local deer was hunted and slaughtered long ago, and with a quiet finality entered a little village leaning off the land into the sea. It traversed a circular path through the village and joined itself again. Here in this village, history feathered the air with the breath of death. Raleigh had once landed here and caulked his ships with pitch. But the site had been lost as the mangrove spread across the swamp at the edge of the coast and the pitch had been excavated until the sea had swallowed up the site in a large lagoon. Now only a large breed of catfish lived there among the roots of the mangrove trees, and small boys hooked them on long, lazy Saturday afternoons and cut off their whiskers before flinging them back again into the murky water.

This village appeared to be at the end of the world, and it seemed as though each day was a deliberate effort. Dawn came slowly; the cold air flowing off the sea, the smell of fish and the wet smell of the nets fading away as the light climbed up the sky. Midday brought a blazing heat that softened the raw pitch with which the road was made in the village. Cars parked too long out in the heat sank slowly, tyre-deep, into the soft asphalt, and the hot sun and the heavy air filled with the smell of cooking drove people into the shade as a torpor settled over the whole village. Evening saw the huge red ball of the sun dipping across the sky into the sea leaving glorious and stunning sunsets that coloured the bay red, burning off the hulls of the tankers that tied up against the long oil-jetty, matching the flares of the oil refinery in the distance as the excess gas was burned off. The evening smell was that of oil.

There was death in the village, but that death was not a final horror, it was not the heart-rending, bitter cry of a sudden and unexpected grief. No! It was the sad, lingering, whimsical death found in the eyes of broken, old men as they patted young boys on the head and considered the foolishness of youth; it was the empty death found on abandoned coasts at the end of small islands dwarfed by the hugeness of the Atlantic; it was the hopelessness of this backwater village, swept clean of talent and vitality, missed and ignored by the political turmoil sweeping the city, dependant upon a poor stony earth and dwindling oil. Death here was a vision of a hopeless future. This sadness filled the air and slowed the movements of the people. It could be seen in the endless game of retired checker-playing fishermen, as they bent over the board balanced on their knees, pondering interminably the next move. It could be seen in the fixed, bulbous gaze of the primary school headteacher, stripped of all purpose and dignity, making his way to Wing's Bar every Saturday morning, his trouser waist hanging below a stomach swollen by beer. And it could be seen in the darkened, blacked-out village that sought forgetfulness in sleep by eight o'clock at night; the sound of a single radio on the High Road only deepening the mournful gloominess of that death.

> Alone I stand in the Autumn cold
> On the tip of Orange Island,
> The Hsaing flowing northward;
> I see a thousand hills crimsoned through
> By their serried woods deep-dyed,
> And a hundred barges vying
> Over crystal blue waters ...
> Under freezing skies a million creatures
>   contend in freedom.
> Brooding over this immensity
> I ask, on this boundless land
> Who rules over man's destiny?[1]

The opening of Wing Luk's Grocery and Bar (Licensed to sell Spirituous Liquors by Retail) every morning was a village ritual, as fixed and as commonplace in the consciousness of the people and as enmeshed in the complex pattern of village ritual as the Indian man named Jadoo, who peed into the open drain outside his shack at 6.30 every morning, and then chewed on a hibiscus stick to clean his stained teeth, and made inconspicuous by its oftenness as the fat, black Shouter Baptist woman who emerged out of her bush-choked gateway at dawn and drew a cross with a bar of red chalk in the roadway outside her hut. Every morning at 6.15 for the many years Wing had lived in the village, he had opened his shop in the same way. The huge barred, wooden door cracked open with a creak of rusted hinges and then Wing floated like an oriental wraith down the two steps in front of the shop and across the small concrete bridge that linked the road to the shop. He stood in the centre of the road, his loose, khaki trousers flapping around his wooden sapats, looking up the High Road towards the imposing structure of the Roman Catholic Church and then down the hill where the High Road curved around the Police Station and a track ran off down a steep slope towards the sea. Every morning Wing looked at the sea, grey in the half-light, his nostrils clogged by the rank smell of fishnets and rotting seaweed, and the faint odour of clay chopped off the coast by the rough night-sea. Then he turned and disappeared into the gloomy cavern of his shop.

Wing had to find strength to start the day. His ritual early each morning was not a blind habit. He had to locate himself again in his surroundings. He had to see the narrow, rutted asphalt street bumping jerkily up the hill, the hard tufts of grass that cracked the thin concrete of the battered pavement that ran along one side of the street. The thin stray dogs hunched against the morning cold, scuttling away from the front of the shop and disappearing under the flooring of the Health Centre across the road all helped to bring his mind back from his night wanderings. For years his dreams had been plagued by scenes of the Old Land; of horsemen flowing up huge mountains, red banners touching the clouds, a red blaze in a frosty sky: he heard the music of Old China and the poetry of its violent history touched him like smoke from the Buddha's nostrils, and he felt the movement of his vast homeland like the churning of a mighty mill of humanity. Often he woke up with a sense of an essential beauty leaping with him across the chasm dividing sleep and wakefulness, and he awoke with an ecstasy that pierced his heart and hung on him like a shimmering robe through all his morning exercises. It sometimes only dissipated when Wing looked at the frothing, grey morning sea which chewed up the land and reminded him of his own mortality.

Throughout the day Wing sat at his ancient till while his wife served at the counter, parcelling out the flour and the rice and the half-pounds of sugar; the sides of salt-fish and the bootblack, the razor blades and the hairnets, the rat-poison and the face-cream, and the thousand other things that flowed out of Wing's shop and helped to flesh out the lives of the villagers whose houses cluttered up the High Road, backed up four to a yard, squashed into almost inaccessible corners of back lots, straggling down to the fishermen's huts by the sea. These people, Wing's customers, mingled curses with their cooking smells and incestuously depended on their physical nearness to each other. They directed a stream of ill-concealed hostility towards the new, concrete houses built by the oil company for its workers at the other end of the village. These houses were serviced by a new-type supermarket owned by Indians who had magically appeared when the housing development was completed. The Indian supermarket, with its little carts which customers wheeled down the aisles between the shelves picking out their own goods, was avoided with grim determination by the residents of Old Village, as the older section of La Negra was called. They preferred to deal with Wing only.

Wing was not fooled by the people's faithfulness to his shop. He knew that they came to him because in their eyes he was neuter. They would not buy from the Indians, and the new supermarket with its efficient check-out lanes and new cash registers robbed them of the contempt they always felt for the shopowners. Wing knew the people well enough after so many years, to be aware of the fact that it was only their contempt for the man behind the counter that kept at bay, for a little while at least, the deep anxiety of seeing their hard-earned dollars disappear for a few paltry, perishable items. So that when they called for a quarter pound of butter (as they called margarine) in loud, impatient tones, Wing cashed their few cents into the jaws of his till with a face as masked and as impassive as a Chinese statue. Wing sometimes matched contempt for contempt and spread their change with a fanning motion of his hand across the counter-top. He sneered then in his mind as he watched washer-women struggle to pick up the small flat coins off the counter with finger-ends swollen, pitted and blunted by too many years in harsh soap.

But sometimes the desperation of his condition forced itself upon him, on rainy days especially, when small children, soaked to the skin, ran in off the street, clutching empty rum bottles to be filled with cooking oil or kerosene, when housewives came in out of the deluge, thick ankles and short, square toes caked with mud, when the open drain between the shop and the road became filled with rushing water choked with the refuse of the village flowing down into the sea, and the air of the dark, untidy shop was warmed with the smell of wet bodies pressed in too close to the stacks of bagged rice and the piled up plastic buckets of preserved pig's meat. Then the talk from the Bar section of the shop grew wild and unsteady as the orders for bottles of rum increased and the small, tattered lives of the village men-folk were laid out before Wing's eyes like sheets of soiled and grease-dirty linen, and his head swam with the closeness of their broken and truncated existence, and his senses longed for the sharp, frozen air of a Chinese winter.

He too was trapped, he thought, in a little humped shop at the end of the world, ten thousand million miles from the snow-swept River Kan and the thousand blurred peaks of Lungkang. His life was defined by the ragged fence-wall of rusted galvanised sheets that ringed his property, and to venture outside this wall was a deliberate exercise in invisibility. Wing lived in squalor while his bank account burst at the seams, and when he drove out in his new Toyota, he slid in and out of the village and into his backyard through the gate in the rusted fence with a sense of negation of self that made him almost invisible. He could never rebuild or modernise the business, he thought, while the shop hummed with stalled customers on a rainy day. His friend Wei Ping, in another village, had built a brand-new supermarket on the site of his old shop. Ping had put in a freezer section along a whole wall and had meat sliced and packaged. He had built shelves along four aisles and had bought twenty small grocery push-carts, he had finished off the front of his shop with a four-lane checkout counter with new registers that rang musically as the totals were made, and had watched his customers disappear without a trace. Ping lapsed into bankruptcy and had wept into his tea one private and grief-stricken night when he confided to Wing that he was leaving San Sebastian and joining a relative in Toronto who owned a laundry. Usually at the end of a day Wing felt strained, used up and exhausted, and during sleep his dreams flashed and flashed memories of China on his mind. And during the morning exercise he felt almost transported in time and place to a more secure and meaningful existence.

Wing exercised early in the morning just before the break of dawn, with just a tiny cup of tea to break the night's fast. His wife who exercised with him could never understand why Wing insisted on that extremely early hour or why the fluid motions of the exercise must be done with the pang of an acute hunger which the small cup of strong tea aroused. But by the time the cold dawn light filtered over the rusted top edges of the battered galvanised sheets that formed Wing's east wall, his naked upper torso was covered with a film of sweat and his wife's small, drooping, puckered breasts pointed to the dawn sky as they leaned back and slow-kicked over the pile of old rice bags that covered the rusted engine of Wing's last car, an old Fairmont. In exercise, Wing experienced each morning, for the twenty odd years he had been married, the pain that lies at the centre of beauty. He could never explain, nor would he ever attempt to do so, what the mornings meant to him – the cold light that gradually filtered over the galvanised sheets and flowed into the ramshackle corners of his yard; the red glow of the eastern sky that he could see at first over the fence, only as he leaped into the air, knee cocked and right arm chopping in the stylised slow-motion karate exercise; the light that climbed rapidly into the sky giving life to the new day; the visions that Mao's lines silently conjured in his head as he swept on across the plain of the Yellow River; and the perfect symmetry in the smooth movements of his ageing wife as she listened with tight concentration to the harmony of her body. This exercise was life, and it made his existence bearable. His children were never included and were never invited to this ritual. Once they arose to watch and were stunned by the intimacy and the power of a hidden and private passion. They never watched again. Wing and his wife exercised, while outside the rusted sheet-wall heavy labourers groaned their way to the oil-fields and the fish vendor blew on his conch calling housewives to the early sell. In the ramshackle chaos of a dying village on the edge of the sea Wing found in light and movement a small part of the harmony of the universe.

> Beware of heartbreak with grievance overfull
> Range far your eye over long vistas.[2]

Saturday evening in Wing Luk's house was a special time. The huge, scarred doors of the shop were banged shut and barred on the inside and Wing himself shot home all the massive iron bolts and placed the padlocks and chains in place. A silence descended on the inside of the shop and a strange atmosphere began to creep into the household as the awareness of Wing, his wife and his two children began to turn away from the realities in La Negra, and be enfolded by the Chinese music that poured from Wing's new stereo system and enticed the senses to the long vistas of the Old Land. On Saturday evening Wing and his family dressed in Chinese silks and ate a special dinner cooked by Wing's wife. No English was spoken during these few precious hours, only Chinese was allowed. Wing's tongue curled around the music of the language and even the commonplace in his conversation became invested with the magic of the strange. On these occasions Wing was treated with extra reverence and respect and as they ate, his senses were filled with the fragrance of the Chinese incense that smouldered before the Buddha on the corner altar. Today Wing felt his joints loosen with satisfied relaxation as he clipped pieces of red pork into his mouth and scooped rice out of his bowl with his bamboo chopsticks. He gazed at the painting hung over the table opposite his chair.

The painting was a stark white background of a quality that reminded Wing of the bleached bones of a dead man. Crowding the left of the frame was a section of mangrove swamp, the exposed roots arching high above the water. The painter's lines were spare and minimal, but somehow the mangrove growth gave the impression of something horribly jumbled and unclean. It was an evil place, a place of shadows and loss of direction. The mangrove roots twisted about each other, choking each other while in the air above the form of the trees rose, outlined murkily against the sky. At times one could hardly tell where the swamp ended and the sky began. And then three birds flew out of the swamp. They were flamingoes, blood-red, necks stretched and wings beating the sour air. Their colour vibrated against the whiteness of the background, and it seemed to Wing that the crimson pulsed against his eyeballs. At times, as Wing gazed at the birds, it seemed that their colour oozed life. The birds sped across the frame, legs stretched taut behind fanned tails, aiming for the middle distance of the picture, a bleak whiteness that spread across to the right of the huge picture. The swamp was on the edge of the sea, and with a few thin lines the painter had created the illusion of a vast sea along the bottom of the painting. In the immensity of that vast white sea, a small skeletal boat sailed, far, far, back in the distance.

Wing seemed to feel his soul rush from him and join the birds in their seeking flight across the vast, white sea. He felt a wind blow across his life, bringing a chill into the very particles of his being. With only part of his mind he heard the music of his wife's voice and the murmur of his son as he answered in imperfect, halting Chinese. The strains of the music died away, halting on a high vibrating note that left a sound in the air even after it had died and gone. Wing looked around the table at his children and at his wife and experienced again that indefinable flow that connected him to a mighty past.

Soon a new week would start. Tomorrow, as usual, he would make his regular trip to the city, to the Association Building. Then on Monday he would again open the shop, floating wraith-like down to the roadway. But tonight he would dream and let his soul wander. The strong anticipation of the dawn exercise began to throb within him. He rose from the table just as the smouldering block of incense crackled and spat a spark high over the small Buddha's head. As Wing turned, the lines thundered in his heart:

> *The yellow crane is gone, who knows whither?*
> *Only this tower remains a haunt for visitors.*
> *I pledge my wine to the singing torrent,*
> *The tide of my heart swells with the waves.*[3]

[1] from: *Changsha*   Mao Tse Tung, 1925.
[2] from: *Reply to Lin Ya-Tzu*   Mao Tse Tung, April 1949.
[3] from: *Yellow Crane Tower*   Mao Tse Tung, Spring 1927.

NOEL WILLIAMS

N.D. Williams was born in Guyana and educated at the University of the West Indies at Mona, Jamaica, where he completed research in African literature. He currently teaches at the 'A' Level College in St Lucia. In 1976 his first novel *Ikael Torass* was selected as the best work of Caribbean fiction in the annual literary awards presented by *Casa de las Americas*, Havana.

Growing up in the Third World is often a harrowing experience. In some ways it is like growing up anywhere: the friendships one finds at school can never be erased; parents with the best intentions seldom understand; but both affect the decisions one finally makes about one's life. *Ilyushin '76* examines the peculiar crises a young man faces as he gropes towards those decisions.

Noel Williams

ILYUSHIN '76

I suppose I could relate this to a psychiatrist, if there was such an anomaly on our island. I know what he would say, though, nurtured on Freud or the finest Scotch. I'd leave his office, I'd stop the first calypsonian I come across and tell him everything. *His* response might be more honest though it would pain me to hear his crude laughter climbing up the Hit Parade.

I know now it was an illusion, a razor-grass path along which you stumble, convinced you've lost your way; not wanting to turn back since that's always an admission of failure or frailty.

All right, we'll try it this way, the familiar recourse, the old blues and rhythm about loss and search.

We'll play the dub side too.

Why do these complications always begin at school, like the knots you get into as you stoop to tie your laces in the playground?

The schoolyard is the first place you find yourself on your own among strangers. You reach back and your mother's warm hand is no longer there. You turn, startled at the vacancy, and she *is* there, smiling into your face, stooping for a second to fix your shirt front; then she's walking away and you notice the funny way she balances on her heels, like masquerade people on stilts at Christmas. Suddenly the schoolyard seems deserted; you discover tears without power, and the wailing gets lost in the playground noise or the sound of father's car as it swings through the gate, already late for the office. Then you're in strange cold hands and water creeps down your cheeks like a lizard.

That was Victor's first stumble into the new world.

Now comes Ivan, who didn't meet Victor until many years later, under circumstances more bewildering than Victor had known. Ivan was from the country. His mother, rumour had it, was a prostitute, an Indian woman, which only explains Ivan's curly hair and his reticence. When the fellows found out they made him feel like the bastard he was.

On the morning the new world broke, Ivan tripped on the stairs as the Maths class hurried not to be late for Mr Collymore. His geometry set fell, spilling everything. That moment Ivan was clutched by all the turbulence he now owns.

He had to stop, brace himself, for the tide was sweeping full force one way; he had no choice but to stoop and retrieve, for which he got a kick in the pants (he never found out who did that) and quickly tears sparkled in his eyes.

It's always awful when your geometry set falls. It clatters and spills everything.

On the stairs, stooping to pick up eraser, bisector, six inch ruler, muddy shoes stamping past your groping fingers, going the other way, you feel as if all the secrets you never wanted revealed to the world had been exposed right there.

The moment was terrifying, the struggle enormous to keep from crying, to fight back shame. Ivan, as he reached for the pieces, wondering if that was all one had in a geometry set, almost choked with blinding rage; he thought the energy it supplied was enough to annihilate, in swift seconds, in one sweeping arc, the school, the island, the whole world.

He said not a word to Victor who'd stopped to help him, who'd heard him choke, saw his eyes glisten. Later he would recall it *was* Victor.

Victor discovered something beyond human kindness, a terrible secret love which he took home as soon as school was over that day and hid in the bottom-most drawer of his heart.

'I'm not sentimental about the past,' Ivan was saying, his eye on the temperature gauge of the car – for he suspected a radiator leak. 'The past is what we must destroy utterly, completely.'

Ivan was fond of adverbs. I remember that about his compositions for Miss Simmonds, the way he used two or three like a fanfare at the beginning of a paragraph when one was enough. *So what?* Some people are just as fond of cricket. Oral sex.

His car was taking me to the airport. Another early morning flight back to the University. On the main road traffic was jammed up, locked in a funereal crawl, bringing workers into the city.

Ivan's workers.

They shot us glances as we hurtled by, envying our free flow the other way. Taxis throbbing with emissions, the passengers tight-packed, bath-fresh on the seats. A clean coiffed serious-faced couple in their first car, their first child in the back seat, his first day perhaps at nursery school.

Ivan's workers. The broad masses of the people.

He would hold up the revolution for as long as it took him to drive me to the airport. This journey was important to us. Since I would be leaving the island within hours it was the best time to reveal frightening secrets. I heard plots, scandal and intrigue that were deemed safe to entrust in my ear only at this point. If word somehow got back to the authorities, if this information *leaked*, it would spell disaster. Thuggery wore the ugliest face on the island.

I listened.

I tried not to worry about missing the plane. Ivan drove slowly, his elbow sticking out the window. It was meant to deceive anyone who might be following, who might get curious about his car racing to the airport, who might set a trap. Wait on an empty stretch for his return. *Ambush the bastard*!

'Hear, when you get back, keep your radio tuned to this side of the world. The fellows organising something heavy.'

I listened.

They were planning to burn down the island prison. Liberate the prisoners. 'Do you know some fellows get busted for twenty five, thirty years? *Youth man*, I talking about. Twenty five years for skanking a tourist; thirty for stealing biscuits in a supermarket. Is like Jean Valjean. Remember that book we had for book review?'

'*Les Miserables*.'

'Victor ——ing Hugo, right. Just like that the baldheads does send you to prison. Mash up your life forever.'

And that was the end of the brilliant scheme he had told me about last year, an adult literacy programme, a volunteer scheme for the prisoners. The authorities had grown suspicious all of a sudden about the whole thing. They put a stop to it. They gave no reason.

'Is that what vex me. Up to now they don't say why they ban me from the prisons. *Crazy baldheads*.'

He glanced in the rearview mirror. It was the last mile to the airport, through the sugar cane fields, the control tower already visible. The road was smooth. He checked his watch and accelerated, remembering we had a plane to catch.

Poor Ivan. Sticking up for society's losers. The islands lost. Ivan, the Saviour.

The whole week back on campus I couldn't sleep at nights. I thought about him. I feared for his life. I kept the radio tuned in as he had said, waiting for the newsflash. Our islands were too far apart, I couldn't pick up his local newscast. I waited.

Famine, nuclear accident, war in the Middle East. Nothing.

Embassy seizure, the silicon chip, a movie star dead at eighty one. Still no word.

'*One man was reported killed and several people injured when* …' That was it, Ivan's declaration to the new world!

'And what about you, comrade?' he would ask, approaching the *Departures* sign, 'How the thesis coming?'

'Still working on the final draft. Should be finished *definitely* next year.'

We laughed, feeling enormously free, buoyed by some hidden understanding, reassured about nothing in particular.

'Then what? They appoint you lecturer?'

'Maybe.'

He smiled and changed the subject.

Never once did he frown, lose his temper, try to change me, bourgeois reactionary, indifferent to the plight of his struggling island masses. It was enough, desirable it seemed, that I dwelt on the other side. I was someone he might appeal to if he fouled up an operation or had to find bail; someone to intervene before the thugs kicked a confession through his bleeding teeth.

Christ, it scared me. I didn't want to be on that side, have to cross over and identify his broken body. Ivan, I could never reach you in time!

It matters to me that you live. You fill that vacancy I feel compelled to reach back to each time I step out to board an aircraft full of strangers taking off for the new world.

'A boy dropped his geometry set on the stairs yesterday,' Victor said at breakfast the following morning, excitedly.

'Which boy?' his mother asked, reaching for the jam.

'A country boy.'

That was the end of the story. From their silence it was evident: the boy was unacceptable for conversation at breakfast. He crunched into his toast.

He had fled up the stairs once he was certain Ivan had retrieved all the pieces. It was an impulse to arrive in the classroom ahead of that boy, get to his seat, then watch him slink in seconds after, alone, shame faced, bearing his own cross.

Something else too. He had glimpsed, as he bent down to help, a frayed collar, a shoe whose sole was peeling; he had heard a choking sound that might have been a nasty cough; there was a scab on Ivan's left hand. It reminded him of his favourite aunt, calling him away one afternoon from a trench in which marvellous tiny fish were swimming. 'Don't play near that dirty water,' she'd warned. He would never play near Ivan.

But he watched him from a distance.

Ivan was the sportsman. Ivan was captain of the football team, the cricket team, the table tennis team. Victor was selected for Head Boy.

From the stone steps near the assembly hall Victor watched him. Waiting for his father's car after school he watched as sadfaced Ivan slipped through the gates, hurrying for the buses at the market square. Driving past the market square he eyed Ivan in his dingy white shirt, queueing with noisy vendors, those women with fat behinds and pumpkin breasts, the vagrants and drunks, the smelly gateway to the country. Ivan's passage home.

'What's at the Drive-In this weekend?' his sister asked.

'Your father is reading the paper. Pass the jam.'

His father was listening to the BBC news and pretending to read the newspaper. If Victor couldn't *possibly* do his homework and listen to the radio at the same time, which was what his father raspingly announced one night, then it didn't seem logical that . . .

It occurred to him that Ivan might drop his geometry set again on the stairs. If that wasn't likely to happen, he might do something equally calamitous. He was probably at his breakfast table, right this minute, or on the bus, squeezed among the baskets, getting ready for his next display of *maladroitness*, Miss Simmonds' word for country boys, uneasy in the city, as if the streets were paved with banana peel.

'What is maladroitness?'

'What is *what?*'

'I can't pronounce it. M-A-L-A-.'

'Look here, boy, you can't eat and talk at the same time.'

Leaning on the balcony on the second floor Victor watched him.

Lunch hour cricket, wickets tumbling fast, fellows taking turns, Ivan on the periphery wanting to play, knowing he wasn't wanted. Bold enough to take a position in the slips. Fought for it, shoving off tall Henderson who made as if to smash his face, then let him stay. Took a catch. Came his turn. Fought for the bat, shoving off Congo Bradshaw who grabbed him by the shirt front, then let him stay. He stayed there as if he would bat forever, as if his dry muddy matchbox village were listening to commentaries; he played shot after beautiful shot; he astonished Victor watching him from the door of the Physics Lab; he beat back all the violence they hurled.

Victor loved the disdain of his wrist, the way he raked back and struck the ball. Ivan, the terrible! Victor loved him.

One ball trapped him right in front the wicket and everyone shouted, knowing they had him now. He fought to stay; he couldn't fight them all. Victor rushed out on to the pitch, his voice crying for justice, holding back the mob, just as the bell rang.

When he saw Ivan the following day, with safety pins in his shirt where the buttons were missing, Victor's stomach hollowed with pain. For the first time he thought of asking Ivan home to play tennis on his table.

'Stop staring like that. You poured too much milk on the cornflakes. Look how he's playing with it. What wrong with you, boy?'

'He's getting skinny,' his sister giggled.

One hot weary morning in August Victor's family strapped their bags, clasped their suitcases, and clutching bright travel folders migrated to Canada.

They took this decision while Victor was in his final year at school, doing his 'A' levels. They announced the decision at dinner one evening, the family summoned mysteriously to the table by Victor's father. He was the Business Manager of a soft drinks factory. For the announcement he had shaven, trimmed his hair and he wore a light blue shirt which gave him a relaxed youthful look.

He spoke solemnly, making rather foolish drama out of a simple statement – so Victor thought, turning away his face, almost offending the old man who paused and asked if he was listening. Right at that point, where he looked up nonchalantly and said, yes, I'm hearing you loud and clear, something, like the cracking of a branch from the tamarind tree, snapped in Victor's skull. He felt cold and shivered and thought it was the February winds calling to him from outside.

His father was saying something about political trends in the island; his mother interrupted to describe how she had caught their maid *sprawled off* on their bed, *in their bedroom*, claiming she was *just relaxing*; his father was saying something about respect for minority rights in a place like Canada.

Victor found he wasn't shivering any longer; it seemed he could take the February winds; his body relaxed as if for a vigorous massage.

After the announcement they had planned a drive to the ice cream parlour, where Victor would make the purchases, sending his sister back to the car to check on the flavours; and then, the Drive-In cinema. That night he made an excuse about having to study; he stayed home with his Gran.

It was Gran who saved him, pulled him back just when it seemed he would slide away to Canada, buckled to his father's fears, without a show of resistance. Gran was a grey, slippered presence in the house; she knitted, she listened to the radio, she had little to say except at Christmas. Now she announced she didn't want to die in Canada.

It chilled his father's heart. 'Who's talking of dying? We're going there to start a new life,' he said.

Rock firm she resisted: no, she didn't feel threatened by island politics; she was too old for socialism; she would not abandon the house. In an alarmingly casual way she added that she had only ten more years to live.

Brave old Gran, refusing to scuttle ship! Victor would stay with her. He turned truculent all of a sudden, spoke of his freedom to use his life as he chose, his right to die in the house where he was born. It held up preparations for departure. For months they tried to pry Gran away from her obsession.

His mother pleaded, as she gave away old clothes to the Salvation

Army; his father scowled and wrote countless letters; his sister spent hours on the telephone. Victor promised to join them later: he would stay behind to feed the dogs, defend the house from woodworms and the socialists, the menace of the poor.

He drove back from the airport in the family car and on an impulse went in search of Ivan. He found the village but no one knew where Ivan lived. He'd always thought everyone knew everyone in these villages. The car got stuck as he turned around, wheels spinning in the mud; he signalled to the youths lounging by the roadside; they watched him; he got out of the car and approached them, feeling somehow exposed and vulnerable, they muttered in patois, their faces hard and sullen, but they agreed to push him out. A scrawny dog chased his car until the wheels outstripped it.

Racing back to the city, shooting through the cane fields, the wind blubbering at the window, the sky a pitiless blank blue, he thought of his family strapped in their seats, jetting overseas to Ontario. *Christ, Ivan, if you were there this wouldn't have happened.* He imagined his father hours later at Immigration sorting out the passports, supervising everything.

They wrote, anxious letter from a Toronto address. His mother wrote. At Christmas, remembering Gran's tireless preparations, they sent cards and snapshots; there they were, grouped tight for the camera, near-smothered in winter clothes, faces beaming and beefy. Dutifully Victor answered. All was well he indicated. One of the dogs had died. He was working at Barclays Bank.

Ivan would learn later of Victor's visit to his village. He was overwhelmed and apologetic. He explained that just an hour before, he was standing at his gate with his cricket gear waiting for the bus that would take him for his weekend cricket match. Ivan would develop into a cricketer of great promise, moving from village matches to playing for a club in the city. Sometimes Victor offered to drive him back after the game. It soon became a ritual.

Victor turned up fifteen minutes after stumps, blew his horn, watched as Ivan, looking professional in blazer, emerged from the pavilion where the rest of the team were sinking beers. *They* would cycle home later, still arguing about the match, their boots hanging by the laces from the handle bars.

Once Victor arrived one hour before the end. He saw Ivan making his way to the wicket: Ivan gloved, capped, his body lean, his shoulders arched. Ivan the terror, going out to do battle at sunset. He watched him play and thought he moved like a dancer with the bat.

His interest in the game deepened. He followed scores and results in the newspapers. He turned up hours before stumps and sat among the spectators in the stands. He discovered Ivan was their hero.

They commented on everything he did, every stroke he played; they speculated on his future. They're his people, Victor thought, it's him they come to see every Saturday afternoon: these old men with their twisted spectacles, their cropped heads bulging with dates and records. He is their idol.

Driving Ivan home, he would repeat their comments, describe the dreams they spun. Ivan laughed and affected indifference.

Slowly he came to resent all that seemed to thrust Ivan in the centre, there to perform and radiate, while he sat on the periphery, waiting to offer simple kindness, unable somehow to stand up, applaud, slap the back of the man next to him in the stands as Ivan, crouched in the slips, brought off an amazing catch.

One morning Ivan's face surprised him from the sports page. His team had pulled off a spectacular win. Ivan was described as a promising player; his had been a patient knock; island potential for the Test series if ever there was one, the sportswriter said.

That afternoon as he watched Ivan something occurred to him. There he was at the wicket, playing another patient knock, as if now that was always expected of him. Occasionally his dancer's body, tight and neat, came erect as he pivoted on his toes. His people shouted and clapped. Ivan seemed effortless, impeccable, correct. In the stands they were speculating now about his chances for the Australian tour. The sportswriter pulled at his crotch and painted visions of Ivan striding out at Lord's, in Melbourne, in India. Only then did it occur to him that Ivan was not a century maker. Persistently he fell short.

He kept falling to unplayable balls; he walked back to the pavilion, to ragged warm applause, the victim of another forgivable error. Ivan, the stroke player of promise, not yet the centurion.

It probably wasn't a point worth raising. Ivan must have known that for all his dazzling play he was yet to score a first class century. Yet Victor felt he ought to mention it, wedge it firmly somewhere in his mind. It would shield him from those wild hopes hatched in the stands. Give him clear purpose.

He never brought it up. He drove Ivan home, he repeated the opinions of the sportswriter that day; he couldn't bring himself to place that peg on Ivan's ground; for here was Ivan waving to the villagers, his face tired and triumphant. Here was Ivan, home.

Driving back alone once more, braking for little boys who rounded up goats or chased cows, Victor rehearsed with the empty seat what one day he knew he would say: 'You're not a century maker, Ivan. You're too full of your people's idle dreams. You who loved the loud *poc* of bat striking ball, you've lost your spunk and defiance. You cock an ear for shallow gossip from the stands. Once you listened to the fierce beating of your heart. You knew then what you had to do. They'll carry you high on the shoulders of their dreams then one day they'll grow weary and put you down and you'll be one of them forever, you bastard.'

The bitterness of his thoughts alarmed him. The point perhaps really wasn't worth raising. If Ivan asked him to explain what he meant his bitterness might rise like a blade and betray him. Watching him play, feeling this terrible resentment, gave him no pleasure. He stayed away at weekends. He suggested Ivan make his own arrangements for getting home.

His mind turned to thoughts about his future. He couldn't see himself working at the Bank the rest of his life. Gran tried to persuade him to enter University. She didn't like him hanging around like a crow waiting for her to die. The campus was on another island; flying home in an emergency wouldn't be difficult; she was quite capable of taking care of herself.

When the Test team to tour Australia was announced Ivan had not been selected. The sportswriter abused the selectors in his column. It was a gesture of pure contempt for young men of the islands.

Victor met Ivan in the streets, playing his part, collecting commiserations from everyone. When he learnt that Victor was leaving for university his face looked pained, frightened, as it did that day he walked into class with his geometry set.

Ivan wrote him one letter. In it he said he'd changed his job. He'd always wanted to be a school teacher. He'd give up club cricket too. He added, finally, that he was now a revolutionary, fighting for oppressed peoples all over the world.

Ivan and I share anxieties about airports. It begins as we approach the terminal building.

In some countries airports are like bus stations, with people sitting around in lounges, reading magazines and waiting for the airbus to call. On our island the airport might have been a launching pad for scheduled landings on the moon.

It is a grand occasion. The place is charged with sad energy and hope. Families and relatives assemble at this point for farewells; everyone is well dressed; sometimes it's hard to distinguish the travellers.

What disturbs Ivan, what sours him to the core, is not just the spectacle of his people forsaking their homeland, preparing to risk the perils of capitalism. It is something more painful, closer to the heart; that he should be witness to that awful fracture within families, that he should sense beneath the tense rituals that sad wrenching apart of lovers, fathers, mothers, children. He spoke to me, as if he were explaining a map, about the long journey to the land of hope, the postal orders sent back, the passing of the years, the loneliness of the aged, the frustrations of the abandoned.

I listened. I didn't expect him to tread tactfully on a matter like this. I wondered about *his* relatives, the people in his village whom I'd always imagined lived full communal lives.

He takes off for the car park and is long in getting back. Usually I've checked in my bags and I'm idling, curious as to where he's disappeared to. My anxiety stirs with the whine of the jet motors as the flight comes in. I flounder on the other side of the terminals, on that lonely walk to the aircraft, clutching my boarding pass as if it were a life jacket, stumbling up the steps, my body stiffening for that insertion into the carrier, into the new world.

'What took you so long. I thought you'd left,' I said.

'Something funny going on here. They have soldiers patrolling the airport. I count twelve so far. Want to see?'

He showed me the soldiers: three of them, marching in a ragged line, slack and jaunty in floppy hats. Ivan's face was grim as he considered them. He was wearing his Che Guevara beret that year and along with his army surplus pants he looked more fashionable than fearful.

I glanced at the soldiers, I looked at him: the island guerrilla, the forces of fascism. It seemed out of place on our island, like neon, too vivid to be real. I thought of the flight delay, the wet hands of heat around my neck, the dry empty days that relentlessly bleach our lives.

'The plane has been delayed,' I said. 'A strike at the other end. It might not come at all.'

I was right. They soon announced that the flight had been cancelled. Faced for the first time with the prospect of turning back, going home, I found myself none too pleased. There *was* a flight, four hours later, on a Cuban airline. It didn't appeal to me. Ivan was suddenly excited, wanting to know what kind of plane it was. 'It's an Ilyushin'. The word assumed magical properties. It was the closest he had come to the Soviet Union and the international struggle. 'It's here already,' the girl said, 'you can look at it from the east end of the building.' We rushed off like schoolboys to have a look.

'That's it? Errol Flynn used to parachute from something like that during the Second World War. Watch them propellers, huh?'

Ivan was captivated and didn't answer. I told myself this was what happened when some little boys didn't receive toy planes in their Christmas stockings. Lacking his passion I held back, mistrustful of so many things. He stayed with me for an hour, talking about the Cuban revolution and the great sacrifices of the Cuban people, until, responding to the time he had sacrificed in persuasion, I relented. I would do it for his sake. I would write him a long letter about the trip. Inflate his heart.

Back at the ticket counter Ivan was so effusive the girl thought for a moment he was travelling. 'Does he talk so much all the time?' she asked, smiling and clipping. Ivan leaned on the counter and remarked on her lovely oval face. She flinched from those words spilling through his beard and withdrew beneath layers of makeup.

I walked him back to the car park. We must have looked an odd pair: the short man with the fearsome beard, a Che Guevara beret, slapping his thigh rhythmically with a paperback on class struggle (as obligatory to his person as a pistol): and the other, tall, thin, clean shaven, hunched slightly and hovering with affection over his every word.

Our leave-taking is usually overdone: a fumbled handshake, a compensatory friendly jab, a wave, an almost simultaneous turning away as of pugilists returning to neutral corners. This time, with one quick glance in the direction of the Ilyushin, Ivan gave me a Soviet embrace.

'Hasta, companero!' he said, squeezing my chest. 'Don't forget to call on my Granny now and then' I said.

I confess tears came to my eyes, urged there by a foolish schoolboy sense of confusion, summoned by the beatings of a schoolboy heart. I watched his little car with the leaking radiator flogging its way back to the city.

The demons that drive us, the dramas we enact on this tiny island, with Russian built planes and paperbacks of political history! The yearnings we stifle! How could long dead Marx send Ivan tearing away from me, back to the revolution, to the plots he would hatch among the coconut trees?

I sat in the lounge and gazed through the plate glass at the landing strip. I felt worse than ever. The soldiers marched past, the line more ragged this time. They were sharing a joke; the joker glancing over his shoulder was shaking with mirth. these were the defenders of our landspace. *What possesses you, Ivan, what drives you on and on like this? Why am I not so blessed?* Impossible, out of all this, to make a pattern: call those noisy airport employees 'the workers' (two were sparring now, making a scene, like overgrown boys) and those soldiers, carrying their rifles like hoes.

Wanting to talk to someone, to stop this breaking of biscuits in my mind, I put through a call to Nina.

'You haven't left yet?' she asked, her astonishment a little forced.

'In a few hours. The flight was cancelled. Has Ivan reached back yet?'

'No. He might be in the city, but he's not here.'

There was a long silence. I was phoning from a different zone. I shouldn't be phoning at all. Even the dead move on after you've buried them.

'Don't forget to write,' she said, her voice fixing something in my stomach, like a tie that wasn't straight. I put the phone down and went back to the table.

I vowed never to write to her. I vowed never again to be trapped like this. If only I could flow, if only I could stop this fearful scrutiny, this peering through at the microbes we are on this island.

In the lounge, seated at another table, facing me, was a stranger for our flight. She was sealing an airletter she had just moistened with her tongue; now she took out a book and got ready to annotate. Her face was part oriental; her spectacles sat on her nose in a way that reminded me of the Head Librarian in town. She had that air of someone official, a *politburo official* (the phrase borrowed from one of Ivan's improbable conversations seemed to fit) and she was evidently taking the Cuban flight.

Who are these people? Why do they come to our island?

She looked up and caught me staring; her smile was affectionate but disapproving. Ivan's ideal companion, matched perfectly, I thought, for obduracy, that quiet preparation for the future. Had he walked in that minute he might have been drawn to her table by her sense of purpose. I could picture them together whispering and nodding, the rest of the world momentarily banished. These possessed people, my God, these leaders for the revolution.

At moments like these I want simply to leave it all, let the drama of individual lives and frenzy play to itself, as really it does. These island theatres, their travelling players, the quickly magnetized crowds! For as long as I sat staring, as often as the soldiers slow-marched outside, spasms of wretched feeling overcame me.

The second stranger had dropped his bag heavily on the floor and had pulled out a chair before he caught my attention. He was youthful and dark-haired and moustachioed in a manner I considered Spanish.

Just one hour to wait.

I heard the music of the guitar and looked up to find his head lowered over the instrument, his fingers feelings for chords. So he would use his time making music! This Cuban – why couldn't he be Cuban? – was going home.

He played the same melody, a song from the heart of his island perhaps. At one point the strumming was so vigorous, the rhythm winding up to such a pitch, it was as if his soul had taken off, was flying through the sky.

I knew no songs of this island. My heart flicked off the minutes as they expired. My heart, a ticking digital of the days and nights of our lives, could not sing of these islands.

Always, when travelling home from the campus, I anticipated Ivan would meet me at the airport. I would send him cables with the flight number and arrival time. (I imagined his excitement as the messenger on motor cycle handed him these urgent messages from overseas and asked him to sign.) He never came to meet me.

I would grip my bags and burst through the swing doors into the waiting smile of Nina. 'Where's Ivan? I'd ask, failing to hide my disappointment. Called away suddenly, she'd say. At the other end of the island. Organising the workers. It sounded urgent, fraught with risk – and I couldn't be expected to understand.

So here once more was Nina, garrulous as we walk to the car, in her African-print robe and African head-dress, costumed like the man she lived with, sharing his running passion for the poor. I didn't trust her airport excitement, the way her body quivered under the robe, drawing attention to itself. I held myself discreetly aside until we got to the car.

What on earth did Ivan see in her? They were teachers on the same staff, he explained. Nina was the only woman who *understood* him. I flinched at this huge sentimental claim which he regretted making as soon as he had spoken. Driving back to the city slowly, deliberately, she talked about their relationship, their domestic problems, his frequent absence at weekends.

At first I was startled by these revelations, the profile of intimacy she assembled, then saddened at the thought that this was what the swashbuckling cricketer or promise had been reduced to, this half way house they kept with its common petty problems.

Later I discovered that Nina was really unsure about her place in Ivan's scheme of things. It emerged during the evenings we spent together in Ivan's flat where Nina, playing the part of consort too hard, was always encouraging me to visit, to eat, to sit on fat embroidered cushions, stare at lit candles and join in serious discussions. She seemed curious about the way Ivan and I interacted. When she wasn't being his secretary, reading back – for my delight, Ivan's beard-stroking reflection – details of his adventures with the authorities, she was clearing away plates, tucking her legs under the robe, listening keenly, I felt, to every nuance of our exchanges; hoping for clues to the man she would possess which I, friend from the schoolyard, might have concealed on my person.

I must have disappointed her. My silence, on those trips from the airport encouraged her to gush; she no doubt hoped that disclosure would flow copiously the other way. I was alarmed at the way she seemed to swarm all over Ivan's private needs, knowing precisely what he wanted and attending to it.

Somewhere after midnight Ivan would grow restless and suggest we drive through empty streets, past the sleeping market place, deep into the island's night. She hesitated, waiting to be asked along, her silence boiling with fears that perhaps she wasn't wanted.

At some point, I suppose, she felt distinctly threatened, pushed back into second place, left outside some magic circle where secrets were divulged or rites practised. It was the beginning of subtle attacks on my presence.

Menacing as snake her tongue flicked words intended to puncture my equaminity. 'You in the castle of your skin.' she would declare, quoting Shakespeare or somebody, launching next into theory about the race and privilege on the island. Like Ivan she was a reader, the literary side to his political essays. Nervously I would glance at him, as anecdote pursued theory, and wonder what was passing through his shaggy head, whether he agreed with her shrill foamy opinions.

He was thoughtfully packing his pipe (a new puzzling appendage to his image that year) and though he must have sensed my discomfort he never once interrupted.

I grew suspicious. Was this his clever way of testing me, through her? I squirmed, refusing to be drawn, until satisfied she had nailed me irrefutably to death, she would toss the whole exercise away as nothing but a joke and ask if anyone wanted coffee.

Ivan, the pipe-puffing scholar, would shift wearily on the cushions and mutter something about class relations being fundamental to the problems on this island. 'What classes do we have?' I asked, leaning forward, letting him play more earnestly the academic lecturing to young timid minds about the cruelties of poverty and capitalism.

It never occurred to me that all this time a snake pit was being dug. One evening I stumbled and fell into it.

I should have read the signs, watched my step from the moment I came into the flat. Hailing everyone and getting no reply I was greeted by a miracle in the living room. Someone had performed a feat of housecleaning, a revolution of sorts, for Ivan's flat like Ivan's politics reflected his distaste for bourgeois comfort and order. Now the paperbacks had been put back on the shelf, the cups and saucers picked up from lying around and returned to their place in the kitchen. A refreshing sense of space, a new order swept me inside and closed the door. A different voice called to me suggesting I make myself at home. I looked around me and succumbed.

Nina came out eventually, fixing her hair, her face bath-fresh and gleaming; and now her body introduced itself like a cousin visiting from the country. Her robe was wrapped tight around her bottom, her shoulders were bare, and the slit at the side allowed flashes of clean unsunned limb. 'Ivan isn't here,' she said. 'What happened?' I asked, meaning to find out about Ivan. 'Oh, I thought I'd do a little tidying up,' she said.

I found myself rapidly giving in to her chatter, the crossing and uncrossing of her legs, her frequent trips to the kitchen, for dinner was being prepared, and since Ivan wasn't coming home that evening I'd have to take his place. 'I'm sure you don't mind,' she said.

At the table, fussing with bowls and plates, she encouraged me to start while she darted back to the kitchen. Gradually it came over me as I sat in the straight-backed chair that perhaps this had all been calculated: the overthrow of the old regime, a new Head of State installed.

I tried to pretend nothing extraordinary was happening although evidence suggesting otherwise was all around me, even in our conversation which turned away from a quick angry disposal of Ivan and his escapades to a probing for more personal revelation. 'Why don't you join your parents in Canada?' she asked. I didn't care to say anything about that and was relieved and startled when she announced that, given a chance, she would abandon the island.

'Why don't you *seize* the chance?'

'You mean make a break for it? It's not that easy ... *to escape to the great wilderness* ... There is a warmth here I can't live without. I don't think I could survive for too long out there. Still when I think of all the things I could possibly be ...'

She urged on me more wine. We had opened a bottle and she hated leaving things half finished. We were seated on the cushions, the robe riding up her legs as she gestured and laughed. I leaned on one elbow at first, then fell to full recline on the floor; she went in search of a cigarette; she was sure I was in no condition to drive home; I could spend the night there if I wanted, she added, softly, the great mother to all tired souls. I protested I was in full control of my senses but did nothing when suddenly her hands touched my face.

The snake pit!

All night I'd sensed the almost imperceptible slide into its darkness. I told myself I had the will simply to scramble out, if seriously menaced, before the snakes lashed their ropes around their body and battened me down. 'You needn't worry. Ivan isn't coming home until next morning,' she repeated. Somehow the reminder sounded foolish. Now her body was stretched out beside mine, and I knew I had slipped into the pit. I froze in terror.

I closed my eyes pretending to be in useless stupor and fiercely I summoned Ivan back: *Why are you never here? Why do you let me fall? Pull me out of this. Drive her off.*

Under the pretext of letting me rest more comfortably she led me into Ivan's room. I couldn't help noticing details of his occupancy: those bright shirts on hangers in an open cupboard; two pairs of shoes; a cricket bat shining as if recently oiled. I felt like a usurper, I had arrived for the coronation.

Not content with removing my shoes she now leaned over me, rubbing my chest, my temples, waiting for some signal to be more openly intimate. I made no move; my terror was complete.

Couldn't she see I didn't want Ivan's throne? That no matter how much she threw herself at my feet, willing to be my subject, I could not take Ivan's place, not here, not ever. And I could not take *her*, even if I knew how to, so enormously foreign was the kingdom of her body; so deep too were my suspicions that this had all been cleverly orchestrated by Ivan himself: the snake pit dug, his intention to embroil, humiliate, get back at me for the chances he never had, for the opportunities he imagined my mulatto skin attracted like a magnet.

Eyes shut, thinking hard, I never heard Nina withdraw until a sound as of someone whispering from the bowels of some hidden grief, came from behind the bathroom door. A menacing sound. It slithered under the door and crept to where my heart started racing with alarm. Quickly I pulled on my shoes.

'You're just like him. Both of you ... useless men!' she shouted, as I fled the room.

When eventually she came out, fully recovered, asking perfunctorily whether I wanted coffee, she found me leafing through one of her paperbacks.

'I think I'd better be going,' I said, putting the book back in the hollow of the shelf, turning to look for my keys, as if nothing unusual had happened.

'How do these complications ensnare us?'

'I wish I could tell you. I don't know what to say.'

'I don't talk like this to strangers. Usually I keep myself to myself. Especially on planes.'

'I didn't ask to be put on this aircraft ... what did you call it ... *Ilyushin*? ... Flying with these people makes me nervous.'

'Nothing has happened so far. The stewardess is really helpful.'

'There's a man sitting at the back of the plane. He doesn't act like a passenger ... don't turn around now ... He's acting strange.'

'What does he look like.'

I'd caught her looking at me – pulling her eyes away as if contact with anyone was unwise – as the Cubans checked our luggage under the wings of the plane. I liked the way she stood apart from the tiny cluster, composed and uninterested, gripping her travel bag, so that I guessed she was nervous behind the sun glasses, the pointed chin, determined nevertheless not to show it. She sat in my row, the aisle between us. The way she fussed with the seat belts somehow suggested she was marking out her private ground, boundaries beyond which it was forbidden to enter. I suppose you could describe her as pretty. She had smooth features and a light complexion, those points of beauty our islanders value. You'd think someone like her would come prepared not to be intruded on as well as not intruding. But she'd forgotten her ballpoint for the immigration card, which is how we started talking later. They fired propeller one, two, three and four, and we took off in a frightening roar, bumping a bit at first, then settling down to something fairly reassuring.

You might expect passengers to say something companionably to each other, soothing anxiety, for we were thundering through the sky like a bomber squadron. An elderly couple held hands. If she were strapped into the seat next to mine I might have said I didn't like sitting over the wings. I thought of saying just that whenever she decided to return the ballpoint. I was surprised when she took off the sun glasses and asked if I thought anyone would try to blow up the plane.

'Well, I know exactly what happens next. Final exams. Then I'll do my internship in the Bahamas. Then it's off to the US or Canada.'

'The islands need young doctors like you.'

'The islands need doctors. I will not let them take my youth. That's what your friends can't see ... such a waste of young lives ... a revolution!

'While you're running away ... '

'And why not? There's nothing to keep me here. Nationalism is a skin everybody sheds eventually. As for these islands, they're futureless places. Just one hurricane and we're wiped off the map.'

'I could have gone with my parents, you know.'

'You didn't go. And you think you're some hero. If you ask me, you're funny.'

'We have one thing in common. We both want to lose ourselves. Vanish from the face of all we've grown too familiar with from birth.'

'All I want to do is practice medicine, live comfortably and wait for death to call.'

'I wish it were as simple as that for me.'

'You're a real queer fish.'

At the next island stop they switched off the propellers. The heat rose. There was time enough to stroll as far as the in transit lounge, to linger until we were summoned. She walked with an erect carriage, racing away from me, pushing petulantly against the brisk wind. It was all I could do to keep up with her, though it was fascinating to watch her striding across the landing strip, our island medical scholar, so unerringly sure about her place, our proportion in the world, about the lanes and routes that take you further, let you expand; surprisingly free, too of that interminable buzzing in the head that is every islander's hive of fears and doubts. There were two huge jetliners parked close to the terminal buildings, almost dwarfing them. There were airport employees unloading bags, working with the air of incarcerated men chafing at their chains. I hurried to catch up with her. We were unprepared for what we saw. The place was teeming with travellers, almost all foreign, waiting to board. It must have been a day of frustrating delays. So many people! They swarmed everywhere, squatting on the floor, chewing gum, examining their sunburns. We went to the duty free shops. They were there fingering the craft work. We sought refuge in the restaurant. They sprawled on the chairs, sipping from beer cans, gazing through the plate glass. A few, perhaps not travelling that day, stood around joking, fondling each other. We didn't know why but an inner sense of suffocation gripped us, and when the announcement came, we fled back to the aircraft, walking close, not saying a word.

'It's the way they carry on, as if we're vegetation, backdrop you pay no attention to.'

'They're only tourists minding their own business, living free, just as you intend to.'

'Did you see that girl in the skimpy bath suit, kissing and carrying on in the open. It's downright indecent, I don't care what you say.'

'Maybe it's their idea of comfortable living. Why do half-naked bodies upset you?'

'Who says I'm upset?'

'Never mind. When you get to Canada you'll find everyone covered from head to toe, especially during the winter months. You won't have to come in contact with anybody except at the hospital. I'm sure you'd like that.'

'It will certainly be more civilised than this part of the world. How much more of this horrible plane do we have?'

'About an hour. What's eating you?'

'None of your business.'

Thinking about it afterwards I imagined how much more she hated these islands now, hated airports and Cuban planes, hated people she had to borrow ballpoints from. The memory of our journey burned like live coals in my mind, fanned often to bright flame as more scraps of conversation came back to me. Once I caught sight of her proud figure in white jacket striding across the lawns towards the hospital. It was distinctly possible. I mused, that I might have made an imprint on her feelings in much the same way she affected mine. The circumstances were too special. It bothered me, though, that she might vanish like a ghost. I felt as if I had conquered something which only she could confirm. I made a few enquiries. They were sure she would make a brilliant doctor wherever she chose to practise. I didn't have the courage to show my face on the wards or at her door and asked to be remembered, to be confirmed. The image of her, that body with its untold secrets, hurtling towards its future, kept appearing in my dreams. I'd be sitting in Ivan's flat, a glance through the window, and there she was suddenly she would appear floating through the clouds in a giant balloon, causing commotion on the ground until she disappeared over the next mountain range. I could only fill my eyes with images of her vanishing into several futures. Then one afternoon she phoned. She sounded breathless as if she had just come in from jogging. 'I'm calling from next door,' she said. 'Did you hear the news?' It was unmistakably her voice though I couldn't believe it! 'How did you get my number?' I asked. 'Did you hear the newsflash? A plane exploded just off Barbados.' 'What plane? Where are you calling from?' 'A Cuban plane. Someone blew it up. Killed all the passengers. Can you imagine, all those innocent people blown to bits in mid air? It's monstrous.' 'I haven't heard anything. Listen, can I see you tonight?' 'I don't know why I'm so upset. I had to call you. I mean, who could conceive of doing a thing like that?'

JOHN STEWART

John Stewart was born in Trinidad in 1933 and completed his education in the United States where he attended the California State University, Stanford University, The University of Iowa and U.C.L.A.

He has lectured widely in the U.S. and the Caribbean. His publications include several short stories and the novel *Last Cool Days*, which was awarded the Winifred Holtby Prize in 1972. He has also made a film about ritual stick-fighting in Trinidad.

John Stewart is now Associate Professor in Anthropology at the University of Illinois at Urbana-Champaign.

This story was finished in 1974 while I was living in
Fresno, California, but the gestation began much earlier.
I read the story of Daaga (also called Donald Stewart)
for the first time at the University of Iowa library in
1965. He was executed for having led a rebellion among
African troops in Trinidad in the 19th century. Given
the fervent re-discovery of Africa and black nationalism
taking place in those days, it seemed another instance of
colonial masking that all through my childhood and
schooldays spent in Trinidad I had never once heard the
name Daaga.

A second awakening relevant to this story occurred
some years later when during the course of anthropolo-
gical fieldwork I had opportunity to share in both the
everyday and ritual activities of a community where
stick-fighting is an old and valued art. Having been
originally socialised to regard stick-fighting as a rem-
nant primitive cultural reflex, I was profoundly moved
to discover in it an ethos that is particularly relevant to
the post-colonial nationalism being forged in Trinidad.
There is a poetic challenging of fate in stick-fighting; one
that resonates with the challenge announced by Daaga
and his comrades when they undertook a rebellion that
could not be, for themselves, successful. This, of course,
I can recount in retrospect. The two – and other things
too – came together in my imagination quite without my
fully knowing, and the result is this story.

John Stewart

STICK SONG

The early swarm of flies was over: only a few darting stragglers
were still abroad, winking the solid darkness that stretched and
rolled away behind the houses. At a dip in the road they could
hear dogs barking from the village on the next hill over. Then drums and
voices.

The drums were thick, low, a distant rumble across the quiet valley.
The voices were not sweet, yet even at a distance the stick-song chorus
made Daaga's skin shiver. For a moment it was like being in a dome with
only the drums and naked voices reflecting, and in Daaga an elemental
stir to dance erupted despite his nagging fear of dancing: his fear of the
feelings stirred and their potential power over him.

He had not heard such music in eight years. He had learned to thrive
on the subtleties of Miles Davis, Max Roach; had been many times over
stirred by Coltrane and Elvin Jones, but not this way. He had thrown

rocks at armed policemen; and armed himself with a new name, a new awareness of his historic enormity he had returned to teach, to awaken the peasant mind from which he had once sought deliverance. Awaken to its own dormant power.

But did he really know better then the dimensions of that power? Could economic theory, political awareness, a revised history – could any of these overpower a drum beat?

'Them boys beating good keg,' Stone said, 'but they can't touch we ...'

As the road inclined they could hear the sounds of their village once again, and soon they walked into the tent yard where the men were practising for the carnival. A general noise and bustle blocked out George Village, blocked out the night. Another dome, this one hearty and self-contained, without echo.

'Ah ah, so you come!' the carpenter shuffled forward short and supple, big veins cording his arms and forehead, his face gleaming an enormous smile. So you come! As if some subtle travail by which Daaga was innocently directed had at last succeeded. The carpenter took him by the hand and led him through the thicket of coarse arms, sweat-drenched bodies pressed and humidifying in the electric glare of a naked bulb. Leading him aggressively through the thickened clamour of village men who an hour ago were humble johns or worked-wrestled lashleys back-sore and spirit-weary from the unceasing peasant days.

But now!

Now, as if something had dissolved the cagedness around their reserve, it is exuberance, mettle in their voices, an expansive flash to their eyes. As though they not only knew how heart first came to beat, but were the acknowledged substance of its magic. Who under the glare of this one bulb light fluttered by moths and other forage of the night were boasting, arguing, challenging each other, all the while sharing the ritual flasks of mountain dew strong still with the vapour of molasses. Homage to king cane. Which with the scent of herbs crushed down where dancing feet had tramped the yard joined an odour that reached away for Daaga. Faint yet persistent, an odour he must have known in the past, pleasantly.

'Aie, aie', the carpenter was gleeful. 'Come, come,' he said, tugging Daaga through the crowd. 'Aie, Conga Man!' the carpenter called as they burst through to a circular space ringed in by the clamour but itself vacant except for one man.

'Aie, Conga Man!'

And from the centre of the ring Conga Man watched them approach without replying. In khaki pants and long white shirt untucked, a cricket cap on backwards over a white headband, he hulked at the centre of the ring with his chin propped on the tip of his stick.

'This we king,' the carpenter said. And Conga Man affected it. The same who to Daaga had been more formally Robert of two bends down the road, husband, father of seven, workman at the factory – now king. Silently awaiting their approach, eyes steady in his concave black face and red.

'Where that?'

'St Madelaine.'

'Yeah when I was a little boy we used to have stick there too ... '

'Yes, I know,' the carpenter suddenly becoming wise.

The drum rattled, and someone sang – 'When ah dead bury mi clothes ... ' Conga Man, leaning once more on his stick rocked back, closed his eyes and smiled.

'I know,' the carpenter said. 'I used to have a ladyfriend over there, a long time before you born. I know they used to have stick. Your own grandfather brother, he was a tiger. But you 'ent know him. He dead before you born. I know they did have stick there, but that before your time.'

'I remember carnival days, and the stick-men singing ... '

'Bois!' an unexpected voice exploded behind Daaga, and he turned to see tall Mr Gray dancing before Conga Man, his empty fingers rigid, circling the air like some wrestler's. 'Bois!' Mr Gray lunged at Conga Man, who ducked and came up in time to catch the older man in his arms. The two men embraced and laughed full in each other faces.

'Gray,' the carpenter called. 'Look Mr Daaga.'

And Gray turned slowly to survey, an unsmiling scrutiny but not unkind. 'So, Mr Daaga you come to pass some time with the boys,' he said.

'A little bit.'

'I just telling him,' the carpenter said, 'I just telling him this the place where stick born.' And old Gray nodded his head in concurrence, without taking his eyes off Daaga.

'But his grandfather village had one or two good stick-men too, you know.'

'Oh yes? Who his grandfather?' Mr Gray asked.

'Old man Grant, used to pastor that Baptist church outside Usine.'

Mr Gray's eyes narrowed, then his frown relaxed as though he had just solved a problem. 'Is so? Boy,' he said to Daaga, 'you a Grant?'

'Look Conga Man, look. Is mi boy. Mi boy come!' the carpenter said.

Then Conga Man pulled himself straight, and smiled. 'Well Mr Daaga, you come to play a little stick?'

Daaga wanted to stop himself from grinning but could not. 'Just to watch,' he said.

'Well we not having much right now, as you could see,' Conga Man said.

'I see,' Daaga said, looking around.

There were three drums abandoned on the ground, though several of the men held sticks, the weave of intercourse was syncopal except for a shouting match or two within clusters for the most part engaged in drinking.

'I tell you he woulda come,' the carpenter said. Conga Man smiled, his face nevertheless losing no sense of presence. Like a serpent. 'I tell all you,' the carpenter continued, 'from the first day I see him that he was a gentleman, but that he was one a we. You taking a drink?' Conga Man said, accepting the already proffered flask from the beaming carpenter. He took a little to wash his mouth and spray, then a medium swallow. Daaga accepted the flask and did likewise to the carpenter's glee.

'You drink like one a we, man,' the carpenter said ... 'Make my heart feel glad.' As he completed the triad.

One drummer had returned and now he rattled his skin a little to call the others.

'So you come back from America,' Conga Man said. 'They does have stick over there?'

'Naah ... ' Daaga replied.

'This is the place where stick born!' the carpenter said, doing a quick kalina step. 'You ever heard of Congo Barra? He born right here. This his grandson.' Which Conga Man did not deign to acknowledge.

'They used to have stick in my village too,' Daaga said. Daaga smiled. 'The old man was my grandfather.'

'Who you for – one of his daughters or his son?'

'His son.'

'And how you 'ent carrying the name?'

Daaga smiled.

'I've been saying to myself all this time,' Mr Gray announced at large, 'I know this man's blood.' And back to Daaga, 'I used to court one of your tanties, boy.'

'He 'ent know bout that,' the carpenter said. 'That before he born.' And turning to Daaga he asked, 'When you went to America Mr Daaga? What time it was when you leave Trinidad?'

'Nineteen-fifty-eight.'

'And you 'ent come back till this year?'

'That's right.'

Again the drums rattled, and someone raised 'Sergeant Brown calling mi name ... ' but he did not get a chorus. As Mr Gray returned to scrutinising.

'Young fella,' he finally asked with force, 'You know where you get that name?'

To which Daaga smiled, 'Sure.' Never forgetting how he had self-consciously selected it from the dusty shelves of a North American library, at a time when many like himself had begun to renew, reaffirm, reconstitute the black African in their person. 'Sure.'

'Hmmm,' Gray grunted. 'Daaga was a hell of a man, you know. Where the bottle?'

'Yes,' Daaga said. Wondering however did old unlettered Gray, back villager that he was had come to know anything about the first Daaga.

They drank and Gray went on. 'How you get the name, somebody give it you or you pick it up yourself?'

'I picked it out,' Daaga said. And it should have been pleasant encountering another who knew of and obviously respected the first Daaga, but it wasn't.

'That's what I'm saying,' Gray's voice was almost amused. 'Because only few people in Trinidad know anything about Daaga. Where you get it, in America?'

'Yes.'

'You see!' cried Gray, announcing once more to the crowd at large. 'America 'ent only for making money – you getting history there too, man. History.'

And how did the history of that first Daaga ever come to old Gray's attention?

'When you know, you know.' Gray spoke like one privy to a mystery, and Daaga offered him a smile, hoping to ignite some feeling of kinship, comradeship, some contact beyond the mere breath of their voices. But the old man's eyes would not let him in.

'You ever heard about Daaga?' Gray said pompously to the carpenter.

'No. But the name sound like a stick-man to me.'

'Stick-man! Daaga was a warrior! In the eighteenth century when the Spanish still keeping slaves, Daaga turned on them. Man, look! Right there in St Joseph, oui! And if it wasn't for a kiss-mi-ass traitor he woulda take over this whole island. Yes! The whole island. But turn his backside gi them, man. They want to see him look sorry and hang-dog, but he turn his back gi them as if to say "Kiss my ass!" You think they know what to do with that?'

'He must've been a bold man.'

'He was a tough man.'

'Anybody with a name like that bound to be dangerous. You going up?'

They drank and the flask was empty.

'Kiss mi ass, he tell them,' Gray said, pursuing the story or history of that first Daaga with emphasis, as if at one time he might have taken such a name himself, handled such deeds himself.

'Where you get all that Gray?' the carpenter asked.

'The priest.'

'What priest, that *maracon* at the Presbyterian?'

'I'm telling you, man,' Gray spoke with forebearance, 'these Americans 'ent stupid like all you think.'

'What that priest know about Daaga or anything in Trinidad?'

'Them Americans know everything man. They smart too bad. You 'ent heard this Mr Daaga here say that where he get his name?'

'That priest only have a lot of books.'

'That's knowledge!' Gray's voice rose like a drum clout. 'Knowledge!'

Then the drummers were reassembled, and the heavy keg picked up a heartbeat. A strong, steady, muffled beat.

'Book knowledge ain't no kind of knowledge,' someone said. 'How about the lost books of the Bible,' Gray came back vigorously. 'You imagine what is in them?'

The light drum cut into the deep-toned keg, and soon the third drum picked up a second off-rhythm, until together they were sounding memories which caused Daaga to rock with a smile on his face.

All talk trailed to an end.

Conga Man, eyes closed, aloof, slowly raised his arms above his head, stick pointing to the sky. Daaga, Gray, the carpenter, they all moved back leaving Conga alone in the circle. A voice raised . . .

> 'My mama gon pay the bail
> Don't let me sleep in the royal jail . . . '

and several immediately chorused –

> 'Tell the sergeant
> Mi mamma gon' pay the bail . . . '

Conga Man began his dance. He leaped in the air, arms outstretched, to land softly on his toes and stalk the circle like a panther wrathfully in search of prey. The cutting drum saluted. Conga weaved, flicking his stick to a defensive position, then abruptly he stood rock still, a challenge to any who dared attack. An agony in his stance, but forever belligerent. Vulnerable he may be, but fearless, and with a price for whoever would find out.

In between the drums a singer chanted his call again, and the chorus answered. Like liquid memory the vibrating beat quivered Daaga's belly and arms, his feet. Aroused to an anciently imbedded dance, he wanted to leap like Conga, stomp the earth, bend the sky. A tremor of fearlessness electrified him.

'You want to play?' the carpenter shouted in his ear above the drums and singing. And Gray was still looking at him, an intensely neutral scrutiny.

Daaga only smiled. When uneasiness, when fear is conquered, man carries out the eternal with nothing but ease. Daaga only smiled.

All the men singing, their voices came sweet. Several danced, though taking care not to confront Conga where he was planted shimmying, his stick crossed and ready. They danced around him, beside him, in complement to his contained power, but never confronting him. The drums rumbled and clapped like sweet thunder, and when Daaga closed his eyes they pounded right in deep beneath his skin and massaged his viscera, so that a power steamed from his head distinct as the smell of sweat, fresh earth, crushed leaves, and something that didn't have a name but was bright and blue in colour. Deepening to black in moments. A discovery of peace in terror. Demon, benevolent, brave martyr, but above all fearless; at work, peace, or play, fearless; divided, conquered, fearlessly emerging, reassembling, dominating; fearless. Daaga sang with the chorus, rocked his head and bounced where he stood; but waited for himself to calm down.

Then with a flourish the drums came down and the song ended. The men went back to palaver and drinking, several thrusting flasks towards Conga who, once more pleasant and benign, shook the sweat from around his eyes, joined in the laughter, and drank.

How you like the boys?' Stone asked, materialising before Daaga. 'They good?'

'Yes, yes ... '

'I did tell you so. I see they make you hot too,' Stone grinned, 'little bit again and you would've jumped in, right?'

To which Daaga could smile and say, 'This music is sweeter than anything I've heard in a long time.'

'I tell you though,' Stone confided, 'if you get hot and want to jump in, don't take on Conga Man. He's very dangerous ... '

To which Daaga smiled, 'Who should I take on, you?'

'Who me, I don't play stick. I don't want nobody busting my head open.' Stone lifting his hat to stroke his head. 'This coconut good just as it is and it gon' stay that way till I get to New York. Only way I get mi head buss is if a New York police hit me in a riot ... '

To which Daaga smiled, relaxed now. Maybe one day Stone would find a library – perhaps the very one Daaga had known – and re-emerge with a new name. Then his cultivating Daaga would have been worth it. But again, he might just get lost on Brooklyn Avenue. There was no way Daaga could prepare him for all he would encounter even living the way they did as brothers before his departure. Maybe one day he would come back with something more than the bravado of a big city street corner. To this same village, and be just the finite dream of his ancestors incarnate.

The rum was new and a little bit smokey, but it drank well. The men praised the hand that made it. They talked ... the babble of men in good spirits because of knowing that weakness and fear would sometime before the gathering broke be exorcised, and they would live sharing the vision. They talked, until the talk divided itself between just two and the others listened. Old Gray's voice shrieked to make a lion pause. 'Daaga is a wicked name, oui!'

The others fell frozen sand on the ear – 'I don't believe none of that stupidness ... ' And Crazy Desmond's eyes looked sharp with contempt.

'Is a wicked name ah telling you ... '

'So what it got in that – my name 'ent wicked too?'

'You? Go on! You ever start a revolution? You ever tell white man kiss your ass? You gon stand up like a man when they point the gun at you? A chicken like you ... '

'So ah is chicken: a chicken fowl-cock! Well buss mi head, nuh! Look it deh – buss it. Ah is chicken. Well get a stick – Ah want to see you buss chicken head ... '

'Damn Trinidadian so blasted stupid, you can't tell them nothing. Where a stick?'

A waiting voice raised the song again –

> 'Mi mamma gon pay the bail
> Mi mamma gon pay the bail
> Tell the sergeant
> Mi mamma gon pay the bail ... '

and the drums overtook the melody

Buh gu duk/Buh gu duk ... '

And Daaga, Mr Daaga, relaxed now. Another rum: the drums. And uncontrollably out of context the memory of himself on a toilet seat in Idylwild. It is a mountain resort in Southern California, flat board cabins between the rustic redwood trees, and the company of a brown woman. It is the summer season, with a blue sky, golden sun, high in the desert atmosphere, and bronze-blond teenagers everywhere eager for experiments to exploit the vulnerabilities ordinarily buttoned down below. It is a porthole toilet: the 'closet' of an earlier childhood. With the sun striated through waving fir branches in a sky blue, deep and eternal. What is it? What is it being sucked into a solitude above the world, becoming pure?

What is it – being sucked into the ephemeral darkness which yet echoes a voice, a warmth, arms clasping.

On the barren ground of an idle hilltop it is the lover embracing his mate beneath the silhouette of empty avocado trees and many unmoved stars in the distance saying *Call my name I want to hear you call my name*. And even further than the stars across the treetops, the ocean washes languidly alike for lovers, dead fish or the melancholy seaman laying down his seine.

All women were one. For a fleeting uncontrollable moment he missed

Woman, mermaid of the liquid night. And in a moment resolved to the excruciating sweetness of their future embrace.

Another rum: the drums.

And Daaga, Mr Daaga, dancing like an ancient warrior before his totem. With a stick in his hand, and the dance coming easily. So that his nostrils burned, and the bones of his face could feel the atmosphere. Daaga dancing in the one-bulb electric light, and the men making room for him, backing off into the traditional circle where it is the drummers, himself, and in a corner the hole where the blood for each night is collected. Daaga dancing. Leaping as lithe as Conga Man on his toes, and the drums filled on dew from the mount following him everywhere, commenting, instructing, sometimes compelling his motion.

The drums tell you what to do.

'Aie, but look, the American dancing!'

'He ent no American: He's a born Trinidadian.'

'Aie, but he's dancing sweet, man.'

'Bound to. No Yankee could dance this dance. Besides, he Daaga.'

'Who that?'

'The fella what did kill all the Spanish and them before your grandfather time.'

'He come back? He spirit come back?'

'Spirit like that don't bury you know ... '

Buh gu duk/Buh gu duk ...

'Aie ah aie! Ah go buss a head tonight! Tonight, tonight!'

It is Crazy Desmond: in his ten-dollar shirt with the cuffs rolled back, sharkskin pants, alligator shoes, and a brims-up felt hat on his head. Dancing left foot, right foot, marking the ground with his stick. For a second, Daaga would have melted into the night, flowed on back to being idle and wild. But Desmond's scent enveloped him like a woman's perfume edged with a touch of rawness, and behind his back the drums rained thunder from a peak. In his right eye Conga Man stood judiciously, his stick grounded like a staff between his legs; and before him Desmond played his stick like an obeahman jabbing spirits, then prepared a carré.

Daaga heard the drums inside his head. He danced. Before him Desmond stretched and retracted like a cobra, his stick cocked above his head. Daaga danced: then planted his feet and took a stance. Immediately there came a blur between his eyes and a knocking dullness. In a single voice the men roared. They broke the circle, and several rushed by him to hug Desmond. The blood was warm coming down his face, as Conga Man led him over to the hole and forced him to bend his head over it. Stone's voice said, 'But all you wicked, oui! All you let Desmond cut the man?'

The rum bath brought a sting to his forehead. His vision came instantly sharper, as did his ears, so that all around him slowed down, and from the core of an impenetrable calm he waited while they worked on stopping the blood.

'He ent cut bad,' said Conga Man.

'But he coulda get his eye dig out!' Stone said. 'The man come quite from New York, and all you let him jump in here to get his head buss!'

'Well why din't you get a stick and stand up then, eh?'

'Me ent tell nobody I is stick-man. But all you let Desmond take advantage man.'

'Take advantage, what? When time comes, jackass have to bray. Besides Daaga or whoever his name is aint from New York. He from right here.'

'Yes. And I believe he gon cut Desmond good, good,' Conga Man said. 'You'll see. If Desmond didn't swinging sideways stick he done cut already!'

'You 'ent see the way Daaga measure him with his eye?'

'I tell you, Desmond done cut already.'

'He gon take him on again.'

And in the old days it was terrifying to watch the grown men play. Terrifying to hear their challenges, then see the fierceness on one face turn to blood. Chilling, the vision of dominance and humility in a dance that always ended the same; chilling, the odour of fear when a man knew he was going to be bled, the lust in the eyes of the bleeder. As a child Daaga had cried for weeks on the vision of losers struck down. But tonight he was quite calm.

It would have been better if there were a song of his own. He was going to cut Desmond tonight, and it would have been nice if he had a song to which this verse could be added. Daaga made a mental note to compose one. The cut between his eyes was dressed, and someone had put a petit-quart of the clear rum in his hand. He raised stick and rum above his head and a few men cheered. He did not turn immediately to look for Desmond.

Not too deep in his past it is daylight saving time in Los Angeles, and the town is on fire. Black men women and children on rampage in the streets, harvesting their due from foreign businesses, dancing a bloody ballet to the rat-a-tat of National Guard fire. And at curtain call nobody knows how many dead, God alone how many left wounded, but no mourning. No applause, no mourning, only an argument left between the wrong and the wronged, into which she could not but induct him, falling back into his life suddenly after all the cha cha chas and bossa novas he had spent in quest of a true lady companion asking What are you going to do about it? As if that were indeed a question! Challenging him on the mount in Griffith Park, Haven't you thought about it? Two brown legs, smooth, unyielding – never mind the weekends as companion in Beverly

Hills – breathing in his ear the native promise everyone knows is but a dream; which nevertheless bears him away promising, promising, promising. What are you going to do? she had asked. Aren't you scared? From the mount in Griffith Park, looking down on a pastel world one corner of which billowed black smoke.

The drums began again and a chantrèlle raised the lavwé –

'Mamma look ah 'fraid
Mamma look ah 'fraid the demon ... '

and got an immediate chorus

'Mamma look ah 'fraid
No stick-man don't 'fraid no demon ... '

Daaga swallowed and handed back the empty petit-quart. He wiped his stick, burnishing the metal cap on the end, then he prepared to pit. The drums rumbled, the circle re-formed. The drums climbed; he started a slow dance. And there was Desmond: leaping tall already, swaying and retracting. Daaga watched him steadily. They circled. Desmond feinted once, twice. They circled again, then Desmond charged, Daaga saw all clearly: and although Desmond was swift Daaga gave ground evading the blow, then brought his own heavily down upon Desmond's skull a split second before their two bodies crashed together.

It was a mighty roar from the men, with someone screaming distinctly, 'Oh God! He kill him'. But Desmond was not dead. On the ground his eyes were glazed, and before friends could remove his hat blood ran from beneath it freely down his left temple. They lifted him and without any help from his legs dragged him to the blood hole. The drums played sweet thunder, then broke, and Daaga found himself lifted in the air by many hands.

The men, elated, Conga Man among them, leaped and shouted. They talked aloud in each others' faces and in a short time reached consensus. Daaga was too rare a phenomenon. When last did anyone see stick play like that? When last did anyone see balance, brains, and fearlessness like that? It was too much for the village to contain that night, and like a compulsive fire going forward, they commandeered the four cars resident in the village, crammed into them singing fresh songs, and set out to show, to share this rare phenomenon in George Village across the hills, or any other where men may leave the safety of their homes and come out in the night to see, to challenge this new hero – Daaga. Behind they left Crazy Desmond sitting under the one bulb light still dazed, with a friend or two feeding him rum, shaving the hair from around his wound to lay a patch on it.

I USED TO LIVE HERE ONCE

This story comes out of a return visit to Dominica made by the author in the 1930's. Jean Rhys's descriptions of the river with its stones, the wider but carelessly made road, the glassy sky and the indifferent children before the changed house are painstakingly realistic and precise. The tone of the remembering character looking for her place, however, gives to almost every item a symbolic character and an emotional charge. This wonderfully compressed and moving story of a person's discovery of placelessness is also an act of courage and a testimony of inner possession in spite of the socio-political facts. Having *lived* here once, the remembering character continues to do so in her mind.

Kenneth Ramchand

I USED TO LIVE HERE ONCE

She was standing by the river looking at the stepping stones and remembering each one. There was the round unsteady stone, the pointed one, the flat one in the middle – the safe stone where you could stand and look around. The next wasn't so safe for when the river was full the water flowed over it and even when it showed dry it was slippery. But after that it was easy and soon she was standing on the other side.

The road was much wider than it used to be but the work had been done carelessly. The felled trees had not been cleared away and the bushes looked trampled. Yet it was the same road and she walked along feeling extraordinarily happy.

It was a fine day, a blue day. The only thing was that the sky had a glassy look that she didn't remember. That was the only word she could think of. Glassy. She turned the corner, saw that what had been the old pavé had been taken up, and there too the road was much wider, but it had the same unfinished look.

She came to the worn stone steps that led up to the house and her heart began to beat. The screw pine was gone, so was the mock summer house called the ajoupa, but the clove tree was still there and at the top of the steps the rough lawn stretched away, just as she remembered it. She stopped and looked towards the house that had been added to and painted white. It was strange to see a car standing in front of it.

There were two children under the big mango tree, a boy and a little girl, and she waved to them and called 'Hello' but they didn't answer her or turn their heads. Very fair children, as Europeans born in the West Indies so often are: as if the white blood is asserting itself against all odds.

The grass was yellow in the hot sunlight as she walked towards them. When she was quite close she called again, shyly: 'Hello'. Then, 'I used to live here once,' she said.

Still they didn't answer. When she said for the third time 'Hello' she was quite near them. Her arms went out instinctively with the longing to touch them.

It was the boy who turned. His grey eyes looked straight into hers. His expression didn't change. He said, 'Hasn't it gone cold all of a sudden. D'you notice? Let's go in.' 'Yes let's', said the girl.

Her arms fell to her sides as she watched them running across the grass to the house. That was the first time she knew.

MY GIRL AND THE CITY

I left Trinidad in 1950 to live in England, and six years later wrote *My Girl and the City* in two days on a surge of inspiration. The rhapsodical and lyrical style (as described) meshed naturally for me into the theme of the heightened emotions one undergoes in love, the city suddenly springing to vibrant life with the experience. Originally it was to be published in the *London Magazine*, but as it appeared first in *Bim*, the Barbados literary magazine, the editor decided to use another story instead: *Cane is Bitter*.

Samuel Selvon

MY GIRL AND THE CITY

All these words that I hope to write, I have written them many times in my mind. I have had many beginnings, each as good or as bad as the other. Hurtling in the underground from station to station, mind the doors, missed it! There is no substitute for wool: waiting for a bus in Piccadilly Circus: walking across Waterloo Bridge: watching the bed of the Thames when the tide is out – choose one, choose a time, a place, any time of any place, and take off, as if this were interrupted conversation, as if you and I were earnest friends and there is no need for preliminary remark.

One day of any day it is like this. I wait for my girl on Waterloo Bridge, and when she comes there is a mighty wind blowing across the river, and we lean against it and laugh, her skirt skylarking, her hair whipping across her face.

I wooed my girl, mostly on her way home from work, and I talked a great deal. Often, it was as if I had never spoken, I heard my words echo in deep caverns of thought, as if they hung about like cigarette smoke in a still room, missionless; or else they were lost for ever in the sounds of the city.

We used to wait for the 196 under the railway bridge across the Waterloo Road. There were always long queues and it looked like we would never get a bus. Fidgeting in that line of impatient humanity I got in precious words edgeways, and a train would rumble and drown my words in thundering steel. Still, it was important to talk. In the crowded bus, as if I wooed three or four instead of one, I shot words over my shoulder, across seats; once past a bespectacled man reading the *Evening News* who lowered his paper and eyed me that I was mad. My words bumped against people's faces, on the glass window of the bus; they found passage between 'Fares please' and once I got to writing things on a piece of paper and pushing my hand over two seats.

The journey ended there was urgent need to communicate before we parted.

All these things I say, I said, waving my hand in the air as if to catch the words floating about me and give them mission. I say them because I want you to know, I don't ever want to regret afterwards that I didn't say enough, I would rather say too much.

Take that Saturday evening, I am waiting for her in Waterloo station. When she comes we take the Northern Line to Belsize Park (I know a way to the heath from there, I said). When we get out of the lift and step outside there is a sudden downpour and everyone scampers back into the station. We wait a while, then go out in it. We get lost. I say, Let us ask that fellow the way. But she says No, fancy asking someone the way to the heath on this rainy night, just find out how to get back to the tube station.

We go back, I get my bearings afresh, and we set off. She is hungry. 'Wait here,' I say under a tree at the side of the road, and I go to a pub for some sandwiches. Water slips off me and makes puddles on the counter as I place my order. The man is taking a long time and I go to the door and wave to her across the street signifying I shan't be too long.

When I go out she has crossed the road and is sheltering in a doorway pouting. You leave me standing in the rain and stay for such a long time she says. I had to wait for the sandwiches I say, what do you think, I was having a quick one? Yes, she says.

We walk on through the rain and we get to the heath and the rain is falling slantways and carefree and miserable. For a minute we move around in an indecisive way as if we're looking for some particular spot. Then we see a tree which might offer some shelter and we go there and sit on a bench wet and bedraggled.

I am sorry for all this rain, I say, as if I were responsible I take off her raincoat and make her put on my quilted jacket. She take off her soaking shoes and tucks her feet under her skirt on the bench. She tries to dry her hair with her handkerchief. I offer her the sandwiches and light a cigarette for myself. Go on, have one, she says. I take a half and munch it, and smoke.

It is cold there. The wind is raging in the leaves of the trees, and the rain is pelting. But abruptly it ceases, the clouds break up in the sky, and the moon shines. When the moon shines, it shines on her face, and I look at her, the beauty of her washed by rain, and I think many things.

Suddenly we are kissing and I wish I could die there and then and there's an end to everything, to all the Jesus-Christ thoughts that make up every moment of my existence.

Writing all this now – and some weeks have gone by since I started – it is lifeless and insipid and useless. Only at the time, there was something, a thought that propelled me. Always, in looking back, there was something, and at the time I am aware of it and the creation goes on in my mind while I look at all the faces around me in the tube, the restless rustle of newspapers, the hiss of air as the doors close, the enaction of life in a variety of forms.

Once I told her and she said, as she was a stenographer, that she would come with me and we would ride the Inner Circle and I would just voice my thoughts and she would write them down, and that way we could make something of it. Once the train was crowded and she sat opposite to me and after a while I looked at her and she smiled and turned away. What is all this, the meaning of all these things that happen to people, the movement from one place to another, lighting a cigarette, slipping a coin into a slot and pulling a drawer for chocolate, buying a return ticket, waiting for a bus, working the crossword puzzle in the *Evening Standard*?

Sometimes you are in the underground and you have no idea what the weather is like, and the train shoots out of a tunnel and sunlight floods you, falls across your newspaper, makes the passengers squint and look up.

There is a face you have for sitting at home and talking, there is a face you have for working in the office, there is a face, a bearing, a demeanour for each time and place. There is above all a face for travelling, and when you have seen one you have seen all. In a rush hour, when we are breathing down each other's neck, we look at each other and glance quickly away. There is not a great deal to look at in the narrow confines of a carriage except people, and the faces of people, but no one deserves a glass of Hall's wine more than you do. We jostle in the subway from train to lift, we wait, shifting our feet. When we are all herded inside we hear the footsteps of a straggler for whom the operator waits, and we try to figure out what sort of a footstep it is, if he feels that the lift will wait for him; we are glad if he is left waiting while we are shooting upward. Out of the lift, down the street, up the road: in ten seconds flat it is over, and we have to begin again.

One morning I am coming into the city by the night bus 287 from Streatham. It is after one o'clock; I have been stranded again after seeing my girl home. When we get to Westminster Bridge the sky is marvellously clear with a few straight patches of beautiful cloud among which stars sparkle. The moon stands over Waterloo Bridge, above the Houses of Parliament sharply outlined, and it throws gold on the waters of the Thames.

The embankment is quiet, only a few people loiter around the public convenience near to the Charing Cross underground which is open all night. A man sleeps on a bench. His head is resting under headlines: *Suez Deadlock.*

Going back to that same spot about five o'clock in the evening, there was absolutely nothing to recall the atmosphere of the early morning hours. Life had taken over completely, and there was nothing but people. People waiting for buses, people hustling for trains.

I go to Waterloo Bridge and they come pouring out of the offices and they bob up and down as they walk across the bridge. From the stations green trains come and go relentlessly. Motion mesmerises me into immobility. There are lines of motion across the river, on the river.

Sometimes we sat on a bench near the river, and if the tide was out you could see the muddy bed of the river and the swans grubbing. Such spots, when found, are pleasant to loiter in. Sitting in one of those places – choose one, and choose a time – where it is possible to escape for a brief spell from Christ and the cup of tea, I have known a great frustration and weariness. All these things, said, have been said before, the river seen, the skirt pressed against the swelling thigh noted, the lunch hour eating apples in the sphinx's lap under Cleopatra's Needle observed and duly registered: even to talk of the frustration is a repetition. What am I to do, am I to take each circumstance, each thing seen, noted, and mill them in my mind and spit out something entirely different from the reality?

My girl is very real. She hated the city. I don't know why. It's like that sometimes, a person doesn't have to have a reason. A lot of people don't like London that way, you ask them why and they shrug, and a shrug is sometimes a powerful reply to a question.

She shrugged when I asked her why, and when she asked me why I loved London I too shrugged. But after a minute I thought I would try to explain, because too a shrug is an easy way out of a lot of things.

Falteringly I told her how one night it was late and I found a fish and chip shop open in the East End and I bought and ate in the dark street walking; and of the cup of tea in an all-night cafe in Kensington one grim winter morning; and of the first time I ever queued in this country in '50 to see the Swan Lake ballet, and the friend who was with me gave a busker two and six because he was playing *Sentimental Journey* on a mouth-organ.

But why do you love London, she said.

You can't talk about a thing like that, not really. Maybe I could have told her because one evening in the summer I was waiting for her, only it wasn't like summer at all. Rain had been falling all day and a haze hung about the bridges across the river, and the water was muddy brown, and there was a kind of wistfulness and sadness about the evening. The way St Paul's was, half-hidden in the rain, the motionless trees along the Embankment. But you say a thing like that and people don't understand at all. How sometimes a surge of greatness could sweep over you when you see something.

But even if I had said all that and much more, it would not have been what I meant. You could be lonely as hell in the city; then one day you look around and you realise everybody else is lonely too, withdrawn, locked, rushing home out of the chaos: blank faces, unseeing eyes, millions and millions of them, up the Strand, down the Strand, jostling in Charing Cross for the 5.20: in Victoria station, a pretty continental girl wearing a light, becoming shade of lipstick stands away from the board on which the departure of trains appear and cocks her head sideways, hands thrust into pockets of a fawn raincoat.

I catch the eyes of this girl with my own: we each register sight, appreciation: we look away, our eyes pick up casual station activities: she turns to an automatic refreshment machine, hesitant, not sure if she would be able to operate it.

Things happen, and are finished with for ever: I did not talk to her, I did not look her way again, or even think of her.

I look on the wall of the station at the clock, it is half-past eight, and my girl was to have met me since six o'clock. I feel in my pockets for pennies to telephone. I only have two.

I ask change of a stander with the usual embarassment: when I telephone the line is engaged. I alternate between standing in the spot where we have arranged to meet and telephoning, but each time the line is engaged. I call the exchange: they ascertain that something is wrong with the line.

At ten minutes to nine I am eating a corned beef sandwich when she comes. Suddenly now nothing matters except that she is here. She never expected that I would be waiting, but she came on the offchance. I never expected that she would come, but I waited on the offchance.

Now I have a different word for this thing that happened – an offchance, but that does not explain why it happens, and what it is that really happens. We go to St James' Park, we sit under a tree, we kiss, the moon can be seen between leaves.

Wooing my way towards, sometimes in our casual conversation we came near to great, fundamental truths, and it was a little frightening. It wasn't like wooing at all, it was more discussion of when it will end, and must it ever end, and how did it begin, and how go on from here? We scattered words on the green summer grass, under trees, on dry leaves in a wood of quivering aspens, and sometimes it was as if I was struck speechless with too much to say, and held my tongue between thoughts frightened of utterance.

Once again I am on a green train returning to the heart from the suburbs, and I look out of the window into windows of private lives flashed on my brain. Bread being sliced, a man taking off a jacket, an old woman knitting. And all these things I see – the curve of a woman's arm, undressing, the blankets being tucked, and once a solitary figure staring at trains as I stared at windows. All the way down to London Bridge – is falling down, is falling down, the wheels say: one must have a thought – where buildings and the shadows of them encroach on the railway tracks. Now the train crawls across the bridges, dark steel in the darkness: the thoughtful gloom of Waterloo: Charing Cross bridge, Thames reflecting lights, and the silhouettes of city buildings against the sky of the night.

When I was in New York, many times I went into that city late at night after a sally to the outskirts, it lighted up with a million lights, but never a feeling as on entering London. Each return to the city is loaded with thought, so that by the time I take the Inner Circle I am as light as air.

At last I think I know what it is all about. I move around in a world of words. Everything that happens is words. But pure expression is nothing. One must build on the things that happen: it is insufficient to say I sat in the underground and the train hurtled through the darkness and someone isn't using Amplex. So what? So now I weave, I say there was an old man on whose face wrinkles rivered, whose hands were shapeful with arthritis but when he spoke, oddly enough, his voice was young and gay.

But there was no old man, there was nothing, and there is never ever anything.

My girl, she is beautiful to look at. I have seen her in sunlight and in moonlight, and her face carves an exquisite shape in darkness.

These things we talk, I burst out, why mustn't I say them? If I love you, why shouldn't I tell you so?

I love London, she said.

ACKNOWLEDGEMENTS

The editor and publishers are grateful to the following for permission to use extracts in this book: André Deutsch and Michael Anthony for ENCHANTED ALLEY and DRUNKARD OF THE RIVER; Mrs Hope McKay Virtue for CRAZY MARY by the late Claude McKay; Earl Lovelace for SHOEMAKER ARNOLD; Janice Shinebourne (née Lowe) for THE BRIDGE; Wilson Harris for BANIM CREEK; David Higham Associates and John Hearne for AT THE STELLING; Wayne Brown for BRING ON THE TRUMPETERS; André Deutsch for LET THEM CALL IT JAZZ and I USED TO LIVE HERE ONCE by the late Jean Rhys; Geoffrey Drayton for MR DOMBEY, THE ZOMBIE; Davis Poynter Limited and Samuel Selvon for CANE IS BITTER and MY GIRL AND THE CITY; Clyde Hosein for HER HOUSE; Noel Woodroffe for WING'S WAY; Noel Williams for ILYUSHIN '76; Davis Poynter Limited and John Stewart for STICK SONG; and Jonathan Cape for RED DIRT DON'T WASH and LOOK OUT by the late Roger Mais.

The editor and publishers are grateful to the following for permission to use photographs in this book:

André Deutsch for the photograph of Jean Rhys; Jonathan Cape for that of Roger Mais; Faber and Faber for the photographs of John Hearne and Wilson Harris; Clyde Hosein, Noel Williams, Samuel Selvon, Wayne Brown, Geoffrey Drayton, Noel Woodroffe, John Stewart and Michael Anthony for the photographs of themselves. The photograph of Janice Shinebourne is by Penni Bickle.

The publishers have made every attempt to contact holders of copyright material included in this book, but in some cases all attempts to contact such person or persons failed. The publishers will be pleased to hear from any such person or persons and will endeavour to rectify the omission at a later printing.

Designed by Malcolm Farrar